Merrilynne

BLOOD PROOF

Books by Bill Knox

The Thane and Moss police series:
Deadline for a Dream (1957)
Death Department (1959)
Leave it to the Hangman (1960)
Little Drops of Blood (1962) ✓
Sanctuary Isle (1962)
The Man in the Bottle (1963)
The Taste of Proof (1965)
The Deep Fall (1966) ✓
Justice on the Rocks (1967)
The Tallyman (1969)
Children of the Mist (1970) ✓
To Kill a Witch (1971)
Draw Batons (1973) ✓
Rally to Kill (1975)
Pilot Error (1977)
Live Bait (1978)
A Killing in Antiques (1981) ✓
The Hanging Tree (1983)
The Crossfire Killings (1986)
The Interface Man (1989)
The Counterfeit Killers

**The Webb Carrick fishery
protection series:**
The Scavengers (1964)
Devilweed (1966)
Blacklight (1967)
The Klondyker (1968)
Blueback (1969)
Seafire (1970)
Stormtide (1972)
Whitewater (1974)
Hellspout (1976)
Witchrock (1977)
Bombship (1980)
Bloodtide (1982)
Wavecrest (1985)
Dead Man's Mooring (1987)
The Drowning Nets (1991)

Other crime fiction as Bill Knox:
The Cockatoo Crime (1958)
Death Calls the Shots (1961)
Die for Big Betsy (1961)

With Edward Boyd:
The View from Daniel Pike (1974)

Non-fiction
*Court of Murder. Famous trials at
Glasgow High Court (1968)*
Tales of Crime (1982)

**Written as Robert Macleod
Talos Cord investigator series:**
The Drum of Power (1964)
Cave of Bats (1964)
Lake of Fury (1966)
Isle of Dragons (1967)
Place of Mists (1969)
Path of Ghosts (1971)
Nest of Vultures (1973)

**Jonathan Gaunt 'Remembrancer'
series:**
A Property in Cyprus (1970)
A Killing in Malta (1972)
A Burial in Portugal (1973)
A Witchdance in Bavaria (1975)
A Pay-off in Switzerland (1977)
An Incident in Iceland (1979)
A Problem in Prague (1981)
A Legacy from Tenerife (1984)
A Cut In Diamonds (1985)
The Money Mountain (1987)
The Spanish Maze Game (1990)

**Andrew Laird marine insurance
series:**
All Other Perils (1974)
Dragonship (1976)
Salvage Job (1978)
Cargo Risk (1980)
Mayday From Malaga (1983)
Witchline (1988)

BLOOD PROOF

Bill Knox

Constable · London

First published in Great Britain 1997 by Constable & Company Ltd
3 The Lanchesters, 162 Fulham Palace Road, London W6 9ER
Copyright © 1997 by Bill Knox
The right of Bill Knox to be identified as the author
of this work has been asserted by him in accordance with
the Copyright, Designs and Patents Act 1988
ISBN 0 09 477170 7
Set in Linotron Palatino 10pt by CentraCet, Cambridge
Printed and bound in Great Britain by Hartnolls Ltd, Bodmin

A CIP catalogue record for this book
is available from the British Library

For Fraser

As always, this story varies in some aspects of procedural detail from the real-life Scottish Crime Squad's operational methods. They prefer it that way. I have been told why and I agree.

BK, Glasgow, 1997

1

Prelude

The first time Iain Cameron heard the noise, it hardly registered. Little more than an outside creak and a brief thud, it was a sound which could have been a gust of wind or a prowling fox.

Iain Cameron kept on reading his book, reached for his mug of coffee, and took another sip from the lukewarm liquid. The book was unexciting to the point of being boring. His eyes needed a rest, his body demanded some exercise. A yawn stole up on him and he set down the coffee mug then glanced at his wrist-watch.

It was midnight. He wasn't even half-way through his nine-hour shift as night-watchman at Broch Distillery. In five months in the distillery job – 'Drink Broch, the most exciting single malt whisky north of the Highland Line' – the most exciting thing that had happened to him was when two forestry workers with too much liquor had crashed their van one night and had hobbled in at two a.m., gashed, bruised, and seeking help.

But it was a job, and there weren't too many around for a man in his late forties, particularly a man paid off from his last job merely for thumping the foreman at the end of a modest argument.

Still, it could be worse. Iain Cameron was single and lived on his own, and the job didn't involve much in the way of effort. His duties mainly involved a patrol around the distillery every hour or so, and the rest of the time he stayed in his little security office, read, drank coffee, sometimes listened to the radio, or just plain dozed. It would do until something better turned up. Maybe his cousin Willie, who earned big money as a labourer on the off-shore oil rigs, would be able to help as he'd been promising. There was always big money waiting out on the rigs . . .

That sound came again, outside somewhere, reasonably close, and louder. Frowning, puzzled, Iain Cameron laid down his book, got to his feet, and ambled over to the door. He opened it, stepped out into the dark night, and looked around at the familiar, unlit outlines of the other distillery buildings.

At first, he heard only the low murmurs and rustlings of the wind. Then there was more of the other, puzzling sound and this time Iain Cameron placed it as coming from the big two-storey warehouse building which sat on its own at the bottom of a small slope, isolated from the rest of the distillery site.

Iain Cameron felt worried and wanted someone else to know it. He went back into the little office and lifted the telephone. The line was dead, and he cursed as he replaced the useless receiver, knowing he was totally on his own.

'Damn it to hell,' he told himself bitterly. 'All right, you'd better do something. But no way are you trying for any medal, Iain, man – not on what you get paid. You go, you take a quiet look, then, no matter what it is, you get back here, close the door again, and keep your fool head down!'

His ancient leather jacket was hanging on a peg and he pulled it on over the heavy grey wool sweater he teamed with army-surplus khaki trousers. Taking a large rubberized torch, gripping it like a club in one hand, he went outside again and set off at his own cautious pace. He could hear only the wind and the occasional soft crunch of disturbed gravel as he headed down the path towards the black silhouette of the warehouse. Then, at the foot of the slope he had a first clear view of the front of the building.

He froze, a cold fear clawing. The main loading doors lay open and the interior of the building was ablaze. The flames, some yellow, others blue-tinged, were growing and spreading by the second, expanding into hungry tongues of roaring, sparking fire. They were starting to throw nightmare patterns of light and shadow along the high-stacked rows of giant wooden casks which filled the warehouse.

Then the whole world seemed to explode in his face.

Iain Cameron was lucky.

He was killed instantly.

*

Minutes later and only four miles away, Andy Kerr was driving through the night along the narrow, twisting and totally empty ribbon of the Glen Laggan road, heading for home. His wife Joan was curled up in the passenger seat beside him. Half asleep, head resting on Kerr's shoulder, she made a mumble of protest each time their veteran Peugeot station wagon jolted on yet another pothole. Andy Kerr was a telephone linesman, Joan worked part-time in the Broch distillery office. They had three young children, his mother was baby-sitting, and the couple were returning after a rare Saturday evening out with friends.

A good evening. Now it would be equally good to get home, and they were travelling under a night sky which sparkled with stars in that special September way unique to the lonely northern rim of Scotland. He began to hum under his breath.

That was one moment. The next, Andy Kerr stared ahead, gave a startled grunt, gripped the Peugeot's wheel, then braked and stopped.

'Andy?' The startled protest ended there as Joan uncurled from the depths of the passenger seat and saw for herself. 'Oh, God!'

The Peugeot had just topped a long rise on the twisting Laggan road. Ahead, at the far edge of the long glen, a black ridge of hill was silhouetted against an eerie blue backlight which was still spreading, still growing in intensity.

'What is it?' asked Joan.

She already knew. They both did.

'The Broch,' said Andy Kerr in something close to disbelief. In their lonely corner of the world, where deer outnumbered people several times over to every square mile, only Broch Distillery lay behind that ridge. 'The whole damned lot must have gone up. But don't worry about the kids. They'll be safe.'

He started the car moving again, heading along the road towards the strange blue light, while Joan Kerr sat upright beside him.

Then it happened. She gasped and made a frantic, instinctive clutch for her husband's arm as a sudden, raking, close-up glare of powerful headlights almost blinded them. The vehicle which had erupted out of nowhere ahead was travelling towards them fast and stayed that way. The lights remained on remorseless full beam while the distance between the two cars shrank at a frightening rate. As the glaring lights and head-on rush continued, Andy Kerr took the only course open to him. He swung the Peugeot's wheel and sent their car in a skidding, bouncing lurch onto the broken verge of rocks and heather. As the Peugeot stalled to a halt, the mystery vehicle roared past.

'Bastard!' howled Andy Kerr. Looking round, he saw the other car speeding away, those dazzling headlights still lancing the night. He knew he was trembling. He howled it again. 'Bastard!'

'He could have killed us.' Kerr's wife still gripped his arm. 'Andy, the fool could have killed us.'

'Did you see who was driving? Or anything about the car?'

She shook her head, and Kerr sighed. That made two of them. It had happened too quickly, had been too frightening, for any details to register. When he looked round again, the strange vehicle was still heading away as fast as ever – then even the shrinking tail lights had vanished into the night.

But the blue glow ahead was still growing. The Peugeot's engine started when Kerr tried the ignition key. Then, lurching and swaying, suspension protesting, the elderly station wagon crawled back across the badly churned verge and reached the road. He looked at Joan, she nodded, and once again they began driving towards the glow.

The stranger vehicle which had blinded them could only have come from the direction of the glow. There was no side-road of any kind ahead until after the Glen Laggan road reached the distillery.

Putting two and two together usually made four, even in the Highlands.

A few minutes more travel took their Peugeot to the private side-road which led off on the left to the distillery buildings. Turning into it, crawling the last short distance, the Kerrs were awed by what they saw. The main warehouse block was a seething, crackling wall of blue flames, an inferno loudly punctuated by flat, fierce explosions as a steady series of whisky casks detonated in the inferno.

But at least they were no longer alone. The lights of two other cars were now approaching from the road behind them, both local and belonging to neighbours.

Andy Kerr stopped the Peugeot and the other drivers followed his example, pulling in behind him. Nobody aboard any of them seemed to want to leave their vehicle.

A sudden new series of detonations sent more wooden casks of whisky blasting up like rockets through what was left of the warehouse roof. Some, relatively intact, exploded in a scatter of ignited liquid and a shrapnel of staves and iron hoops as they hit the ground again. All around, fierce blue-white flames raced along new streams of blazing whisky or burned in trapped pools.

Andy Kerr opened his driver's door, felt a wave of heat scorch in, and slammed the door closed again. The remains of another giant cask crashed down near the Peugeot and an instant river of burning alcohol gushed towards his vehicle. He cursed, slammed the car into reverse gear, and backed to where the two other cars waited.

'What about the watchman?' asked Joan suddenly. 'Andy, where's Iain Cameron?'

'Hell. I'll look.' Kerr reluctantly opened his car door again, and stepped out into the heat. The night air was acrid with smoke and the heavy, overpowering reek of burning alcohol stung at his eyes and throat. Another string of casks began exploding and soaring from inside the blazing warehouse, and two of them crashed down to his right, spewing new flames and scattering liquid.

Then Andy Kerr felt sick. This new outbreak was flowing to join an earlier, dying glow. A charred shape lay in the middle of that dying glow, a shape which had once been a man.

He had found Iain Cameron.

It was all Andy Kerr needed. What the hell was he supposed to do next?

Police were few and far between in the northern Highlands. The nearest one-man police station was about thirty miles away, where the sole constable who manned it covered a beat which stretched over five hundred square miles from mountains and lochs to even a stretch of Atlantic coastline. God alone knew exactly where he was or how long it would take him to arrive at the Broch.

'Why me?' despaired Andy Kerr.

Yes, he was a telephone linesman. But he had another hat, one he shared with Joan. They were both volunteer Special Constables.

He swallowed hard, turned his back on the inferno, and walked towards the other cars.

Hell, he was a Special. Maybe he could ask them to park in an orderly line – or something.

Thirty-six hours later, at noon on the Monday, Detective Superintendent Colin Thane was at Glasgow Airport and ready to board the scheduled morning flight to Inverness when a voice over the Tannoy asked him to report to the airline gateway desk. He grimaced towards the young and red-haired woman detective sergeant who was travelling with him, left her, and went over.

'For you, superintendent.' A harasssed blonde in a ground service uniform nodded towards a telephone. 'Someone named Moss.' She frowned at her wrist-watch. 'Can you make it quick? We're ready for boarding.'

Colin Thane, a tall, grey-eyed man in his early forties, thanked her and lifted the receiver. The warrant card in his pocket identified him as deputy commander of the élite Scottish Crime Squad. Any call from Phil Moss, a detective inspector and the Squad's new line manager, mattered. Moss seldom wasted anyone's time – including his own.

'Thank you.' He waited until the ground service uniform made a frosty retreat. 'Phil?'

'There's a new update faxed from Inverness.' As usual, Moss didn't sound like he was singing or dancing. 'No happy thoughts.'

'Go on.'

'First, they've got the autopsy report on the distillery watchman. Call it accidental murder. His skull was smashed in by a chunk of exploding whisky barrel. 'A wisp of mournful humour crept into Moss's voice as it came over the line. 'Blame the Demon Drink again.'

'You're talking best quality single malt whisky,' reminded Thane sadly. 'Show respect.'

'High grade Demon Drink.' Moss was unrepentent. 'Next, there's still no lead about the team involved, but it was an arson job and it could be professional. Northern found traces of three separate start-up locations in the warehouse.'

That much Thane had expected. But he knew that Moss always kept something bad for last. He shifted his grip on the receiver, aware that the blonde ground service uniform had returned and

12

was frowning at him from only a few feet away. In the background, he could see other passengers fidgeting.

'What else?' he asked resignedly. 'Keep it short, Phil.'

'Short?' Moss paused and gave a low-key belch which thundered over the line. 'Broch Distilleries have finished doing their sums. The whisky that went up in flames had a duty-free value of three million pounds sterling. Duty paid, it would have been eight million.'

'Dear God.'

'I thought you'd be pleased,' said Moss placidly. 'Have a good trip.'

'Go to hell,' said Thane.

There was a mild chuckle, then the line went dead. Thane sadly replaced his receiver, went back to where Detective Sergeant Sandra Craig was waiting and just had time to give her a murmured version of Moss's update before the Inverness flight was being called.

The small turbo-prop commuter Jetstream had every seat filled. The eighteen passengers were a mix of locals returning home, business travellers with order books, and a trio of football fans. The fans didn't mind who knew that although their team had lost they'd stayed on and had had a hell of a good weekend in the big city.

Passengers sat in rows of three abreast, with an off-set aisle, and Thane had a window seat. He had unashamedly used rank to claim it, consigning Sandra Craig to the middle seat. She hadn't been amused when the aisle seat was occupied by a fat and talkative middle-aged male who had heavy dandruff.

Thane ignored his sergeant's scowl as the aircraft took off. Part of his mind was on the case waiting ahead, the rest of his attention was fascinated by the changing scenery below. Climbing rapidly, leaving Glasgow and the Clyde Valley behind, the Jetstream levelled at 20,000 feet then headed north on its one-hour flight to Inverness. First the farms and historic old castles around Stirling gave way to the stern upland green of Perthshire. Then that in turn was behind them and the turboprop gave an occasional shudder as she met the first of the thermals spawned from the high country of the Cairngorm mountains.

Looking down, at the same time vaguely aware that the man beside Sandra was plying her with unwanted smalltalk, Thane could see a thin ribbon of tarmac which was the backbone A9 trunk route, a ribbon busy with tiny ant-sized vehicles. Then the A9 had twisted away, and he was left with ranks of tall, bald mountain peaks scarred by deep gullies, and no visible sign that human life had ever come their way.

Much of the Cairngorm range was naked granite rock, sometimes streaked with purple heather, or glinting where occasional veins of quartz broke through. A few sheltered corries held year-round patches of snow. Lesser reaches were skiing country in the winter, others brought adventurous hill-walkers trekking in the summer. But most were an emptiness of high country, where even the ubiquitous tree-planting Forestry Commission knew when to give up.

At last, the Jetstream banked in a slow turn and gradually began to lose height. Briefly, her shadow dancing across a sunlit slope below sent a herd of red deer fleeing and Thane smiled at the sight. Probably the herd saw more overflying aircraft than they saw people – and didn't know how lucky that made them.

The man sitting next to Sandra was persisting with his earnest chat-up campaign, based around the idea they meet for a dinner date in Inverness. Her patience had worn thin, her curt replies were icy but inaudable.

Thane could have told him he was living dangerously. But Sandra could take care of herself, and he forgot about the man as a distinctive, typically lonely group of buildings caught his eye on the ground below. Only distillery buildings had such a combination of high roofs and those unmistakable still-house chimneys. Moments later he could see two more similar groups ahead. They had reached Speyside and one of the recognized 'whisky trails' where more than a score of whisky distilleries produced some of the world's most revered malts.

His particular distillery, his reason for coming north, lay somewhere miles away to the west. With a bill of one dead and three million pounds sterling damage, any distillery jokes he knew had gone sour.

The little Jetstream shuddered in a new patch of turbulence, shaking hard. Beside him, Sandra seemed to be thrown towards her neighbour and Thane heard a near scream of pain come from the man, who suddenly clutched both hands at his groin while Sandra casually rubbed at her elbow.

Thane caught his sergeant's eye and met a totally stony stare. Then Inverness, the grey historic capital of the Highlands, lay ahead. Five minutes later the aircraft had landed at Dalcross Airport and her passengers were disembarked at the toytown-size terminal.

'Interesting flight, sergeant?' murmured Thane as he and Sandra crossed the arrivals hall together while her travelling companion disappeared off at a hurried limp in the opposite direction.

'I warned him,' she said grimly. 'He kept pawing my knee.'

'You came close to making him an instant soprano,' warned Thane gloomily. 'It gets us a bad name. You should have broken his hand off at the wrist. It's more feminine.'

'Sir.' She called a truce. 'Would I get that in writing?'

'No way.' Thane shook his head. 'I get into enough trouble without looking for more.'

Sergeant Sandra Craig gave a grin, knowing that was often true.

A man with thick, dark hair and regular features, Colin Thane combined a muscular build maybe just a few pounds over-weight with a deceptively easy-going air. He was wearing a lightweight Lovat suit, a blue shirt, and a maroon-knitted silk tie which had been a birthday present from his wife. His shoes were a pair of brown leather moccasins, old enough to be comfortable.

What was just hinted at in the few crowfoot lines around his grey eyes was a police career which spanned the long rise from Glasgow beat cop to becoming number two in the hand-picked Scottish Crime Squad.

Sandra Craig, by comparison, was still in her twenties. Tall and slim, with attractive looks and green eyes, her red hair a warning of a temper to match, she had earned promotion to sergeant a few months back. For her career future, though Thane knew better than to hint it, she was accelerated promotion material. Her travelling outfit was a white silk roll-neck sweater topped by a blue corduroy jacket. Faded tailored blue denims were teamed with a broad metal-studded leather belt, a present from an admiring armed robber she'd once arrested. Her feet were in black leather lace-up training shoes.

Carrying the overnight bags they'd taken as cabin luggage, they headed towards the welcoming party – a woman constable in uniform, small, young, and well-built, with dark eyes, raven-black hair and an attractive pert-nosed oval of a face.

'No other luggage, sir?' The unmistakable Highland lilt in her voice was brisk as she nodded at the bags they were carrying.

'Only these,' confirmed Thane, wondering how she had got through Northern's minimum height requirements. 'What do people call you, constable?'

'Maggie, sir – Maggie Donald.' The dark eyes twinkled. 'That and other things. I'm Traffic Department.' She escorted them out to a parked and mud-spattered blue Range Rover which had Northern Constabulary badges on its doors and gave an apologetic gesture as they started to get aboard. 'Sorry there wasn't time to run her through a car wash, sir. Things have been a bit busy with us.'

'We'd heard,' agreed Thane stonily.

'I suppose you would, sir.' She watched Sandra as she got aboard, frowned, and the lilting voice raised a little, 'Sergeant, could you oblige me by not kicking that parcel on the floor beside you too often? That's our Chief Constable's best uniform. I'm bringing it back from the dry-cleaning.'

Then they were on their way. As the Range Rover began moving, Thane heard their dark-haired driver singing under her breath. The tune was straight out of the Top Ten.

From the airport, located a few miles out to the north-east, it was only a few minutes' drive into the heart of Inverness. The Highland capital, home to a population of around 40,000, another claim to fame its elusive, legendary Loch Ness Monster, had its streets jammed with slow-moving queues of tourist cars mixed with tour buses and the occasional embattled local vehicle.

'Business seems good,' murmured Thane. 'Maybe too good,'

'This is our peak season for visitors, sir.' Maggie Donald shook her head. 'We can't have it all ways.'

'True.' Thane nodded. 'How's the Loch Ness Monster?'

'Fine, sir.' She beamed at him through the rear-view mirror. 'There was a new sighting reported last week – two German back-packers claim they saw her close inshore down near Fort Augustus, whatever the truth of it.'

Sandra Craig showed her strong, white teeth in an amused grin. 'A Tourist Board gift. Do many people still fall for the Monster nonsense?'

'Monster nonsense, sergeant?' Their driver's manner froze. 'I don't think I could agree with calling it that.'

'Come off it, Maggie!' Puzzled, Sandra blinked in surprise. 'How many people honestly believe they've seen the thing?'

'I could give you a list, sergeant.' The raven-haired girl had both hands tight on the steering wheel. 'What kind of names would satisfy you? And would you want ages and occupations?'

Sandra glanced at Thane, hoping for a way out.

'What do you think about it, Maggie?' asked Thane mildly.

'Me, sir?' Lips pursed, she weaved the car through a sudden small space in the traffic. 'Yes. I believe in her – and who can prove she isn't there?'

Thane did the wise thing, left it alone, and soon they reached Northern Constabulary headquarters, a modern building which sprouted VHF aerials and telecommunications dishes.

They were in luck. Another police car drew away from the parking area at the main headquarters door. The Range Rover slotted into the vacated space, then they left the vehicle and followed Maggie Donald into the building, past the public counter. The counter was quiet, the only customer a large drunk with a bleeding and badly split lip claiming he'd been assaulted by his wife. She was there too, equally large, telling two listening, grinning cops that she was ready to do it again.

Their overnight bags were taken and stowed away. Maggie Donald led Sandra off towards the force canteen, and a pimple-faced orderly took over as Thane's guide.

He followed the youngster along a corridor, then a stairway brought them into executive territory where there were job titles on every door. They stopped at a door marked Chief Superintendent, Operations. The orderly knocked and there was a muffled shout from inside. Opening the door, the orderly ushered Thane into a large, well-furnished room.

'Colin! Good!' Beaming, emerging from behind a large yellow pine desk, a tall, thin middle-aged man in a dark green gabardine suit crossed quickly to meet him. 'Thanks for coming.'

'Nobody told me I had a choice,' said Thane dryly. As they shook hands, he noted that most of one wall of the office was occupied by a large-scale map of the North of Scotland, a map thinly scattered with marker pins. He didn't often cross paths with Detective Chief Superintendent Mick Farrell, the head of Northern Constabulary CID, and this was the first time they'd met on Farrell's home territory. 'But someone said you had a problem.'

'Somebody got it right.' Farrell grimaced. 'Somebody also said your people will take it on.' He considered Thane with a critical eye. 'You've put on some extra beef, haven't you?'

'And you sound like my wife.' Thane considered Farrell in turn. The Northern CID chief had a long-jawed face, close-cropped grey hair, and slightly hooded blue eyes. 'What's going on up here, Mick? What's the panic?'

'At Broch Distillery? Good question, and I'm damned if I totally know.' Farrell grimaced. 'How much of a briefing did you get?'

'Not a lot,' said Thane. 'There wasn't time.'

'There's never time – I've booked that as my epitaph.' Farrell thumbed at one of the armchairs beside his desk. 'Sit down while I check on something. Then I can give you a starter. I've got the Broch Distilleries sales director in the building causing general chaos. We needed another formal statement on what happened, we were unlucky, and he turned up.'

'The awkward kind?' Thane settled in the chair.

'Today's understatement,' said Farrell with feeling. 'Believe me.'

The Northern chief superintendent went back to his desk, punched a couple of buttons on his internal telephone, then had a brief conversation with someone who answered at the other end. As he did so, a car departed outside in a noisy scatter of gravel and somewhere nearby another telephone began ringing. Strong sunlight was coming in through the window behind Farrell's desk in a way that emphasized a tiredness around the man's eyes. The Northern detective had now been living the Broch case for a full day and a half in addition to whatever else he had on his plate.

Thane caught himself thinking back that same amount of time. For once, he'd had a reasonable weekend. Being able to take his wife out for a meal on Saturday evening had been a small luxury. He'd been in a good mood when he arrived at Scottish Crime Squad headquarters that morning to find Jack Hart, the leathery-faced squad commander, was waiting for him and that Sandra Craig had already been put to work organizing two flight tickets to Inverness. She had dragged out the overnight bag Thane kept in his office, and was checking her own bag for essentials like spare knickers and iron-ration chocolate bars.

'Northern Constabulary want help,' Jack Hart had said it simply. 'We owe them.'

Owing could mean anything, and if you didn't know and if it wasn't being volunteered then it could sometimes be better not to ask. But there had been a file – there was always a file. This one was brand new and very thin, little more than a handful of fax-sheet flimsies. A few more minutes and he had left Hart's office and gone through to the main Crime Squad duty room to brief Phil Moss.

That left one other priority. He had telephoned home and his wife had answered, about to leave to drive their two teenage children to school then go on to the local medical centre where she was now part-time practice manager.

'I'm going north,' he said.

'Till when?' asked Mary Thane.

'I don't know.'

'I'll survive.' After marriage to a cop for almost twenty years, she was used to most situations. 'I've got a new book from the library – *Cooking for the Single Woman*.'

Which didn't sound like a caring farewell, but they didn't always need to talk in words.

'That's done.' Farrell finished the call and slammed down his receiver. The Northern man looked slightly happier as he perched his thin body on the edge of his desk. 'Now your sales director. His name is Morris Currie, he'll join us briefly, then he has to get to the airport – thanks be to God.' Farrell scowled. 'His usual way to solve a problem is to threaten to thump someone.'

'Has he done it?'

'Thumped someone? Unlikely, but he talks big.' Farrell shrugged that aside. 'Broch Distilleries may not be giant-sized in the malt whisky production league, but they rate as prosperous independents. They take their name from Broch Castle, which their chairman owns, and which is a few miles further along the glen road from them. They also own a couple of smaller distilleries along Speyside, a major blending and bottling plant down in the Lowlands, then a little bit of this and a little bit of that—'

'But right now your Mr Currie is not a happy sales director?' suggested Thane.

'Indeed he's not.' Farrell sighed. 'Being down three million pounds has to hurt, even if insurance will pick up the tab. Losing a night-watchman worries him a lot less.'

'How about Customs and Excise?'

'Losing a few million doesn't make them happy,' mused Farrell. 'But the liquor was still in bond – no duty paid. There's not a lot they can do about it.'

'Hard luck.' It didn't break Thane's heart. 'Anything yet about the car seen driving away?'

Farrell shook his head.

Thane tried again. 'How about motive?'

'For this?' Farrell sucked hard on his teeth. 'I don't know.'

Then they heard voices approaching them along the corridor outside.

'Leave it till later,' said Farrell quietly.

There was a knock on his office door. It opened as Farrell growled a response and two men entered. The first, aggressssively in the lead, had thick, collar-length dark hair. The other, older and balding, maintained a face empty of expression and closed the door again once they were in.

'Finished, Mr Currie?' asked Mick Farrell in a neutral voice.

'So I'm told.' Morris Currie gave a short nod. Thick set and medium height, he had a broad face with an impatient, thick-lipped mouth, hostile brown eyes, and a small nose with wide nostrils. He wore an expensively tailored charcoal grey business suit, a white shirt with a button-down collar, and a floridly patterned silk tie. Seeing Thane, he frowned. 'Well, now – who are you?'

'Hired help, Mr Currie,' said Thane laconically, getting to his feet.

Mick Farrell made the introductions which Currie acknowledged with a grunt but ignored Thane's offered handshake.

'We'll see what your people can do, Thane,' he said. 'I'm not thrilled with what I've seen of police progress so far,' continued the distillery executive with heavy sarcasm. 'Hell, half the locals don't seem to have all their switches working – either that, or their backsides need kicking. You won't find it hard to do better.'

'It's early days, Mr Currie. Bringing in Crime Squad expertise will significantly strengthen our investigation.' Maintaining a forced civility but flushing, the Northern CID chief turned back to Thane. Drawing a deep breath, he indicated the bald-headed man. 'Andy Mack, one of our detective inspectors, has been acting as case collator.'

'Sir.' Andy Mack, a blue-eyed man in a baggy tweed suit, gave a flicker of a grin, as if reading this new arrival's mind. 'Somebody had to draw the short straw. It was my turn.'

'It happens,' said Thane with some sympathy. 'I know the feeling.'

'That's cosy,' said Morris Currie derisively. 'But how long do you plan to hold hands around here, Thane? Shouldn't you be getting answers where it all happened, over at Broch?'

'Once I'm ready,' said Thane, refusing to be ruffled. 'I don't try for answers until I have questions.' He considered Currie with a deliberate interest. 'But I could start with some for you, right now.'

'Me?' Currie stiffened with instant suspicion. 'How? I've gone through everything with Mack.'

'So, now tell me,' invited Thane. 'Just two simple questions, Mr Currie. Have Broch Distilleries stirred up any new business enemies lately, or have they been involved in any kind of local fall-out?'

'"Simple answers,"' countered Currie. 'Number one. No, we haven't. Number two. No, nobody. At least, not that I know about on the sales side of things.' He took a white handkerchief from his top pocket, blew his nose with some care as if also taking time to think, then deliberately tucked the handkerchief away again. 'If you're wondering about some kind of local Highland vendetta, ask someone else.'

'Like who?'

'Try Finn Rankin – our chairman.' An edge of sarcasm returned to Currie's voice. 'If and when you finally decide to go out to Broch you'll find Rankin there, superintendent. Speak with him.' He glanced at Andy Mack. 'Agreed?'

The Northern detective inspector gave a reluctant nod.

'Exactly.' Currie wasn't finished. 'I'm business, not production, superintendent. You'll only waste time if you ask me about things up here. I'm based in Edinburgh, I only came up yesterday because of what had happened and to see how I could help.' He paused and very deliberately looked at his watch, a gold Rolex on a leather strap. 'Now what's important is that I make the afternoon flight back to Edinburgh.'

Farrell nodded. 'Inspector Mack has a car waiting.'

'Good. Almost surprising.' Currie smirked towards Thane. 'And you, superintendent? Finished for now?'

'Almost.' Thane controlled his temper for the sake of the local men. 'Did you know Iain Cameron?'

'No.' Currie looked almost surprised. 'Watchmen aren't my department.'

'Then maybe this is,' said Thane doggedly. 'You lost a lot of whisky in that fire.'

'Around three million pounds' worth, duty free.' The round-faced, city-suited figure sighed. 'Thane, please keep this short. I must make that flight. I've an evening meeting arranged in Edinburgh with an American who buys for a New England chain of liquor stores.'

'Will the fire loss hurt any of your existing business?'

'No.' Currie impatiently shifted his balance from one foot to the other. 'Look, you've made it clear you know damned little about the whisky trade. So I'm going to spell this out, then I'm on my way. One, we're only middling-size players at the quality end of the whisky trade. Two, we lost about three quarters of a million litres of Broch malt whisky in that blaze.' His mouth shaped a slight sneer. 'If you're happier, think of it as over one hundred and fifty thousand gallons – you don't look the metric type.'

'Maybe not.' Thane suddenly realised it would have been very easy to hit the man and not feel sorry afterwards. 'Either way, it's a lot.'

'Maybe, to the the average punter who buys by the bottle—'

'Or even by the half-bottle,' murmured Mick Farrell, wooden-faced.

'Very funny.' Currie grunted derisively, in no mood for interruption. 'Your question, Thane? We could have done without this. We've had one whisky warehouse badly damaged, partly destroyed. But we're insured, and we've at least five times that amount in other warehouse storage within the distillery area.' He made a vague, dismissive gesture. 'On top of that, we've maybe another four million litres of single-malt and blended whisky stored in bond outside of this region.'

'It still sounds like a large splash in anybody's loch,' said Thane stubbornly. 'It had to hurt.'

'It hurt,' admitted Currrie. Then his salesman side shone through again. 'But we're shuffling stock around, reassuring

22

customers we'll meet deliveries, so what the hell?' He shaped an assured smile. 'What happened to us was probably the work of a plain and simple nutcase – a nutcase with a grudge and a liking for arson.'

'He also killed a man, Mr Currie,' said Andy Mack stonily, hands stuffed deep into the pockets of his baggy tweed jacket. 'That makes him a dangerous nutcase.' He took a deep breath and glanced at Mick Farrell. 'Sir, if I'm going to make the airport in time—'

There was a brief mutter of farewells and of token handshakes – this time Thane found himself included – then Morris Currie was escorted out by Mack. As the door closed again, Mick Farrell dropped into the swivel chair behind his desk. There was relief in his hooded blue eyes as he gestured Thane to drag his armchair nearer.

The Northern chief superintendent nodded, opened a desk drawer, and brought out a whisky bottle, two glasses, and a small jug of water. There was no label on the bottle.

'This is research, Colin,' said Farrell, a small smile relaxing his long-jawed face. He poured two careful measures of very pale, almost colourless liquid from the bottle. 'What we've got here is first-run overproof single malt from Broch distillery – the stuff you can't buy.'

Thane took a first careful sip and Farrell did the same. The whisky was smooth as silk, delicately smoky in flavour, yet with an almost sweet malt undertone.

'Sheer angel's breath.' Farrell gave a long sigh. 'The girl who picked you up at the airport also brought Andy Mack back from the distillery this morning. Andy brought the bottle.'

'Research,' repeated Thane with respect. He added a small measure of water before he sipped again and saw Farrell did the same. Only a fool did more than taste that strength of liquor neat. Not if he wanted to think straight for the rest of the day – or longer.

'About Currie,' said Farrell suddenly. 'He's either a fool or a liar. That's why I hesitated when you asked about motive. We've heard hints about some kind of trouble shaping around Broch Distillery for the last two or three months.'

'Trouble?' Thane took a new sip and let it linger. 'What kind?'

'The kind they haven't reported, so officially it isn't any of our damned business,' scowled Farrell. 'Things we hear about, from

23

what could be plain vandalism to vehicles sabotaged, a couple of men beaten up who won't say why – and not just at the distillery. They've had problems outside, some in other force areas.' He stabbed with a finger. 'You Crime Squad people have the luxury of being able to raise two fingers to things like Scottish force area boundaries, go where you like as you please. Sooner or later, even without the fire, this was probably coming your way.'

'Currie said talk to Finn Rankin, the company chairman,' reminded Thane.

'Rankin is a trouble-making old devil. But I'd try him.' Farrell shaped a grin. 'He has three daughters, all damned good-looking, all directors in the company.' The grin became a chuckle at some memory.

Whatever he was about to add he left unsaid as his telephone rang. Farrell lifted the receiver, answered, then listened for a full couple of minutes without interrupting the voice at the other end. Thane watched his expression change from initial doubt to something close to satisfaction.

'Good,' was all Farrell said at the finish. 'Keep in touch.'

He hung up, hummed briefly to himself, emptied the rest of the whisky in his glass at a single swallow, then set the glass down with a firm thump. The bottle with no label had vanished.

'Something going on?' asked Thane.

'Yes.' Farrell gave an apologetic gesture. 'It's in the "need to know" category, and you're not involved, Colin. But it is still partly why you're here. I've got a separate major operation on the go, I'm short of resources from manpower onward. I need this Broch caper like I need a hole in the head.'

'So you dump it on us.' Thane gave a lopsided grin. 'Is the "need to know" going well?'

'So far.' Farrell saw Thane glance towards the large wall-map. 'And there's nothing marked there.'

The map was large-scale, covering the whole of Northern Constabulary's vast territory. It could only be described as different. Northern's patch totalled one sixth of the total land mass of the United Kingdom, including the whole of the Highland Region, which on its own was the size of Belgium. It also took in the whole length of the Western Isles, the Orkneys, and the Shetlands – and that sixth of land mass was covered by a total force of only six hundred and fifty regular officers.

'We were working out something the other day,' mused Farrell. 'Any of our officers out in the Shetlands are working nearer to Bergen in Norway than to headquarters here in Inverness.'

He warmed to the theme and went over to the map, slapping a hand on its surface. 'But where you're going is to the west – about fifty miles if you were a crow, nearer seventy if you've got wheels.'

'I've a sergeant who'll pack survival rations,' said Thane wryly. 'Where's the distillery?'

'Here.' Farrell pointed. 'Three or so miles more along the same road and you're at Ardshona village and Broch Castle. Miss them, and you count sheep or climb mountains.' His hand swept on. 'Before you ask, the nearest police station is thirty miles or so away. That's over here, at Fadda Village, where we've a constable.'

There was a knock at Mick Farrell's door again and an orderly brought a tray of sandwiches and coffee. The sandwiches were thin-sliced Aberdeen Angus beef on lightly buttered brown bread. While the two men ate, Farrell returned to his theme.

Whole vast stretches of Northern's territory depended on the isolated one-man stations, where what might be marked as a village on the map could in reality mean less than a handful of cottages. At Rhiconich, in north-west Sutherland, a constable in his twenties had Britain's largest beat – six hundred square miles of empty mountains and wild sea-coast. His nearest back-up was at either the one-man stations at Fadda or Lochinver, both around forty miles away from him by road.

'It's different.' Thane took another of the fast disappearing sandwiches.

'You're thinking fishing salmon and chasing deer, and how city cops would queue to swop jobs – even before they knew the sergeant maybe visits once a fortnight and an inspector makes a royal tour once a month?' Farrell shook his head. 'Take Fergus Gordon, our cop at Fadda. He's married with a six-month-old child. Last month young Fergus had a call-out to a shepherd's cottage five miles along a single-track forestry road. The shepherd had a shotgun, he'd gone berserk, he'd already blown his wife and his dog away, and there was a teenage daughter screaming for help on the phone.'

But it had been sorted out. Without back-up.

'I need a name,' said Thane. 'Who told you about the troubles around Broch?'

'You're going to meet him,' said Farrell simply. 'It was Finn Rankin. He came to see me totally off the record, we've spoken by phone a couple of times since.' He smiled at Thane's surprise. 'For now, it still stays confidential. Rankin can tell you why.'

Although it wasn't much, Farrell had provided what little he could in the way of resources. Farrell had assigned the same plump young policewoman and the same four-wheel drive Range Rover as transport for his visitors. Although Northern's scenes of crime team had been withdrawn from Broch Distillery, Farrell had managed to leave one spare detective constable as a presence. As the local uniformed man, Constable Gordon had also been drafted in from his post at Fadda.

'When I've more spare bodies, and if you need them, you'll get them,' promised Farrell as they parted.

Thane nodded. His own Crime Squad team were on their way up by road, but it would be a few hours before they could join him. Then Farrell's telephone was ringing again, and the thin, long-jawed chief superintendent barely shook hands before he was galloping back into his office and closing the door.

'Need to know' still ruled.

But Detective Inspector Mack was waiting when Thane reached the ground floor, and the bald-headed veteran had a buff-coloured Northern Constabulary file to hand over. It was a total update on the whole Broch situation.

'Were you told who you've been given as a DC?' asked Mack. He chuckled when Thane shook his head. 'Well, you've got Harry Harron, sir. Some folk reckon he's slightly mad, but don't let that worry you – he knows his mountains.'

Then, as if reckoning he'd already said too much, Mack vanished.

Thane found his sergeant and their police driver waiting in the headquarters canteen. Sandra Craig had been busy. She clutched a paper sack filled with packaged sandwiches, chocolate bars, and fruit.

'Will that be enough?' asked Thane resignedly. It was one of life's mysteries that Sandra would snack her way around the clock yet never seem to gain as much as a pound in weight in the process.

'Just being prepared, sir.' The redhead indicated the dark-haired uniformed figure opposite. 'I talked with Maggie about where we're going. They haven't many corner shops.'

'But plenty of corners, superintendent,' said Maggie Donald warily. 'You treat the roads out there with respect.'

'How long will it take us?'

'A full couple of hours, sir.'

'Then move.' Thane thumbed them to their feet. 'Now. Before either of you take root.'

The two women officers exchanged a suffering glance and rose. On the way out, Thane discovered that the overnight bags had already been taken back out to the Range Rover again. The vehicle had also been washed and refuelled. They got aboard, Thane and Sandra in the rear, Maggie Donald back behind the wheel.

'Maggie' – Thane leaned forward as she started the Range Rover's engine – 'did you bring Morris Currie down with you this morning?'

'No, sir.' She shook her head. 'Broch laid on a car for him.'

Satisfied, he sat back and they began moving, leaving the Northern headquarters parking area and heading through busy traffic until the Range Rover joined the A835 Ullapool Road.

For most of the first hour after that it was travel along a good road busy with traffic of every kind. Place names began to click past, from Lovat Bridge and Muir of Ord to Marybank and Loch Garve. Other traffic thinned away. Open moorland gradually faded and a change to loch and mountain closed in.

Thane had concentrated on the detailed incident file he'd been given, passing each page to Sandra Craig as he finished, scowling as she dripped tomato sauce from a fish sandwich onto some fax flimsies, but noticing that she was still keeping an impeccable shorthand note of each and every query he raised. Then, suddenly, the Range Rover turned off the highway, joined a narrower road on the right-hand side, then seemed to be heading straight for the nearest mountain.

'We're really on our way now, sir,' said their driver cheerfully. She half-turned in her seat and glanced round. 'There are some good viewpoints along here – and you'll probably see some deer.'

'Forget the scenery and the damned deer,' snarled Thane as the Range Rover took a swerve. 'Keep your eyes on the road, will you!'

Constable Maggie Donald said something under her breath which was totally insubordinate, but obeyed while the new road they were travelling took a curve around the mountain, climbed over one ridge then another, and kept on that way.

They were travelling into a wilderness where sparse grass clung to thin soil amid broken rock, where the few and small, weather-blasted trees had gnarled, twisted trunks thick with moss and lichen. The rest was tough, low heather and thick bracken. If there were deer around, they were in hiding. But there were sheep. There were sheep on the hills and sometimes ambling on the unfenced road, where the squashed remains of untold rabbits littered the broken tarmac. The sparse traffic on their route amounted to a handful of work trucks or four-wheel drives.

Sandra Craig tackled a chocolate bar and passed a banana over to their driver. Thane watched the road, watched the mountains, and was struck dumb as he saw the majestic wing-span of a golden eagle riding the high thermals above one ridge.

It seemed like they'd been travelling on this winding, snaking road for a very long time, always at the same, steady pace, before Maggie Donald cautiously glanced round again.

'Almost there, sir,' she announced. 'We're at the start of Glen Laggan.'

'And I'm glad—' began Sandra Craig, then changed to a groan. ' – Oh God, not another one.'

There had already been the occasional dead sheep by the roadside, and this one, like the others, had obviously been hit by a vehicle. But, whatever had happened, there were traces of wool and blood and worse scattered clear across from the other side of the road to its mangled remains.

There were also the marks of a fierce skid across the tarmac . . .

'Pull in,' ordered Thane as they went past. 'Now!'

Puzzled, Maggie Donald brought the Range Rover to a halt.

'Back up.'

'Sir.' Frowning, she reversed the vehicle to where the sheep was lying, and braked to a halt when he tapped her shoulder.

'Now wait.' As Maggie Donald switched off the engine, Thane opened his rear door, climbed out, and looked around.

He was standing under a clouding sky, there were insects buzzing all around, and the Range Rover's exhaust had begun making a first occasional crackle and spit as it cooled. Thane

28

sucked his teeth and looked again at why he'd stopped. The skid marks began on the other side of the road, where the sheep must have been hit, and where he could see small fragments of headlamp glass. But the skid marks ran in a wild curve across the tarmac, vanished into the coarse light brown soil of the verge where it dropped steeply away, and did not reappear.

Out of the corner of his eye, Thane saw Sandra Craig leaving the Range Rover. His sergeant came to join him as he walked to the edge of the verge and looked down a steep, scrub-covered slope. Something had ploughed its way down that slope and recently, scarring through the coarse soil and small stones, uprooting a path through scrub and heather, then disappearing lower down.

'Let's do it, sergeant,' he said resignedly.

She gave a small sigh for her black leather training shoes, then followed as Thane began scrambling down the slope. Thorns from the scrub clutched at their clothes, sharp-needled grass stung, and still the ploughed-up trail continued downward, the broken vegetation showing all the signs that it had not happened any great length of time before. Here and there they passed more splinters of broken glass and occasional anonymous pieces of twisted vehicle.

That all stopped where a raw outcrop of rock had acted like a barrier with the wreck of a blue Nissan coupé crumpled against it.

Thane signalled Sandra Craig to wait, made a careful way down the last short distance to the wreck, pulled aside a leafy section of tree branch, uncovered part of the Nissan's smashed windscreen, brushed away some buzzing insects, and looked inside the car, which lay on its side. There was a dead man in the driver's seat, almost impaled on the buckled steering wheel.

He saw more blood on the passenger side. The passenger door had burst open, the glass smashed, the metal obscenely twisted around the upper body of a second dead man. Thane looked back up the way they had come and could see no trace of the road above.

But for the dead sheep and those skid marks, the wreck and its dead could have lain undiscovered for a very long time. Where it had come to a halt beneath the rock was black bog mud carpeted with plate-sized red-crowned mushrooms crawling with insects.

'Sir—' Sandra Craig had joined him to look inside the Nissan. She pointed at the tumbled contents in the rear of the passenger compartment.

The dark metal shape of a sawn-off shotgun was jammed against a khaki travel bag which had burst open. Thane could see what looked like two balaclava masks with eye slits, gloves, and an assortment of tools including a boltcutter. There was a crumpled, blood-stained map, a smashed Thermos flask and two plastic-bodied torches.

They'd found the arson team from the Broch Distillery.

'Sandra.' Thane thumbed towards the slope. 'Leave them. They're not going anywhere.'

His sergeant nodded and started upward, tackling the slope in the kind of effortless way which Thane envied more than she would ever know. Taking a deep breath, he started valiantly after her.

Whoever got the task of recovering the Nissan and its occupants wasn't going to find it easy. But at least that would be for someone else.

And his Crime Squad team would have several positive things to do.

2

'Ever had a day when you'd have been better off to stay in bed, sir?' Harry Harron, the lanky, sad-faced Northern officer left on sentry duty at Broch Distillery, had a resigned gloom in his voice. 'The way I see it, one body at a time is ample for anyone.'

'I won't argue.' Colin Thane wondered if the man expected an apology. 'Suppose we get on with things as they are?'

'Sir.' Detective Constable Harron had sense enough to leave it there.

'Good.' Thane considered the Northern officer again. Harron was an unattractively angular man in his late thirties with a long thin face, mousey hair, and a horse-like mouth with large, badly chipped teeth. He wore an expensive-looking green wool suit with an immaculate khaki shirt, a plain green tie, and brown ankle boots. But DC Harron wasn't going to like it when he discovered that his shirt tail was flapping out from under his jacket. 'Then we'll get back to work.'

They were standing in warm sunlight at the open door of Broch's gatehouse hut. The hut still offered several reminders of the dead night-watchman, including a book which Iain Cameron had been reading, left open and face down. But one thing Cameron hadn't done was leave any kind of indication to explain why he'd set out on his final, fatal inspection.

The night-watchman's hut had been taken over as incident centre, and the doorway gave a direct view across towards the partially gutted warehouse. A fire protection wall and a sprinkler system had saved a portion at the rear, but much of the rest had been reduced to charred roof beams and blackened brickwork. The air held a lingering reek of burned liquor and tiny flakes of whitened ash still drifted on the breeze.

Half an hour had passed since Thane had arrived. His car had driven straight into the distillery compound, past an open and unmanned main gate in a perimeter fence. He had begun by surprising Harron, who had been taking it easy in the watchman's hut, drinking tea with Constable Gordon, the local uniformed man.

'Local' was relative. Fergus Gordon was young, fair-haired and eager to help. He had driven thirty miles from his one-man station at Fadda and brought along two of his nearest Specials. Thane gave him back one of them, a hill shepherd in workaday tweeds and boots, and sent them off to guard the wrecked Nissan coupé. Maggie Donald had gone along to act as guide. Now the other Special, a retired banker, was ambling around as nominally in charge of the main gate.

The telephone line to the hut had been repaired and was working again. Thane gave Sandra Craig the task of calling Inverness to tell them about the Nissan and requesting the back-up help that was needed. The news wasn't going to make Mick Farrell a happy camper.

That much under way, he had taken Harron and had at last visited the gutted warehouse, where workmen were starting salvage preliminaries. The men watched impassively as Thane and Harron went into the charred gloom of the building.

Inside, conditions became worse. They splashed through shallow, scum-streaked pools of liquid, or crunched over debris while the lingering stink of burned whisky clawed at their

31

nostrils. Beyond that, they reached a wilderness of fallen tiers of fire-damaged whisky barrels.

The Scenes of Crime team, long since gone, had removed any firebomb traces they had found. But Harron produced the warehouse foreman, an elderly, ruddy-faced man named Ferguson. The foreman could show where suspicious fragments had been collected from two sites and where a small, burned-out torch battery and melted fragments of electrical flex had been recovered at a third.

Thane thanked the man. Then, the fume-filled air making his head throb like a drumbeat, he led Harron into the open again and back to the security hut. Sandra Craig's round of telephone calls was finished, and she had somehow coaxed the retired bank manager Special into organizing a fresh pot of coffee.

'I spoke with Chief Superintendent Farrell at Inverness, sir.' She poured coffee into a badly cracked mug and gave the mug to Thane. 'He wasn't singing and dancing.'

'That's no surprise.' Thane was glad to settle into what had been Iain Cameron's chair. He gulped at the coffee, the drumbeat still throbbing in his head. 'Any more about our own team?'

'Well on their way.' The redhead took a moment to bite into a sugared biscuit from her private store. 'They'll reach Inverness within the hour, check in there, then they should be with us before dusk.' She saw Harron eyeing the coffee pot and nodded an invitation. 'Help yourself.'

'Thanks, girl.' Harron's horse mouth twisted into a chipped-tooth grin.

'Call me sergeant.' The redhead's voice chilled several degrees in an instant. 'My rank, constable. Any problem with it?'

Harron flushed and didn't answer.

Thane kept out of it, sipping at his coffee, looking away from them. But he knew exactly what the redhead was about – and why. Dinosaur attitudes still lurked in some dark corners of the Scottish police culture. Any woman who reached detective sergeant rank in the few years it had taken Sandra Craig to get there had made it the hard way. If she believed in establishing ground rules now and again, then he wasn't going to get involved.

'Did Inverness run a PNC check on the Nissan?' He used the question to bridge the silence.

'Like you asked, sir.' Sandra ignored the luckless Harron. 'They've a listing of a blue Nissan with that registration number, no report of it being stolen. The apparent owner is a Glasgow woman – that's being checked.'

Thane shrugged. He was almost ready to gamble on what the city cops landed with that inquiry would find. But it was a preliminary to another item on his mental list.

'I've a job for you, Harry.' He waited until Harron faced him. 'Start with the distillery workforce. Try for anyone who remembers seeing a strange blue Nissan, two men aboard, driving around here.'

'When, sir?'

'Any time over the past few days.' Thane was patient. 'I'm presuming that pair weren't local. They didn't just drive all the way north, shout hooray, then break into that warehouse cold. They'd need time to check basics – things like the best way in and the best way to leave again.'

'That could maybe include meeting up with local help,' murmured Sandra Craig.

'I'd put money on that.' Thane put down the coffee mug and got to his feet. 'If you get lucky and want to contact either of us, try the distillery office. I need to talk with Finn Rankin. He told your headquarters people he'd be at his desk all afternoon.'

'He must have changed his mind, superintendent.' Harron shook his head. 'I saw him leave at about the same time as you arrived. It looked like he was heading home.'

'Then I'll have to try there.' Thane allowed himself a scowl.

'One of his daughters is still here,' volunteered Harron.

'Which?'

'I'm not sure, sir.' Harron shrugged. 'They're all boss cats of some kind.'

'Women in high places,' mused Sandra Craig. 'Even in a distillery?'

'It's becoming that kind of a world, sergeant,' said Harron with a gloomy resignation. 'God knows why.'

'I suppose She does,' said the redhead innocently. The man froze.

'Give over, both of you,' said Thane wearily. 'Harry, you were here yesterday, correct?'

'Most of the day, sir,' confirmed Harron. 'Why?'

'Did you meet Morris Currie, their sales director?' Thane saw

33

Harron's cautious nod. 'What did you make of him? An honest opinion, Harry.'

'I didn't like him much, sir.' Harron grimaced. 'I don't think I'm alone. He got here late yesterday afternoon, within the hour I heard him in a shouting match with his chairman.'

'About what?'

'No idea sir.' The Northern man shrugged. 'It was through a closed door. But neither of them sounded happy.'

'Harry.' Sandra Craig spoke again as Harron made to leave. 'Do me a favour?'

Harron hesitated, instantly suspicious. 'Yes, sergeant?

'Smarten up,' she said stonily. 'Your shirt tail is hanging out.'

Harron flushed, swallowed, and left, quickly.

Five minutes later, leaving the retired bank manager to guard the security-hut telephone, Thane and Sandra Craig walked across towards the grey stone and slate roof of the main distillery building.

It was pleasantly warm, there still wasn't a cloud in the sky, and his head had totally cleared. The fire-ravaged warehouse block was out of sight. Ahead, dominated by the traditional pagoda-style chimneys over its malt kilns, the Broch main building followed the usual basic pattern of its kind.

Most distilleries now used fringe touches of electronic technology, but everything about the Broch showed that it still mainly followed the almost sacred distilling process built around water coming direct from a hill stream.

The rest, declared any distiller, was no secret. Simply a kind of magic.

Brought in by the truck-load, barley grain was soaked in mountain water for days, then hand-shovelled and stirred on special drying floors for several more days to allow the barley seed time to sprout and germinate. That was when the starch in the barley released some of its sugars – and at a precisely timed moment the barley was moved on, dried in a peat-fired malting kiln, then ground down, to a fine grit.

Again the hill water was added to produce a sweet wine called wort. Then native skills developed by generations of distillers took over. The wort wine, with yeast added, became an alcohol which was distilled then distilled again in giant glinting copper stills like those that Thane could see shining inside tall, narrow, almost cathedral-like windows. It was the prelude to another vital stage. With only simple gauges to tell them what was happening, the distillers had to judge when to isolate the first raw distillate and the last, low-grade, tail-off dregs. The newly distilled single malt whisky, pure and colourless, torrented on to be measured through final spirit safes and into giant vats.

More hill water was added to bring it down in proof strength, then the result went into wooden casks. Scottish law demanded malt whisky matured undisturbed for at least three years. Most of the casks were old sherry casks, and the whisky could gain its final colour from the sherry residue which had soaked into the wood.

Time was the final secret. A maturing less than the three years rated as close to a hanging offence. The average maturing could be eight or ten, fifteen or even twenty years.

'Like to hear what they say about whisky?' he asked Sandra Craig.

'Sir?' she prepared in a resigned way.

'A good whisky is like a good woman – worth waiting on.'

'What do you do when you find a bad one, sir?' she asked mildly. 'Shout hooray?'

Thane grinned. They had reached a heavy oak door which had a well-worn brass plate which said General Office. When he tried a handle it turned. The door creaked open, and he beckoned. 'Come on. We'll find some cages to rattle.'

They went through, into an impressive lobby area with a marbled terrazzo floor. Small spotlights shone on displays of silver trophies, photographs, and framed exhibition prize certificates. Most of the background was a giant fan-like design constructed of whisky bottles, all with the distinctive green and yellow Broch Single Malt label. A closed-circuit security TV camera was mounted on the wall above it, the lens covering the room. A woman appeared from the rear of the lobby. In her late thirties, with dark hair and a pleasant face, she came towards them.

'Superintendent Thane?' She gave a small smile. 'Inverness told us you were coming.' Her brown eyes switched to Sandra, then she turned to Thane again. 'I'm Joan Kerr . . . I host at visitor reception and run the general office.'

Her name connected with Thane. 'You and your husband . . .?'

'We're both Special Constables.' She nodded. 'We were the first people to get here when the fire began.'

'Yes.' Thane remembered her witness statement from the Inverness Headquarters file. 'A bad end to your evening.'

'It could have been a lot worse.' Joan Kerr was wearing a dark green and yellow plaid skirt, a plain white shirt-blouse, and a sleeveless waistcoat in the same green and yellow plaid pattern. They were the Broch whisky label colours, to match her visitor reception role. Tucking her hands into the pockets of the waist-coat, she added quietly, 'And before that, I thought we were going to be wiped out by that other car.'

'You were lucky,' said Sandra Craig bluntly.

'Luckier than our watchman.' The dark-haired woman's mouth tightened as she turned to Thane again. 'They say you've found a crashed car and that two people aboard it were dead?

Thane nodded. 'True.'

'And neither of them was local?'

'It seems that way.' Thane sucked his teeth appreciatively. 'Three right out of three, Mrs Kerr. Who says? Inverness or the local grapevine?'

'I can't remember.' The woman smiled. 'But then, I'm not involved and neither is Andy, apart from getting the phone lines working again. Chief Superintendent Farrell got word through to us yesterday – because we were witnesses, he says he can't use us any other way.'

Thane might have played it differently, but it was Farrell's decision to make, so he didn't comment.

'Just as well,' said Joan Kerr, taking his silence as sympathy. 'What happens this morning? I 've a sales director screaming for sets of production figures he won't admit he could have asked us for weeks ago! We had to work flat out to complete them in time.'

'I met him,' said Thane neutrally. 'How about yesterday? Didn't he have some kind of quarrel with your chairman?'

'I heard there was something.' She shrugged. 'But it wasn't while I was here – I took the afternoon off. Anyway, they have a small war most times he comes up.'

That was all she knew. Thane talked the woman again through the main details of her statement, confirmed that her linesman husband would be home by evening, then warned her that someone might call round to talk with them.

'Fine, superintendent,' she agreed, unperturbed. 'But don't send anyone round too early – we've two children to put to bed.'

'Not before nine,' promised Thane. He took a half-step nearer. 'Joan, I want you to have a talk with my sergeant, totally off the record. Things you know, things you've heard.'

'Meaning she'll be trawling for gossip?' The dark-haired woman pursed her lips. 'That's not my scene, superintendent.'

'We may come up with something that matters,' urged Sandra. 'Just you and I, Joan – no one else.'

'The woman-to-woman approach?' Joan Kerr grimaced at the thought. 'Sergeant, don't forget I'm a Special. I've seen the "Female Interview" training video.' She glanced at Thane, who was studying a large colour photograph which was part of the publicity display, then sighed. 'Anything else, superintendent?'

'Curiosity.' Thane thumbed at the photograph. 'Is this the namesake?'

'Our Pictish broch – how Broch Whisky got the name.' She nodded. 'You'll see it just behind Broch Castle. Two thousand years old, minimum – no drains, no mod. cons then, superintendent.'

'When people were hardy or died young.' Thane considered the photograph again. Resembling a giant circular beehive, the Pictish broch had been photographed with the sun giving a pinkish hue to its rough, time-worn sandstone blocks. Most Scots still learned about brochs at school. Back in the Iron Age, the Picts who had inhabited the north-west of Scotland had built their brochs as forts and watchtowers. The Picts had vanished, only a handful of their brochs still survived in the most isolated of Highland locations. 'Joan, why did Finn Rankin leave so soon after I got here?'

'He didn't tell me, superintendent. He usually doesn't,' said Joan Kerr dryly. 'Ask Lisa, his daughter. She's here.'

'Where?'

'Right now?' The woman shrugged. 'Lisa's with the distillery manager. She's production director, they're sorting out a problem at one of the washbacks. If you want, I'll take you over.'

Thane gave a sideways glance at Sandra Craig.

'Find someone else for that, Joan,' suggested his sergeant. 'You stay, and that way we can have our talk.'

Joan Kerr left them, headed back into the general office, then returned accompanied by a tall young Indian girl who had her jet black hair in two long plaits tied with tartan ribbon.

'Jazz can take you over, superintendent.' She turned to the girl. 'Jazz, take our visitor to Miss Rankin in the washback hall. Remember he's a policeman. Try not to lose him.'

'I won't, Mrs Kerr.' The girl, who wore faded denims and an outsize white wool sweater, gave Thane an easy-going smile. 'Right, superintendent, let's go!'

Thane followed as she set off. Leaving the reception area, they went through the general office, where two middle-aged women tapped at keyboards. Then their way was out through a side door into an open courtyard. They crossed the courtyard, their footsteps noisy on stone slabs, then reached a sliding door which said No Admittance.

'In here, superintendent.' Ignoring the warning, the dark-skinned girl hauled the door open and beckoned. 'We'll take a shortcut through the production hall. It saves time.'

Once they had stepped through, she closed the door. The production hall was vast and cathedral-sized, with raw granite walls, a high-vaulted ceiling and a concrete floor. He followed his guide past giant copper stills and softly purring furnaces, then around gleaming spirit safes where torrents of newly condensed alcohol were pouring past glass inspection hatches. But the only other people in sight were technicians in white overalls. Modern distilleries operated with a modest workforce.

'Seen any of this before, superintendent?' asked Jazz.

'Some of it.' Thane faced his guide with a twinkle of curiosity. 'How does anyone get a name like Jazz?'

'They say there's a first for everything.' She chuckled. 'It started off as Jasmine, superintendent – Jasmine Gupatra. I'm from Liverpool – in Liverpool, call yourself Jazz and life is easier.'

'How long have you been at Broch?' he asked.

'A few weeks.' She considered him shrewdly. 'I'm a student in disguise, this is a university work-experience posting – I'm doing a Masters course in food technology. Does it matter?'

'To me, yes. It makes you neutral,' said Thane. He rested his hands on a polished barrier rail, feeling the cool of the metal. 'There's a story that some workforce trouble had been building over the past few weeks. How much do you know about it?'

'Maybe a little. I've heard talk.' Jazz hooked her thumbs into the waistband of her denims and gave a wary frown. 'Most people don't worry too much about me – I'm just the "here today, gone tomorrow" student kid.' She paused. 'You could say the natives have been restless – but that doesn't mean a revolution was scheduled.'

'Was anyone special doing the stirring?'

'Some of it was down to Iain Cameron.' Jazz frowned and spent a moment fingering one of her long plaits of black hair. 'But you need someone alive who could be bounced off walls. Right?'

'Yes.' Thane waited.

'I'd try Donny Adams,' she said slowly. 'Adams was a foreman, till he was caught faking timesheets for his pals. Now he's a maltman with a shovel. He hates the world—'

'And he makes trouble?'

'Sets it up,' she corrected. 'There's a difference.'

They set off again down the production hall, past more of the copper giants and their throbbing unseen contents. The air grew warm. All around, the purr of the spirit-still furnaces blended with the muffled background roar of exhausts escaping through the overhead chimneys. A solitary distillery hand, stripped to the waist and making notes on a clipboard mouthed a greeting. They reached a door in a partition wall, went through it, and as it closed again most of the noise was left behind.

'You wanted Lisa Rankin.' Jazz gestured. 'You've got her.'

Thane let the new scene register. The washback area of the production hall was filled with large, low-set wooden vats, each partly sunk into the stone floor. Each washback tub had reinforcing bands of broad copper, each was topped by a sectional wooden lid, and the air was heavy with the strong, sweet odour of fermenting barley.

Two figures were standing beside a tub, deep in conversation. One was a tall, long-legged blonde Viking of a woman, wearing a white laboratory coat. The man beside her was smaller and middle-aged, dark-haired and balding. He was dressed in khaki trousers, a red plaid shirt and a dark grey tie and, whatever Lisa Rankin was saying, he nodded as he listened.

'Coming, superintendent?' asked Jazz with a mild impatience.

Thane let her lead the way. Lisa Rankin saw them coming and nudged her undersized companion. They waited for Jazz and Thane to arrive.

'More police, Miss Lisa,' announced Jazz brightly. 'Superintendent Thane. Joan Kerr told me to bring him over – she's getting the third degree from a woman sergeant.'

'That won't worry Joan,' said Lisa Rankin in a husky voice. 'Our Joan eats sergeants.' Seen nearer, the Broch production director's looks were marred by an old scar which began somwhere above her hairline and ran down most of her left cheek towards her mouth. She indicated her companion. 'Superintendent, this is Alex Korski, our distilling manager.'

They shook hands, Lisa Rankin's contact a light touch, Korski's a confident grip.

'So how can I help this time, superintendent?' The woman didn't hide her low threshold of patience.

'Originally, I wanted to see your father—'

'He went home.'

'We know he was expecting trouble,' persisted Thane. 'Even before the fire.'

'Which means you've been talking with his top cop friend Farrell over in Inverness.' Lisa Rankin had deep blue eyes and they had hardened a little. 'My father enjoys gloom and despair. But just this once it looks like he was right.'

'Your father has never been anybody's fool, Lisa.' Alex Korski gave a small, dry laugh. 'As his daughter, you should know that.' The small, balding distillery manager looked at Thane. 'This story about a car with two dead men aboard – is it true?'

Thane nodded.

'I'm glad,' said Lisa Rankin almost viciously. The long scar on her cheek deepened with anger. 'I hope they rot in hell, whoever they were. The lost whisky doesn't matter. Maybe Iain Cameron was no great shakes at anything – even as a night-watchman. But even so . . .'

'Nobody deserves that kind of dying.' Thane finished it for her. 'Do you usually have only one watchman on duty at night?'

'That's the normal. But he wasn't always alone. There's often a night-shift team working in the distillery.'

'But not last weekend?' Thane scraped a thumb along his chin as she shook her head. 'How long in advance do you give warning of night shifts coming up?'

She sighed, understanding. 'Usually at least a month.'

'And they're easy enough to find out about?'

'Very easy.' She bit her lower lip, frowning.

'Any other security?'

'For the main distillery building, yes – we have automatic alarms linked to Broch Castle. There's a video security camera at the reception area.'

'But not for anywhere else inside the perimeter fence?'

'No.' She shook her head. 'I take it you don't think much of our security, superintendent.'

'I don't,' he agreed. 'What about the main gate?'

The blonde woman shrugged. 'In daylight hours, it just lies open. The rest of the time, when it's closed, the night-watchman turns away visitors.' She gave a defensive frown. 'This isn't the city, superintendent. The perimeter fence is meant to keep out deer from the hills, not people. We – oh hell, understand it, will you?'

'I'll try,' said Thane.

Lisa Rankin sighed. 'Around these hills the worst insult people can still hand a neighbour is to lock their own house door – whether they're in or out. Plenty of doors haven't been locked in years. We call it trust, superintendent. It's still not totally extinct.'

'I've heard of it.' And envied a fading way of life. He switched to something else. 'What about today? Why did your father leave the way he did?'

'Ask him. I don't know.' She pursed her lips. 'He simply walked into my office, said he had to go home and was gone. Then ' – she gestured towards Korski – 'next thing Alex had this problem turn up.'

'It's not a big deal, superintendent,' murmured Korski. 'Sometimes there's a fermentation problem, like now. We're agreed what to do.' He indicated the washback tub. 'This batch is being lazy. We'll give it a little quality time and maybe an extra dusting of yeast' – he grinned – 'which I would deny under oath.'

'I won't tell,' said Thane stonily. Most of his attention was still on Lisa Rankin. He mentally slotted the blonde woman as in her early thirties. Even that cruel facial scar failed to destroy her striking good looks. Those clear blue eyes were set in a firmly boned face, she had strong white teeth, and she had the kind of generous mouth which should have been meant to enjoy laughter. Build perfectly proportioned to her height, she had good muscle tone, firm breasts, and a slim waist—

'Superintendent? Are you with us?' Her voice brought him

back him to reality. Korski had switched his attention back to the washback tub. Whatever Lisa Rankin had said and Thane had missed, she was waiting for an answer.

'Sorry.' He gave an apologetic grin. 'My mind drifted.'

'It doesn't matter.' She was frowning, meaning it did. 'I said if you want to meet my father I'll drive you over to Broch Castle. It isn't far.'

'I'd appreciate that.' Thane nodded. 'I should let the sergeant know.'

'Jazz.' She turned to the girl. 'Tell the sergeant we've gone over to see my father. She can collect her boss later.' She let Jazz leave through another door, then switched her attention to Korski. 'Alex, sort out this washback thing. Then have a team run a full diagnostic check on the rest. One like this is enough – however it happened.'

'I'm on it now,' Korski promised.

'Hold on.' Thane stopped him as he made to turn away. 'In your job, you keep an ear close to the ground, right?'

'I – uh – suppose so.' The small, balding manager was obviously uncomfortable.

'Then you know what I'm talking about, Mr Korski,' said Thane softly. 'What hints of trouble coming did you pick up?'

'Me?' Korski made it a startled squeak. His face flushed red, almost as red as his shirt. 'None. At least, none that – that I thought mattered!'

'Nothing from Iain Cameron?' pressed Thane. 'Nothing from Donny Adams, with his grudge about losing his foreman's job?'

'Donny the Shovel?' Lisa Rankin gave a harsh hoot of disbelief. 'No way. Not him!'

'A few of the lads maybe talk wild at times.' Alex Korski moistened his lips. 'But talk is cheap, superintendent. Talk doesn't light fires or kill people. Donny Adams can shout and yell. But that's where it ends. I know him!'

'Think about it,' said Thane softly. 'Then tell Adams we'll be round to see him later.'

Swallowing, Korski nodded and beat a retreat. Lisa Rankin considered Thane for a moment then offered what came close to an apology.

'Alex isn't much of a management pillar of strength,' she admitted wryly. 'But he's a damned good technician.'

42

'And you don't think much of Donny Adams as part of your trouble?'

'It's like Alex says. Adams likes making a noise – he'll make bullets as long as someone else will fire them. But he's too dim to be much of a conspirator.' Lisa Rankin dismissed the thought then glanced at her wristwatch. 'If you're ready to go, I 'll collect a jacket from my office – I can get it as we leave.'

They went out through the door Jazz had used. There was a blank-walled corridor on the far side.

'We were told that you Crime Squad people were coming up from Glasgow,' said Lisa Rankin as they walked along. 'Isn't it overkill?'

'Sometimes we're like the cavalry,' began Thane. 'It's called mutual aid—'

He broke off. The scream and the noise of a scuffle came from beyond a turn in the corridor just ahead. Glass smashed. There was another scream, a man's cursing yell of pain – and by then Thane was already on his way, charging along the corridor's concrete floor, Lisa Rankin close at his heels.

Another moment, and he skidded around the corner. The length of corridor ahead was a line of office doors, one of them lying half off its hinges, a glass upper panel smashed, two people wrestling in the opening. One was a tall, thin man in overalls and with a balaclava mask with crude eyeholes hiding his face. He was struggling with a noisy, yelling Jazz Gupatra – and it was the girl who would not let go.

Thane raced to close the gap, his mind registering that the man was wearing bright yellow household rubber gloves. But suddenly, the stranger shifted his grip, straightened, lifted his slightly built opponent off her feet, and threw her bodily out across the corridor. Jazz Gupatra gave a startled yelp, thudded into the opposite wall, then went down. The stranger didn't wait. Turning, ignoring Thane racing towards him, he sprinted down the corridor, reached a fire door and slammed his way through, leaving the door swinging wildly.

For Thane, things suddenly began to go wrong. He tried to hurdle the sprawl of Jazz's denim clad legs and promptly collided hard with Lisa Rankin. The tall blonde grabbed at him for support as they both almost went down.

'Look where you're damned well going!' The woman made it

43

a near snarl, clung to Thane as she regained her balance, then thrust him away. 'I'm all right. Get him!' Thane galloped on again, reached the swinging fire door, charged through it, and immediately collided with someone new who tried to grapple with him. As a fist swung towards his head, he instinctively blocked the punch, slammed his right at the other man's unguarded middle, then cursed and tried to take the worst of the force out of his blow before it connected.

'Back off, you idiot!' he raged. 'It's me!'

'Sir – I'm sorry . . .' A confused, partly winded Detective Constable Harron staggered clear. 'I thought—'

'Don't even try thinking,' snarled Thane. The corridor was empty. 'Where did he go?'

'Through there.' Harron pointed vaguely at an archway gap in the line of office doors. 'I – I thought you were another one—' Then the Northern man's discomfiture was complete as Sandra Craig came dashing from the other end of the long corridor. Joan Kerr, who came close behind her, was armed with a whisky bottle held like a baton.

'Out of the way!' Thane shoved past Harron, reached the archway gap between the doors, then found himself in a small extension stub to the main corridor. There were two doors at the end, the right-hand closed and marked Toilets, the left-hand lying open.

He chose the left, plunged out into open air at the rear of the distillery building then came to a breathless halt as Sandra Craig joined him. They looked around at an empty hill wasteland of heather and stunted, yellow-tipped gorse. He could see nothing that moved.

'Over there!' Sandra pointed. 'The birds!'

A noisy flock of irate crows were exploding out of one patch of gorse and circling angrily – then a moment later their cawing was drowned by the start-up howl of a high-revving engine. The snarling source appeared, a motor cycle which bounced and bucked along as it gathered speed. The man in overalls was aboard, standing high out of the saddle in trials rider style while the machine clawed for grip on its knobbled cross-country tyres. Engine note rising and falling, it raced off across the rough hillside.

'And that's that!' There was disgust in Lisa Rankin's husky voice as she arrived and glared at the snaking ribbon of dust thrown up as the motor cycle kept travelling. 'Damn him, he's good!'

'Yes.' Thane sucked sadly on his closed teeth. 'Do you know anyone around here who can ride a bike that way?'

'Plenty of them. Half the shepherds and gamekeepers this side of the Highland Line use trail bikes. It's like they were born with wheels instead of feet.'

'Sir?' Sandra made it a query.

Thane shook his head. Attempting any kind of search or pursuit would be a waste of time. He stood with the two women and they watched in silence as the speeding, bouncing motor cycle disappeared from view behind a fold of ground and the sound of the high-revving engine faded. Then they went back into the building, where an uneasy Harron was standing in the corridor with Joan Kerr, who had a protective arm around Jazz's slim shoulders.

'What happened?' Thane asked Jazz.

The young student grimaced. 'Shouldn't you ask how I'm feeling?'

'If that's what you want,' said Thane dryly.

'And that makes you a caring cop?' Jazz flicked a long lock of black hair away from her face and winced at the effort. The young student's pigtails had lost their tartan ribbons and her floppy white wool sweater had been badly torn at one shoulder. 'It hurts when I move, but I don't think he broke anything.' She sighed. 'What happened? I was on my way back to the general office like I was told—'

'Taking a different route,' reminded Thane.

'So I like a change.' Jazz shrugged. 'I heard noises coming from Miss Lisa's room. Because I knew she wasn't there, I looked in – prize mistake number one. Our friend Balaclava Bert was there, going through her desk. It looked like he'd been at the filing cabinets. Then I didn't get out fast enough – prize mistake number two.'

'And he wasn't Donny Adams?'

'No way.' The pigtails twitched an emphatic negative. 'Wrong build, and our Donny has halitosis that kills at fifty feet.'

Stifling a grin, Thane looked in at the open door of Lisa Rankin's office. Then his grin faded. The intruder had come close to trashing the room, which was dominated by her desk and a blank-eyed computer screen. Filing cabinet drawers lay open and their contents had been thrown around. Desk drawers had been hauled out and emptied, photographs were scattered on the floor.

'Can you think of anything he could have been after?' he asked Lisa Rankin, and tried to hide his disappointment as she shook her head. 'Then will you check if anything obvious is missing?'

'Fingerprints, sir,' protested Harron.

'He wore gloves,' countered Thane bleakly. 'Or didn't you notice?'

Lisa Rankin looked into the trashed office, shook her head in disbelief at what she saw. The Northern man swallowed then hastily stepped back to allow Lisa Rankin to go past him and into the trashed office. She crossed over, grimaced, then went in. Some distillery workers had appeared as a background audience at the far end of the corridor, but were content to stay there.

Thane drew a deep breath and sighed. 'Sandra. You first.'

'We heard screams, we came running.' She left it there.

'Harron?'

'I was looking for you, sir,' said DC Harron warily.

'Why?'

'Something I'd been told, something I thought you'd want to know. I – well, I found Sergeant Craig, she told me where you'd gone.' The long-faced Northern detective glanced uneasily for support. 'I was on my way when I heard the screams—'

'I do a good scream,' agreed Jazz cheerfully.

'Screams, sir,' emphasized Harron. 'I came running, in time to see this character with the balaclava mask crash through that swing door and disappear. Then another – uh—'

'Large thug?' suggested Sandra helpfully.

'Another person' – Harron glared at her – 'came crashing through the same swing door. So I – I tried to stop him. I'm sorry, superintendent.'

Thane shrugged with minimal sympathy. First there had been the delay when he and Lisa Rankin had collided, then the way had been blocked by Harron's clumping charge – the lost seconds put together became enough for the motor cycle intruder to make his escape. An intruder who very obviously knew his way around Broch Distillery, and who had also planned his escape route in advance.

'Why come looking for me?' he repeated.

'You told me to question my way around the distillery staff, sir.' Harron made an attempt at a smile. 'Isaiah Six, Eight, sir. "Whom will I send, and who will go for us?" You sent me. I got lucky . . .'

'Miracles can happen,' muttered Sandra Craig.

'Sergeant.' Thane gave her a glare. 'Go on, Harron.'

'One of the warehouse team says he remembers a blue Nissan stopped outside here last Thursday.' Harron rushed his words in his eagerness. 'His name is Peter Bell, he usually heads home during his lunchbreak, which is what he did. He saw the car parked at the side of the road when he was coming back.'

Thane stiffened. 'What else does he remember?'

'That the car wasn't local, sir – Bell certainly didn't know it – and that he thinks there were two men aboard.' The Northern man showed his chipped teeth in a cautious grin. 'It's all he remembers, except that later the car had gone.'

Thane glanced at Joan Kerr. 'Can we trust Bell?'

'He's reliable, superintendent.' She nodded firmly. 'If Peter Bell says the Nissan was there, it was there.'

A filing cabinet drawer slammed shut inside Lisa Rankin's office. Something fell, they heard her soft cursing, another drawer slammed, then after a few moments the blonde woman came out into the corridor.

'It's a shambles,' she declared, anger in her husky voice. 'God knows what he was after – we don't keep cash in there. The only money is in my handbag, which hasn't been touched, there's nothing obvious missing. But it's like a hurricane went through those files—'

'What was in them?'

Lisa Rankin shook her head. 'Everything and anything to do with production data – despatch notes, duplicate invoices, copy export documents. If he took anything, I won't know till I miss it.' She paused and frowned. 'Joan, for anything vital we'll have computer disc back-up, right?'

The older woman nodded.

'So at least that's not a problem.' The blue eyes brightened with relief. 'Well, what now, superintendent?'

'I need to meet your father,' said Thane. 'More than ever.'

He handed things over to Sandra Craig. She could put Harron back to trawling for witnesses – which would please both of them. The pigtailed Jazz volunteered to start sorting out the blizzard of scattered papers in Lisa Rankin's office. Two of the brawnier distillery workers would stay handy against any outside chance of the rubber-gloved raider returning. Sandra would keep tabs on everything else.

'One more thing.' Thane eased her away from the others. 'What have you got from Joan Kerr?'

'So far, not a lot, sir.' The redhead made an attempt to hide a chocolate bar she'd been nibbling, then gave up and gave him a couple of squares. 'But I'd like to keep trying.'

'Do it.' Hungry, Thane bit on the chocolate. 'Don't forget we've got our borrowed policewoman from Inverness—'

'Maggie Donald.' Sandra grinned. 'Not much chance of that.'

'When she shows up again, get her to organize sleeping quarters for our people.' Thane wondered if Sandra knew she had left small tempting crumbs of chocolate at the corners of her mouth. 'They'll need food to match – or they'll start beating Police Federation drums.'

'There's talk of the Federation voting me in as next Crime Squad delegate,' murmured Sandra. 'Francey Dunbar's term is almost up.'

'God,' said Thane gloomily.

Then they left it there as Lisa Rankin joined them. She had fetched a grey suede jacket from her room and wore it draped loosely over her shoulders. She was also carrying a large deerskin handbag.

'Ready?' she asked.

'Ready,' Thane agreed. They headed out.

Lisa Rankin owned a cherry red Lancia sports coupé, and drove with little respect for either her passenger or vehicle. Her tyres scattered gravel as they left the distillery parking lot, a long blast of the Lancia's horn took them past an incoming truck as they reached the public road. Then, making a fierce gear change, she headed north.

'How far?' asked Thane, while the sports coupé's white on black instruments climbed and the engine rasped.

'Minutes.' Lisa Rankin swore mildly as the Lancia bottomed hard on a pot-hole and her steering wheel shook with the vibration. She nodded at the narrow ribbon of road ahead. 'Over that line of hills you're at the start of Glen Laggan – then Ardshona township first, with Broch Castle just beyond it.'

'Fine.' Thane winced and gripped the facia rim as they took a bend in a way that tested the little car's suspension. 'Are we in a rush?'

'No.' Surprised, she eased back on the accelerator.

'Good.' Thane considered the empty moorland scenery for a moment, then turned in the passenger seat to face her. 'Lisa,' – he raised his voice above the engine note – 'what's this all about? What's been going on?'

Taken off guard, she gave him a quick glance. Suddenly, her scarred but beautiful face could have been carved from stone, her blue eyes had become like icechips. Then, just as quickly, her attention was back on the road.

'Ask my father,' she said bitterly. Her right foot hit the Lancia's accelerator and the engine boomed as its rev counter swung and the cherry red sports coupé gained speed. 'How the hell would I know, superintendent?'

They drove on in silence, past some rough grazing jointly shared by a few Blackface sheep and a handful of brown and shaggy long-horned Highland cattle. Then the road topped a long rise of ground and travelled down into a narrow, tree-fringed valley. The sun glinted on a ribbon of a stream from the far end of the glen. A thin scatter of stone-built cottages clung around it, and as the Lancia travelled on, Thane could smell wood-smoke coming from their chimneys.

'Ardshona township, superintendent.' Lisa Rankin ended her silence without looking at him. 'And Broch.'

'Got it.' Beyond the cottages, partly screened by trees, sat an early Victorian-style mansion. Built of grey local stone, it had turret windows at each corner, a modest surround of shrubbed gardens, and the flat roof sported an incongruous satellite TV dish. 'That's home?'

'Home.' The blonde nodded, her manner partly thawed. 'Not exactly a palace, not half as big as it looks, but we like it – and the first year my father had spare cash, we put in central heating.'

The car reached the start of the little township and murmured on. There was a small schoolhouse and a tiny Free Presbyterian church. One of the two other buildings of any size was a modest general store. The other, the Ardshona Inn, was an old two-storey inn with a thatched roof and a painted nameboard. Two women were gossiping in the street, and a child playing outside the general store waved a greeting as Lisa Rankin flashed the Lancia's headlights.

Once past the last of the houses, Lisa Rankin turned off the main road, steered between a pair of stone pillars, and then they were on the start of a narrow gravelled driveway hedged by rhododendron bushes in full flower. At the end, Broch Castle lay ahead. It was fronted by a modest band of grass and shrubs, then there was a parking area where a grey Volvo station wagon shared space with a vintage, travel-stained jeep and small white Ford Escort.

'Better make sure they're awake,' said Lisa Rankin, and gave two short blasts on the Lancia's horn. Then she parked her vehicle next to the Volvo, drew on the handbrake, and switched off the engine. They climbed out of the car, walked across the gravel, then went up six steps to a front archway topped by a carved stone shield. A large door in the archway was dark, solid oak, and was lying open. They went through into a long hallway which was bright with vases filled with flowers. There were colourful scatter rugs on the polished wood flooring. Several rooms led off the hallway, and spiral staircases with metal balustrade rails climbed up at either end.

'Hi, Lisa!' greeted a tall slim woman in her late twenties, coming towards them. She had long, chestnut hair, wore a knee-length black skirt with an open-necked white shirt and brown leather sandals, and considered Thane with some curiosity. 'Company?'

'Police,' said Lisa Rankin. She kept the introductions brief. 'Superintendent Thane, my sister Anna.' She paused just long enough to let her sister smile a greeting. 'Where's father?'

'Here,' said a male voice from above. 'What's going on?'

Thane looked up. A man with a lean, weatherbeaten face and closely cut white hair was frowning down from the top of the nearest spiral staircase. Finn Rankin didn't seem overjoyed at having a visitor.

'I'll come up, father,' Lisa Rankin acknowledged, then faced Thane. 'Please wait.'

She headed for the spiralling stairway and went up. At the

top, she took her father by the arm, spoke briefly, then they vanished from sight.

'You've come from the distillery?' asked Anna. She sighed when he nodded. 'More trouble?'

'A break-in,' said Thane.

'Serious?'

'We don't know,' admitted Thane. 'Not yet.'

'Damn. Haven't we had enough?' She frowned towards the top of the stairs. 'I'm sorry you're being kept waiting. Courtesy isn't Lisa's middle name.'

'I had that feeling,' admitted Thane.

'We're inclined to be that kind of a family.' Anna Rankin paused as another door opened at the far end of the hallway and an attractive woman in her fifties, her grey hair fashionably short, looked in. Anna smiled and raised her voice. 'No problem, Jonesy – just Lisa and a stray gendarme. Lisa's with Dad.'

The woman returned the smile and vanished. The door closed again.

'Another relative?' queried Thane.

'Jonesy?' The brunette shook her head. 'Say housekeeper.' A roguish glint of humour showed in her dark brown eyes. 'At least, for tax purposes. More than that, ask my dad. Will that do?'

'I reckon.' Thane grinned and scraped a thumbnail along his chin. Anna Rankin and her sister, age and appearance apart, shared some family traits in several ways. 'One problem I've got in all this is that I'm an outsider—'

'I'd heard,' she agreed dryly, understanding. 'You're saying it might help if you knew more about us, as a family?'

'It might.'

'All right.' She nodded slowly. 'You probably know most of it. There's Finn Rankin and the three Rankin daughters. My mother was killed in a car crash when I was so young I hardly remember her.' She stopped for a moment, rubbing a pattern on the polished wood floor with the toe of one sandal. 'After that it was just Dad and the three of us for a lot of years. Until – thank God – Jonesy came along.'

'Which is none of my business.'

'No. But it maybe helps that you know.' Anna Rankin said it

51

deliberately. 'So ... the rest is that Dad runs Broch Distilleries as executive chairman. As the oldest, Lisa is his deputy and also production director. Middle sister Gina is blending director. She's located away from here, down in Ayrshire, where we blend and bottle our economy malt, Broch Highland Label.' She gave a small twinkle of a smile. 'Gina is married to a gem of a man, Robert Martin, our head blender. Right now they're happily pregnant and Dad is expecting his first grandchild.'

'And where does Anna fit in?' asked Thane mildly.

'I'm a qualified solicitor and the firm's legal director, God help me.' She used a hand to brush back a strand of that long chestnut hair, shaped her mouth in a comic grimace. 'Don't ask about the rest. I was married, but not for long – it ended messily, I came back to the nest.'

Thane nodded. Anna Rankin didn't look like the conventional solicitor. Thankfully, few of them did any more – and the rest of what she'd told him was enough of a thumbnail CV for the moment.

'How about Lisa?'

'Everyone needs a big sister. We've got one,' said Anna Rankin dryly. 'There's no particular man hanging round her neck, if that's what you really want to know. They come and they go, like the seasons.'

'What about your sales director – is Morris Currie family?'

She blinked and almost laughed. 'Thank God, no – and he's the only other director we've got. There was – well, a reason when it happened. Like we inherited him, you understand?'

'No.' Thane shook his head. 'Just that it isn't all sweetness and light when he's around.'

'He knows his job.' She shrugged. 'He just happens to be an awkward swine.' Then she paused with some relief. 'There we are! That didn't take long!'

Her sister came back down the spiral stairway, her scarred face empty of expression, her blue eyes hard to read. Lisa Rankin stopped on the botom tread, one hand resting on the balustrade rail.

'You've to go up, superintendent.' Her mouth tightened. 'He knows what happened.'

Thane went past her and climbed the winding metal staircase. He reached an upper floor, where framed prints of Highland

52

animal life, from foxes to wildcats, decorated the walls, then saw a narrow, separate flight of steps leading on again.

'Up here, superintendent.' Finn Rankin appeared at the top of the new flight and beckoned.

Another twenty or so steps brought Thane face to face with Finn Rankin. He shook hands with a tall, very thin man who topped him in height by at least a couple of inches. The Broch Distillery chairman looked in his early sixties, with his crop of white hair framing a lean, heavily lined face which had prominent cheekbones, large ears, a beak of a nose, hazel eyes, and a thin-lipped mouth. Whatever his mood earlier, he now seemed more placid.

'We should have met earlier.' The older man, made it a partial apology. 'Something turned up – personal.' He was wearing a blue folk-weave cotton shirt and light-coloured corduroy trousers with a thick leather belt which had a large silver buckle. His feet were in scuffed suede ankle boots. 'Still, let's get on with this.'

He beckoned, and Thane followed him through into a large turret-shaped room, part study, with a desk, computer screen and a telephone-fax, and part personal retreat with a leather couch, deep armchairs, and a small bar. There were large windows. One window looked east over the rhododendrons towards the village. Another, behind the desk, faced north towards hills and heather. But much of its view was occupied by the same giant sandstone beehive he'd seen in the reception area photograph. A fallen section revealed an outer wall of at least twelve feet thick. He guessed the beehive peak was over thirty feet in height. When the Picts built their fortress brochs, they were meant to last.

'You'll have a drink. The proprietor's reserve,' said Finn Rankin, kicking the room door shut behind him. If he noticed Thane's interest in the view, he ignored it. The man opened the bar front, produced tumblers, then another bottle of the whisky which had no label, and poured two generous measures. Reaching into the bar again, he brought out a jug. 'Water?'

'If it's allowed,' said Thane wryly. It was well after four p.m., late afternoon, a long time since his last proper meal.

'This water is – rainwater, straight from our own butt.' Broch's chairman splashed water, gave one tumbler to Thane, and gestured a fractional toast. 'Slainte.'

'Slainte.' Thane savoured an unhurried swallow from his glass, enjoyed the liquor's smooth fire of a journey down his throat, then took a second look at a framed colour photograph he'd already noted on Finn Rankin's desk. It was a group shot of Rankin, the woman called Jonesy, his daughters Lisa and Anna, and a third girl whose identity was easy to guess. Lisa was blonde, Anna was a chestnut brunette, this other girl had glinting hair which was a deep rich brown. The likenesses between all three left no doubt.

'Gina?' he asked.

'Gina,' agreed Rankin proudly. 'And – uh – you know about Jonesy?'

'I know about Jonesy.'

'My wife—'

'Was killed in a car crash,' nodded Thane.

'She was driving. Lisa was in the car – she was seven years old.' For a moment, Rankin seemed to age with the memory.

'I wondered.' Thane thought of the scar.

'Plastic surgeons tried their best.' The man took a deep breath, and showed no sign of sitting down. 'So – you're here, you've questions. Let's have them.'

'For now, they're basic,' said Thane. 'Who doesn't like you – doesn't like you enough to hate your guts?' He raised a slightly sardonic eyebrow. 'Do you still think you could be talking about some crazy brand of Highland industrial relations feud?'

'It still could be possible.' Finn Rankin said it slowly, almost painfully.

'Not business, not personal?'

'The warehouse fire was plain sabotage, superintendent,' said Rankin. He scowled and set down his glass on the desk. 'But why kill a night-watchman I think that was just as much an accident as these men being killed when their car crashed.' The white-haired man chewed his lower lip. A few tiny beads of perspiration had appeared on his forehead and he wiped them away with the back of one hand. 'There's one bottom line nobody can deny. Someone has been making trouble for us – I'm damned if I know who, I'm damned if I know why.'

'You've no notion?'

'None.' Finn Rankin didn't hide his underlying tension. But somehow it wasn't the kind of tension Thane usually identified with anger. Finn Rankin had to be worried, maybe even frightened. At a guess, there was something the man knew, something he was determinedly keeping to himself, whatever its importance.

'There's another mystery, Mr Rankin.' Thane kept his manner friendly, his voice neutral. 'Why would someone want to break into your daughter's office?'

'How should I know?' Rankin scowled. 'Maybe he was some kind of opportunist rat who thought he'd catch us with our guard down.' He jammed his hands deep in the pockets of his corduroys and took a deep breath. 'Look, try to remember I'm the one who went to Inverness and told Mick Farrell we had problems here.'

'I haven't forgotten,' murmured Thane. 'You're friendly with Chief Superintendent Farrell?'

'We fish together. We've gone deer stalking.' The man shrugged. 'No more than that.'

'I understand.' Without waiting to be asked, Thane settled into an armchair. 'Why don't we do the rest of this the easy way? Suppose you sit down, suppose we talk – from the beginning?'

'I've done it already—'

'Not with me,' said Thane quietly.

For a long moment, Finn Rankin stood tight-lipped. The only sound in the turret room was the buzz of a fly as it explored a window. Suddenly the man sighed and sat in another chair.

'Go on.'

'Here's a start,' said Thane in a deliberately amiable voice. 'Morris Currie. You had a shouting match with him yesterday. Why?'

'Business.' Rankin made it a growl. 'And damn all to do with you, Thane.'

'Sorry.' Thane shook his head. 'Not good enough. And I don't fish, I don't shoot. So don't waste my time and I won't waste yours. I asked why.'

Startled anger showed on Rankin's face, then gave way to something else which could almost have been bitter amusement.

'I said business. Currie says he can clinch a new export order if someone gets an extra slice of commission.' He snorted. 'We disagreed on how much of a slice. Maybe things got noisy.'

Thane switched to the initial troubles at the distillery, then on from there while time slipped past for a full half-hour. But the stony-faced whisky executive's story didn't change. Not even in detail – which was unusual on its own. He mentally corrected himself – not unusual, too good to be true.

The telephone on Rankin's desk rang twice while they talked. The first time, Rankin rose, went over, briefly lifted the receiver, then dumped it down again on its cradle. The second time, the instrument gave a single 'ting' then went silent in a way that meant it had been answered in another room.

There was one further interruption. A light knock on the room door made them look round. The door opened, and the grey-haired, good-looking woman Thane had seen earlier looked in. She ignored Thane, her eyes on Rankin.

'Finn?' She made it a simple question.

'Jonesy.' Finn Rankin gave her a slight, reassuring smile. He indicated Thane. 'Did you meet Superintendent Thane?'

'The girls told me about you, superintendent.' The woman stayed at the doorway.

'Which sounds like a problem.' Thane returned her greeting with a slight smile.

'I wouldn't say so.' She switched her attention back to Rankin. 'All right, Finn. I'll leave you in peace.'

She went out and the door closed.

'So—' the woman's interruption seemed to have had an immediate, reassuring effect on Finn Rankin – 'what's left?'

'Let's call it finished for now,' said Thane, knowing he was running out of questions that mattered.

'I know the rest of it.' The man surprised him with a grin. 'If I remember anything, let you know. Right?'

Thane nodded, rose, and went over to the turret room windows. There was still no sign of either Sandra Craig or a police car outside. Crossing to the other window, he looked down at the stone beehive shape of the Pictish broch.

'Do you do a guided tour?' he asked.

'No problem – I'll arrange it.' Rankin added a warning. 'Don't try to explore on your own, superintendent. Stonework so old is loose, dangerous. But take a walk around the outside if you want.'

He opened the door, went with Thane down to the start of the main circular stairway, offered a perfunctory handshake, then left his visitor. The man went back up to his turret room, went inside, and the door slammed shut.

Thane stood where he was for a moment, looked up, then drew in a deep breath.

'You're lying, Rankin,' he told the closed door softly. 'Why, I don't know – but I'm going to find out.'

The other residents at Broch Castle had gone to earth. When Colin Thane went down the spiral stairway to ground level he found the long hall deserted and all its internal doors closed. The main outer door was still open, and he left the grey mock-medieval Victorian building, glad to feel the warmth of the sun again on his back.

The dog had stopped barking, there was only the distant sound of a powered chain-saw. He wandered around the castle garden area for a spell, then saw a slabbed path which led in a wide curve towards the rear of the building.

Towards the rear, and maybe towards the Pictish broch. Curiosity started him walking along the path, which took him through the formal garden area then a vegetable patch behind the castle and snaked on through long grass and scrub. The slabs underfoot became broken, covered with weeds and rabbit droppings.

He was right. The broch lay ahead, an awesomely impressive memorial to an ancient, long-vanished tribe. Years of work had gone into bringing together the vast amount of stone needed to construct that primitive beehive shape, and it was much larger than he'd thought. As he walked around the rough outside wall, a gnarled tree growing out of one crack and another section fallen in, he revised his guesswork. That outer wall was a lot more than twelve feet thick, the dome height was considerably over his guess of thirty feet.

For the people of the Iron Age, a broch had been a strong-hold, its strength its own security. There were a few tiny loopholes, no arrow-slits, no outer defences. Only those great walls with each piece of dry stone placed to match against another, and only one entrance – small and low, framed by three massive slabs of rock, guarded by a twentieth-century door with a large steel lock. A sign nailed to the gate warned 'PRIVATE – KEEP OUT'.

Thane went over to the door, tried rattling it with one hand, then sprang back, startled, as a large black crow exploded out of a nearby gap in the stonework in cawing indignation. As the bird flapped away there was the sharp whip-like crack of a single shot. A bullet slammed into the stonework and gouged sharp chips of rock, then it whined away in a wild ricochet.

He saw a movement and a glint of light over among nearby bushes then dropped down, his face only a hand's width away from a dried patch of deer dung. Dry-mouthed, Thane moved a little – and another shot smashed into the stonework above his head. He went down again.

This time, he stayed where he was. The weapon had sounded like a .22 rifle, the glint could have been a telescopic sight. At that range, even a second-rate shot could have taken him out – if that had been the idea.

A full minute passed. Thane heard rustling from over among the bushes, then a strange, mocking laugh. Something moved very near to him, and he half-turned, to meet the face of a friendly mongrel whose mother had probably been a sheepdog. The mongrel's tail thrashed, it came nearer, then Thane was having his face thoroughly licked.

'Good boy.' He fended the dog off with one hand, listening.

The rustling among the bushes had ended. He waited another full minute then cautiously got to his feet. Nothing happened, except the dog brought him a stick. Sighing, he took the stick, threw it, and the dog went chasing off.

On the way back, he took a route through the bushes. He found a patch where the undergrowth had been flattened, but nothing more. He went on, passing close to Broch Castle again. Whatever they'd heard, whatever they'd seen, nothing stirred.

He went on grimly. Then, as he reached the driveway area at the front of the big house, he heard the sound of a vehicle approaching. In another moment the big Northern Constabulary Range Rover came crunching over the gravel and halted beside him. Maggie Donald smiled at him from behind the wheel, then Sandra Craig opened a passenger door.

'Been waiting long?' asked his sergeant as he got aboard. Then her eyes narrowed. 'What's been happening, sir? You've got mud on your clothes.'

'That's not a surprise, sergeant.' His mouth a tight line, Thane glanced back at the castle but said nothing more.

The policewomen looked at each other, puzzled. Sandra nodded, Maggie Donald thumped a foot on the Range Rover's accelerator pedal, the V8 engine bellowed, and they took off in a scatter of gravel.

'I've a few things to tell you, sir,' said Sandra Craig as the vehicle swayed along. 'You could be surprised.'

Thane nodded. But he had already decided not to be surprised by anything.

3

Dusk was greying from the hills when a convoy of travel-grimed police vehicles finally reached the little Highland township and drew up in a half-circle to one side of the patch of communal grazing ground which acted as Ardshona's centre.

Rested, already fed and watered, leaning on the porch rail outside the Ardshona Inn, Colin Thane knew unqualified relief as some familiar Crime Squad faces showed among the arrivals who came with the vehicles. That went double for the first passenger to emerge. Detective Inspector Phil Moss, small, scrawny, crumpled as ever, looked around with a city dweller's natural distrust of open spaces short on bricks and mortar. Then Jock Dawson, the Squad's specialist dog-handler, appeared from the elderly Land-Rover he'd been driving and opened its rear door. Two dogs bounded out, furiously sniffing the air, tails thrashing.

Two more members of the Crime Squad team came out of another car, to be joined by a handful of Northern Constabulary uniformed men as the remaining vehicles emptied. Thane hadn't expected Andy Mack, the veteran Northern CID inspector, to come up with the convoy, but he was there accompanied by two strangers in civilian suits. Moving around them all were Sandra Craig and Maggie Donald, busily explaining arrangements to the new arrivals.

'Phil!' Thane hailed Moss from the Ardshona's porch and beckoned. 'Over here!'

Moss heard him, saw him, gave a vague half-salute, then plodded over, and arrived on the porch. Uncertainty was written large on his thin face; he considered the ancient frontage of the tiny two-storey inn with unconcealed horror.

'This is it?'

'This – or nothing. Not within an hour's drive.' Sandra Craig

59

and Maggie Donald had carried out their own pre-emptive strike. They had taken over most of the inn, including every bedroom available. They had even found an empty storeroom at the rear which could be used as an incident room. He tried to sooth Moss's gathering frown. 'Things could be worse. The food is good, the beds look clean.'

'People say that about Jock Dawson's dog van.' Phil Moss gave a low-key rumble of a belch. Then, considering Thane again, he let his face thaw into a twist of a grin. 'And we've been having problems, have we?'

'It looks that way,' admitted Thane.

'Weren't you warned?' Moss delivered his own acid verdict. 'This part of the world is inhabited by thick sheep and mad Highlanders.'

Thane didn't argue.

They'd first served together when Thane, as a detective chief inspector, had been in charge of one of Glasgow's toughest waterfront CID divisions. Moss, although older and outranked, hadn't soured at being his second-in-command, and they'd built a reputation as a team feared by the city's dockside gangs. When Thane had been promoted out to the Scottish Crime Squad, that was when Moss had taken a break to have 'cut and weld' surgery for a long-tolerated duodenal ulcer. Afterwards Moss had been assigned to a non-operational desk job at Strathclyde force headquarters. Somehow, even though the surgery hadn't been a total success, he'd then managed a new transfer to an equally non-operational Scottish Crime Squad desk role, and had quickly forgotten most of the 'non-operational' part.

Together, they formed an ideal team. Thane knew the rules of the job and tried to work within them. But he was regularly behind in his dreaded paperwork, he was seldom a diplomat, and every now and again he would land in a situation where he had a hunch about things in a case and little else. Then his instinct was to abandon caution, charge in, and sweat out the results.

Which was when Moss often mattered most. A bachelor with thin, sandy hair, always shabbily dressed to the point where kind old ladies had been known to give him money in the street to buy a meal, Moss could sit, could listen, could assess – and be happily in his element. Dry, complaining, insolent, he could tackle the most tedious research job or analyse a tax return – then as if by magic produce a way that gave Thane a new chance to avert disaster.

It might be an odd partnership, but it worked.

For which fact Detective Superintendent Colin Thane had more than once said a silent, thankful prayer – even if he'd never have admitted it.

'So?' asked Moss, thrown by Thane's silence. 'What next?'

'Everybody gets fed and settled first. It's been a long day, Phil.' Over at the cars, Jock Dawson was already feeding his two dogs. Some of the new arrivals were making towards the Ardshona Inn's bar entrance. After their kind of day, a couple of ice-cool beers would be welcome. Thane watched the dogs for another moment, booting his mind into gear again. 'What's the score with you?'

'Pretty good. We hauled up the Nissan and body-bagged the dead. Everything is swept up and on its way to Inverness for forensic and autopsy tests.' Moss released another low-key belch then scratched pensively under one arm. 'We have a Northern casualty surgeon along with us, and Mick Farrell donated one of his best scenes of crime officers. I said we'd pick up their bar tabs.'

'Dear God!' Thane knew there wasn't much chance that either of the Northern pair were teetotal. 'What we've got is some additional minor mayhem and some thin-ice possibilities.' He sighed. 'Better let everyone know there's some maniac with a .22 rifle – probably with telescopic sights – who was maybe using me as a target.'

Moss blinked. 'What's maybe?'

'He didn't try too hard,' admitted Thane. 'Get some food, Phil – the venison pie is good, no antlers in the pastry.' He paused, glancing at his wrist-watch in the fast fading light. 'We'll have a Think Tank meeting an hour from now. Tell the troops.'

'An hour.' Moss nodded, took another suspicious look around at the shadowed landscape, then padded off.

Left alone, Thane relaxed against the porch rail. The smell of woodsmoke from township hearths was growing stronger on the Ardshona night air and a scatter of house lights were beginning to show. Ardshona – the township's name, he'd been told, was the old Gaelic word for Bliss. Further off, a distant black silhouette against the sky, the Dorsair ridge of mountain rock face translated as the Doorkeeper. Except that the Doorkeeper seemed to have let something other than Bliss slip through.

'A cool evening, superintendent,' said a gruff voice. 'We often get this north chill in the evenings.'

'I'm enjoying it, Andy – and the peace.' Thane considered the stockily built man coming towards him. Joan Kerr's telephone linesman husband had been rounded up by Sandra Craig or Maggie Donald – he wasn't sure which of them – then put to work, running temporary phone and fax lines into the empty storeroom. 'How's the installation work coming along?'

'Finished.' Andy Kerr, a friendly, square-faced man, grinned. 'It lets me feel I'm helping – though I'm still damned if I know why those Headquarters brains at Inverness won't use me or the wife when we're sworn-in Specials.' He took a step nearer, then considered the sky. 'No change yet. We could use some decent cloud and some real, normal rain. Och' – the linesman gave an odd grin then hesitated – 'but there's maybe one thing I should tell you. Now, kind of like in confidence, right?'

'Like in confidence.' Thane nodded. 'Go ahead.'

'It was crazy, but it happened.' Kerr lowered his voice. 'Just about a month ago, Finn Rankin offered me hard cash to check the telephones at Broch Castle and the distillery in case any of them were bugged.' He shrugged. 'I did, they weren't.'

Thane stared. 'Did Rankin say what gave him the idea?'

'Not that or anything else.' The linesman shook his head. 'I didn't ask, and I didn't tell Joan.'

'Does he know you're a Special?'

'Aye. But it isn't any kind of a crime to have your own phone checked, superintendent,' said Kerr placidly. 'Now I'm off home. Though I've a feeling I'll be damned lucky if there's any dinner on the table for me tonight.'

He turned and ambled off, leaving Colin Thane speechless. In another minute the linesman's British Telecom van started up, headlights sweeping down the line of parked police cars, and drove away. As it left, something large and dark and virtually silent swooped across the grazing ground across from the inn. The shape dived on its prey and something small and helpless died with a blood-curdling scream.

Drawing another breath of the woodsmoked air, Thane turned and went into the inn. The public bar was old and dark and busy, mostly filled by his own people, although a handful of sour-faced locals still clung to their territorial rights in one corner.

'Something I can get you, Mr Thane?' beamed the fat, bearded landlord serving drinks behind the bar. His name was Leckie Campbell, his wife, an equally large woman, ran the restaurant. The unexpected law-enforcement invasion was good news to them.

'Not now, but maybe later.' Thane recognized two of the locals as he left, faces from Broch Distillery, then passed the glass door which led into the dining room. He heard a furious clatter of crockery and caught a glimpse of Campbell's massive wife, now with an assistant drafted in from somewhere, serving food around her tables. A dark-haired, middle-aged woman, she saw him through the glass, beamed as broadly as her husband, but didn't stop working.

A stairway further along led up to the Ardshona bedrooms. He went past it, opened another glass-panelled door which led into a dimly lit backyard and crossed to the single-storey storeroom on the other side. The door there was heavy and creaked, but there was bright neon tube lighting inside. Thane stepped in, closed the door, and stared.

There had been a total transformation since his last visit. Then, the storeroom had had bare, whitewashed walls and a grubby concrete floor that had been littered with anonymous cardboard grocery boxes. Now it had been cleaned, with trestle tables carrying a spaghetti tangle of new wiring to link telephones and a fax machine. Chairs had appeared from somewhere, an ancient filing cabinet had been dragged in. A large scale map of Glen Laggan and another of the wider North Highland area had been pinned to one wall. A Mountain Rescue survival poster brightened another.

Sitting in the midst of everything, her red hair glinting like spun copper under the tube lights, Sandra Craig looked unusually pleased with herself – and only partly because of the transformation.

'Does everything work?' asked Thane, mainly to annoy her.

'Everything, sir.'

'Good.' He could see two of the telephones and the fax machine were monitor-proof encrypted Crime Squad equipment, newly arrived with the rest of his team. There were other boxes still to be unpacked. But his eyes strayed to a linked TV set and video player on one of the tables. They'd been borrowed from the Ardshona's public bar, another reason for the resident natives' smouldering wrath. 'Including these?'

She nodded.

'Show me again.'

His sergeant went over, flicked a couple of switches, inserted a tape in the video player's slot, pressed buttons, then stepped back and aimed the remote control unit in her hand. The TV screen quivered then came to life with a fast-moving picture while she watched numbers spin in one corner.

'Now.' She pressed another button.

The picture slowed to regular speed, firmed, and the screen filled with the grainy, jerky tape recorded by the security camera which covered the Broch Distillery main office and visitor reception area. Thane had watched the video twice before, on a small TV set in the Campbells' private sitting room.

They were there – the two men he'd only seen lying dead at the wrecked blue Nissan coupé. On tape, they were alive and smiling, one a fat, round face and close-clipped fair hair, the other older, balding, with a narrow face and wearing rimless spectacles. Both were casually dressed, both blended well into the small group of visitors who were being given an introductory talk by Joan Kerr before being taken on their tour around the distillery. There was no sound on the tape, but the faces showed smiles and silent laughter. The camera was positioned behind the woman and the lens was on fixed focus.

'There,' said Thane.

The remote control clicked and the TV picture froze, showing the group – nine visitors, including the two who mattered. Nine who had gone on the full distillery tour that Thursday morning, plus another man who had just walked in on the extreme edge of the screen and was standing apart from the others. He was flabby in build, he looked in his late fifties, he had long, mousey grey hair, and he wore grubby white overalls. It was a brief appearance. On tape, the man took one look at the visiting group, backed away and was gone. Donny Adams, the distillery's resident troublemaker, had been identified by Joan Kerr.

It had been Sandra Craig who had remembered the security TV camera covering the Broch general office and reception area, her notion to check the time-lapse security cassette around the time when the Nissan had been seen outside the distillery. It had paid off. The tape began as proof positive that the two strangers had visited that day. It established some kind of a link to Donny Adams – Joan Kerr had a vague memory that the man had looked in at the general office on an errand – and it also pointed to that day's entries in the distillery's Visitors Book. Nine names were listed for that morning tour. Four were a family party from Inverness, one was an elderly woman holidaying in the village, then came a German couple with an address in Munich. Last in the list, the two men who mattered, had written the needle-in-a-haystack names James Smith and John Brown, one with a scribbled, indecipherable address – the other with only a Glasgow G33 postcode.

Meaning someone had a sense of humour. Most cops and criminals in Scotland knew that G33 was the postcode address for the city's big, sour-smelling and overcrowded Barlinnie Prison, known to regulars as the Riddrie Hilton.

'Thanks, Sandra.' Thane sucked gently through his teeth as she switched off and the TV screen went blank, his thoughts already going in another direction. 'Any word from DC Harron?'

She shook her head.

Harry Harron wasn't making much progress on the new task he had been given, finding Donny Adams. So far, all that was known was that Adams had done a morning shift at the distillery, then had suddenly announced in the early afternoon that he wasn't feeling well and was going to take a rest break. Adams hadn't returned. He drove an old green Ford Thames pick-up truck, and it had also vanished. Adams was married and lived with his wife in a cottage on the edge of the township, but he wasn't there and his wife didn't consider it unusual for Adams to disappear without warning for a few days at a time.

'The woman is probably glad when it happens,' said his sergeant grimly. 'According to Harron—'

She stopped as one of the newly installed telephones began ringing, the sound echoing inside the bare brick of the storeroom walls. Thane reached it first, lifted the receiver, and answered.

'Colin, good!' A well-known voice came like a bellow in his ear. Commander Jack Hart, head of the Scottish Crime Squad, might have the best of new technology available but he resolutely refused to believe it was possible to hold an out-of-town tele-phone conversation at any level less than a shout. 'Bought yourself a kilt yet?'

'I want the bulletproof model,' said Thane stonily.

'Only if we can afford it,' Hart warned. The Squad commander, a total professional, now had to spend most of his time trapped behind a desk defending his modest budget against government cuts. 'How's it going?'

'The weather is good, so the locals want rain. Can you hold?' Thane glanced round at Sandra, who understood and quietly left. As the storeroom door closed behind her, he turned his attention back to the call. 'Things are getting complicated.'

'I've heard – and I've read everything that has come in.' Hart's peeved voice vibrated over the line. 'For God's sake, Colin, do you have to keep finding dead people? What's wrong with the live variety?'

'I'm trying.' Thane knew Jack Hart's moods. When Hart was annoyed, it could be like being attacked by a Rottweiler, and Hart could be annoyed for many reasons. Mary Thane and Hart's wife Gloria were allies in a couple of animal charity causes and some day would probably be arrested together – when Hart, he knew, would oppose bail. For both of them. He drew a breath and chose his words carefully. 'Your friend Mick Farrell isn't making my life easy.'

'Meaning?' It came as a growl. Hart was probably showing his fangs.

'I thought the Squad took on the Broch case as a favour. But Mick Farrell says no. He says that Northern Constabulary are up to their necks in a major operation – one nobody wants to talk about. We've simply been dragged in to plug a manpower gap.'

'He was supposed to keep his mouth shut,' said Hart, his voice indignant with embarrasment. 'But you've more or less got it right – and plugging gaps is good for public relations.' He fell silent, then gave a soft curse. 'I'm sorry, Colin. I was practically made to swear a blood oath on this one. I couldn't refuse, not when I was leaned on at high-grade government level. We're too near the time for our annual budget review. Northern do have a special operation to keep under wraps, but it really is "need-to-know" stuff.'

'And I don't need?'

'You don't,' confirmed Hart. 'Understood, Colin?'

'Understood.'

'And that's today's lesson in total quality management.' Hart sighed. 'As far as this Broch business goes, you'll get full support. There are some answers you wanted on the way to you now. Anything else you need, ask. Hell, man, think of it as a Highland holiday!'

'Thanks,' said Thane sarcastically.

He heard Hart chuckle, then the line went dead. As he replaced his own receiver, the fax machine came whirring to life. The leader sheet showed the incoming message was from Crime Squad operations desk. In that part, at least, Jack Hart was keeping his word.

Sandra Craig returned a little later. His sergeant came in, took one look at Thane's face and stayed quiet.

The conference team gathered on time, arriving over a couple of minutes, gossiping as they settled into chairs, some still nursing half-empty glasses, most of them obviously hoping that whatever was ahead wouldn't take long.

Out front and facing them with Sandra beside him, Thane gave the others a moment while he ran through a mental checklist. Typically, Phil Moss had stationed himself at the back, almost hidden behind the stout, bushy-haired bulk of a yawning young man who wore a fringed deerskin jacket and who already seemed half asleep. The duty police surgeon from Inverness, Dr David Linton had covered Iain Cameron's death and couldn't be expected to be over-enthusiastic at being hauled out again. The man seated beside him, twice his age and with a flattened nose that was a long-ago souvenir of being hit with an iron bar in a Saturday night Inverness brawl, Nikki Neilson was a Northern scenes of crime sergeant who was also on his second trip to the area.

There were others. Jock Dawson, the dog handler, had the younger of his two dogs, a yellow Labrador bitch named Goldie, lying contentedly at his feet. His other dog, the older and massive Rajah, a tan and black German shepherd, was sound asleep in their Land-Rover van.

Next to Dawson were the two newest Crime Squad members, both detective constables. Dougie Lennox was slim and tall, with a boyish face and fair curly hair. He had joined the Squad from an Edinburgh CID murder team – and with him had come the story that he could charm most females out of their socks and often much more. Slouched down beside him, happily smoking a small Dutch cheroot, Ernie Vass was a solidly built figure in his thirties who had been a CID officer in Aberdeen. That was after he had been eased out of the Grampian force's traffic department for denting one police car too many.

It left a Northern Constabulary quartet seated together like a defensive group. Andy Mack, the bald, sad-faced DI, was surreptitiously glancing at his watch and had already made it plain he wanted home to his own bed in Inverness. Next to him, scratching at a fierce black beard, sat a uniformed Northern Headquarters sergeant named Wishart. They were flanked on one side by Fergus Gordon, the Fadda constable, and the other by a frowning Harry Harron, returned from yet another fruitless sweep in search of Donny Adams.

'That's everybody.' Thane rapped the table top, knowing the rest of the Northern team, including the the activated Specials, were happily entrenched in the Ardshona's bar. 'We can get started.'

'Superintendent' – Harron made a loud, throat-clearing noise to attract attention – 'can I ask a question first?'

Thane nodded.

Harron frowned round towards Ernie Vass. 'One of your Crime Squad officers is smoking. Should we take a vote about whether this should be regarded as a No Smoking workplace area?'

Vass gave a mild blink, his cheroot staying in place. Andy Mack gave his detective constable a glare meant to drop him dead. There were grins from some and stony-faced neutrality from others.

'Personally, I don't care if Ernie smokes or burns,' said Thane wearily. 'The inn allows smoking. Can we leave it?'

'The man's a bampot,' growled Andy Mack. He raised his voice. 'Harron, don't annoy me. Shut up.'

'Sir.' Harron subsided into silence, his long-jawed face flushing.

'Right.' Thane tried again. 'You're not going to hear a lot that's new. But' – he deliberately switched his gaze back to Andy Mack again – 'I don't believe in leaving people working in the dark.'

He paused, then added with a frosty emphasis, 'If I'm working with people, I prefer to trust them.'

The Northern DI's bald dome flushed red, but he gave a vague mutter of agreement. At the rear, Phil Moss fought down a small grin. He and Thane had already discussed a few items which would not be paraded – not yet, at any rate.

'So let's start. We still have no hard motive for what's going on, and I don't buy any suggestion that we simply have some local workers with a grievance against hard-hearted bosses.' Colin Thane took the lead with a tightly edited version of his side of what had happened around him since he'd arrived. At the right moment he nodded to Sandra Craig, and his red-haired sergeant ran the sequence footage from the Broch security tape. It brought grunts of surprise from the part of his audience who had helped drag the blue Nissan and its dead out from the bottom of the roadside gorge. Fergus Gordon said nothing when Donny Adams appeared on the monitor screen, but his mouth fell open.

From there, Thane went on through the trail-bike rider's raid at Lisa Rankin's office, then the apparent marksman who had fired at him outside the Pictish broch, and rounded it off with the way that Donny Adams had done an apparent runner.

'Your turn,' he told the line-up of puzzled faces in front of him, then pointed towards the bushy-haired casualty surgeon. 'Want to start, doctor?'

'I haven't much.' Linton shook his head. 'Your men in the Nissan died not long after the night-watchman was killed at Broch Distillery. That's the best you're going to get, superintendent. The one harpooned by the steering column would die instantaneously, his partner took a little longer – we'll run a full post-mortem back in Inverness tomorrow, but don't look for surprises.'

'You also did the PM on the night-watchman?' queried Thane.

'Cameron?' Linton nodded. 'This morning. Then I was just cleaning up—'

'When you were grabbed again.' Thane finished it for him. 'Anything in the Cameron PM?'

'Mostly what you know already. Killed when his head was smashed in by a chunk of whisky barrel – we dug out some bits. The body was marinated after death, cookbook style – first I've seen like it. Interesting.' The casualty surgeon frowned, fingering some of the fringes on his deerskin jacket. 'But Cameron had been drinking earlier – stomach contents included a quantity of partly digested alcohol. Probably brandy.'

'Not whisky?' Thane accepted Linton's headshake and switched to Neilson, the Northern scenes of crime sergeant. 'Nicki?'

'Bits and pieces, sir.' Neilson made it an apology. 'We'd identified the timing devices used in the warehouse fire. We're talking mildly sophisticated. Three adapted el cheapo stop-watches, battery operated, linked to small chemical firebombs – three used at the warehouse and a fourth, identical device – probably a spare, – found in the crashed car. Where, in addition to the sawn-off shotgun, there had been a pair of bolt cutters used to cut through the heavy padlock which had secured the main warehouse door. The Scenes of Crime Sergeant packaged the rest. Fingerprints taken from the men killed in the car were already on their way by car to Inverness, to be computer-coded down from there to the main SCRO index in Glasgow.

'Both were carrying plenty of folding money, but nothing in the way of ID.' Neilsen gave a confident rub of a finger along the broken ridge of his nose. 'As you'd expect. We'll give the Nissan a full going over tomorrow then see what turns up.'

'What about the Nissan itself?' asked Fergus Gordon. The young constable blushed as several pairs of eyes swung towards him. 'I mean – well—'

'Worth asking,' agreed Thane dryly. He turned it over to Moss. 'Phil, your turn.'

'A new fax arrived half an hour ago.' Moss shrugged. 'It's the way we thought. The Nissan is seven years old, but a reasonable runner. It was bought for £1,500 at a car auction in Glasgow last weekend by a buyer who paid cash.'

'Fake name and address?' asked the Northern uniform sergeant resignedly.

'A Mr Tony Blair. Address, a public lavatory in Pollokshaws Road. Nobody seems able to remember what our Mr Blair looked like.' Moss gave a wearied belch which was loud enough to echo round the brick storeroom. 'Meaning professionals.'

Buying a cheap used car while using a false name made good sense if a criminal had a big enough job in mind. It was ten times safer than using a stolen car, for which police could be searching.

70

Transfer documents were simply forgotten, it remained registered in the previous owner's name, acquiring a stolen tax disc
and a forged insurance certificate were simple enough details.

Colin Thane sat back for a moment, half-listening to the
general buzz of discussion. Then he concentrated on the meeting
again as it moved on to other areas. For the rest of an hour they
discussed detail, and by the end had almost travelled a full
circle. He looked across at Moss, who gave a slight nod of
agreement.

'Time to wrap it, everybody.' Thane brought silence with a
gesture. 'Some of you are heading back to Inverness. Thanks for
your help today' – he paused and gave a twist of a grin – 'and I
don't exactly plan on having you back.'

They broke up. As the Northern officers left, Andy Mack came
over to Thane and they shook hands.

'I'm leaving you another car and a couple more men, but only
for tomorrow,' said the tired-faced Northern detective inspector.
He sighed. 'Right now, that's about all the help on the ground
we can offer. So – well, good luck with it.'

'If anything happens, you'll hear,' promised Thane.

Mack nodded. 'About Harron. He's loyal, he works hard. But
if he gives any more trouble—'

'I'll drown him,' said Thane solemnly.

'Do that,' approved Mack, and left.

Within minutes, most of the police cars which had been lined
up across from the inn had started up and had departed on their
night drive back to Inverness.

Thane saw them go, then went back through the inn to the
converted storeroom. Moss and Sandra Craig were still there,
but she made muttering noises about catching up on sleep and
left.

'Do I get the feeling you haven't had too good a day?' asked
Moss sarcastically as Thane dropped into a chair beside him. He
paused and frowned. 'I was reading those fax originals you've
sent back to Glasgow. You want full checks on every Broch
director, even the sisters? For real?'

'For real.'

Moss shrugged. 'Maybe they're just cream soups – you know,
rich and thick.'

'No chance.' Thane shook his head. 'Daddy Rankin is nobody's
fool, Phil. But he's badly worried, I'm not sure why. Morris

71

Currie, his sales director, is a waste of space. The women—' He grimaced 'I met two of the daughters. Either of them is probably sharp enough to skin you. The oldest would use your hide for a handbag.'

'That's a happy thought.' Moss was impressed enough to stifle a yawn. 'What's top of tomorrow's local list? Finding Donny Adams?'

'He's a reasonable priority – no more.' Thane knew it was part of a scattergun approach, but for the moment he had little that was better. He glanced at his watch. It was only a little after eleven, but this had been a long day. 'We'll shut shop. Get everybody back here for eight a.m., ready for an eight-thirty briefing.'

'Neat, clean, standing at attention. They'll be there.' Moss started another yawn then released a long, raucous belch instead and followed it with a scowl. 'But I still don't care what anyone says, all this damned fresh air can't be healthy. Not unless your lungs are used to it.'

'You'll survive,' promised Thane. 'But watch the milk – up here, it comes from cows, not cartons.'

'That's what I mean,' complained Moss, and shoved himself to his feet. 'Good luck and goodnight!' He headed for the door and went out.

Left alone, Thane used a pen and paper to work out the beginnings of a check-list for the morning. Finished, he folded the sheet of paper, put it into his inside pocket, then hauled one of the telephones onto his lap, lifted the receiver, and dialled his home number in Glasgow.

It rang out briefly, then the call was answered, and for a moment he was almost fooled, then got it right.

'Kate?'

'Me,' agreed his daughter. 'Hold on. I'll get Mum – but don't yack for ever. We're watching a weepy video.'

A few seconds passed, then Mary Thane came on the line.

'How long are we allowed?' asked Thane.

Mary laughed. 'I'll bribe her. How are things?'

'There's one hell of a lot of scenery,' he admitted.

'So it's not a "there today, back tomorrow"?' There was no real surprise in her voice. Mary Thane had been a cop's wife for too long to expect the easy way.

'No chance.' Thane started to give her the incident room

72

number, but Mary didn't need it or the Ardshona Inn number. Maggie Fyffe, a cop's widow who was both Jack Hart's personal secretary and the key player in the Squad wives' unofficial grapevine, had already passed them on. He gave up. 'All quiet with you?'

'Deadly dull. Your son is up in his room, doing God knows what with his computer. But like Kate says, the video is good.' Mary paused, listened to their daughter's voice at her end, then chuckled. 'She wants to know if you've met any good-looking women.'

'They queue outside my bedroom door,' declared Thane.

'She heard. She says you're a liar,' said Mary sadly. 'You've to say hello to her friend Sergeant Sandra, and can she start the video again?'

'Say yes.' Thane gave up. 'I'll call again tomorrow, if I get the chance.'

'Tomorrow, fine. But if you're still away on Wednesday I could be out,' she warned. 'The kids have tickets for the world's greatest rock concert at school, remember? I'm picking them up afterwards.'

To give them a lift home. No parents in their right minds left young teenagers to find their own way home in a nearly twenty-first century city like Glasgow after dark. Tommy was a cheerful pimple-faced fifteen-year-old adolescent, Kate was two years younger and showed every early sign of sharing her mother's looks. For both, there were lurking dangers – just as there were for everyone.

'Take care, Colin,' said Mary softly as the video began loudly in the background.

'You too,' said Thane.

He hung up, switched off the storeroom lights as he left, and went back through the inn, then up the main stairway to his room. It was small but clean, simply furnished, the walls covered in old, bilious Victorian wallpaper heavy with blue grapes and dark vine leaves. Outside, the moonlit view from his window was out towards the distant dark silhouette of Broch Castle. He closed the curtains, got out of his clothes, washed in the room's tiny, added-on en suite bathroom, then slid naked under the thin quilt on the narrow single bed.

The bed was comfortable enough. Once he'd switched off the room light there was silence for a moment then a steady rustling and scratching began behind the dark-brown wainscot wall behind his head.

So he was sharing. It didn't worry him. He lay back for a moment, looking out at the night, listening to the rustling and squeaking and the faint murmur of the wind.

Colin Thane wakened as the curtains of his bedroom were opened and the morning sunlight poured in. A cup of tea had been placed on the small table beside his bed and the landlord's wife, coming over from the window, considered him with an amused interest. She wore a grey sweater and blue corduroy trousers.

'Sleep well, superintendent?' The large woman's deliberate inspection continued. 'That girl sergeant of yours said you'd want to be wakened at seven-thirty.'

'Yes.' His quilt had slipped off during the night. Thane grinned and hauled it back to cover his naked length. 'I did, Mrs Campbell.'

'I'm called Belle.' Her eyes twinkled. 'You're well built for a city man, Mr Thane – pleasingly well built.' She was in no hurry to leave. 'Another fine day, whatever you'll be doing, and still not a rain cloud around. Will you be having another try at putting the handcuffs on Donny Adams, the way they were saying in the bar last night?'

'Maybe at finding him,' corrected Thane. It was hard to be dignified as he tried to take a gulp of tea with the cup in one hand while he kept a grip on the quilt before it slid again. 'Do you know Adams?'

'He drinks here.' She gave a short laugh. 'Everybody in the glen drinks here unless they're dead or teetotal.'

'Where would you look for him, Mrs Campbell?'

'Belle.'

'Where, Belle?'

'No idea. He was born and bred in Glen Faddan.' She shrugged. 'Don't expect much help from his wife. Jess Adams is a natural, lying slut. If she ever told the truth about anything her teeth would turn black. Her son Willie is the same—'

'Willie?' Thane frowned, surprised.

'Willie, whoever the father was – if his mother ever knew

74

herself.' She shrugged. 'He doesn't live with them. You could say Willie travels around.'

Thane set down the cup and forgot about the quilt. 'Does Willie have a trail bike?'

'You wouldn't expect me to know.' She shook her head.

'Belle' – he stopped her as she turned to go – 'did Iain Cameron do his drinking here at the inn?'

'Where else?' The bulky woman tired. 'Tho Bible thumper Detective Harron that you brought along asked me yesterday. I told him—'

'Tell it again,' invited Thane. 'What did Cameron usually drink?'

She sighed. 'Whisky, superintendent.'

'Never brandy?'

'Only sometimes.' The sigh became a chuckle. 'As a special treat – if someone else was doing the buying. But I hadn't seen it happen for a while. Who told you?'

'Someone mentioned it,' said Thane vaguely. 'Thanks, Belle.'

'My pleasure.' She opened the bedroom door then looked back at him, the twinkle back in her eyes. 'You're married, superintendent?'

He nodded.

'Lucky woman,' she said mildly, and left.

Thane had a shower and a shave, chose a clean shirt from his travel bag, dressed, gave his shoes a token shine with some toilet tissues, then went down to the dining room. A middle-aged holiday couple were at a table in the far corner, but his police team had already been and gone. Only Jock Dawson remained, stealing leftover sausages from the breakfast buffet for his dogs.

'Did your pals travel all right, Jock?' he asked.

'No problem, sir. This is as good as a holiday for them,' said Dawson gravely. 'New smells, new trees, strange droppings, all that kind o' thing.'

Dawson gathered up his haul and went out. A freckle-faced and yawning young waiter took Thane's order of orange juice, toast, and coffee, and when it came Thane ate quickly. He was nearly finished when Sandra Craig came in, sat across from him at the table, and helped herself to his last piece of toast.

'Fax, sir.'

She handed over the fax, then spread a thick layer of butter on the toast while Thane read. The night-duty teams had been busy in both Inverness and Glasgow. Fingerprints taken from the dead men found in the Nissan matched with prints held in the main computerized SCRO collection. John Rogers, convictions for armed robbery and assault, and Peter Marsh, convictions for arson and the use of explosives, were listed with Glasgow addresses and had regularly worked as a team. 'Usual follow-ups?' asked his sergeant through a mouthful of toast.

Thane nodded. Any names logged as 'known associates' of Rogers or Marsh would have to be leaned on in the search for any hint about why they had headed north. Meantime, it was still too early to expect any of the background detail he'd asked for on Broch Distillery's ruling family. But that could wait.

'Organize a couple of things, Sandra,' he told her. 'Check how to get to Iain Cameron's place, then do the same for where Adams lives. I think we'll go visiting.'

He finished breakfast with a final mouthful of coffee, then left her. The combined team of Northern and Crime Squad officers were already outside the inn, gossiping in the sunlight beside their vehicles. The gossip ended before he reached them.

'Phil.' He flickered a greeting to Moss, who was leaning against the front of one car. Moss had shaved – the evidence was a streak of dried shaving cream down one cheek. He could also have used a clean shirt, but that was an incidental. 'Everybody here?'

Moss nodded, and Thane beckoned them nearer.

'We've a morning mostly made up of things to check, people to see.' He looked towards Nikki Neilson, the Northern scenes of crime officer. 'How do you feel about dogs?'

'Sometimes I think I married one, sir,' said Neilson woodenly. 'No problems.'

'Then I want you and Jock Dawson to check around where that trail bike was hidden during yesterday's office break-in. Move on from there to around the Pictish broch, where that rifleman cut loose at me. You're looking for anything.'

'Sir.' The broken-nosed scenes of crime man nodded his understanding.

'You two.' Thane switched to Lennox and Vass, and the new Crime Squad members brightened hopefully. 'You know we've talked to distillery workers already, but do it again. I need any possible local sightings of the men killed in the Nissan. They've been identified as John Rogers and Peter Marsh, both Glasgow, both known criminals.' He ticked the rest of their general tasks off on his fingers. 'You're also trying to find out why Donny Adams has gone AWOL, and where he has gone. And another Adams has popped out of the woodwork – his son Willie. Knock on doors, wear out shoe-leather. Understood?'

Lennox and Vass exchanged a wry glance.

'Great,' muttered Lennox under his breath, but they nodded.

'Right.' Thane turned to Harry Harron next. 'Harron, you're on trail bikes – names of local riders, where they were yesterday afternoon, the kind of machines they use. Then I want a list of people who own any kind of rifle – with or without a firearms certificate.'

'I' – Harron showed his large, chipped teeth unhappily – 'I'll try, sir. But the guns list might not be easy. Some Highland folk – well, you could say they're constructively forgetful when it comes to paying for gun licences and certificates. The same goes for any kind of vehicle licensing—'

'You know them,' snapped Thane. 'I don't care if they come after you with claymores or chain saws. If it helps, sing psalms at them – but do it.' He relented a little. 'Take Fergus Gordon along to assist. Stay together and you won't get lost.'

'And what would be wrong with that?' murmured Phil Moss.

Thane went through the rest of his mental checklist. If the same two mobilized specials from the previous day showed up again at Broch Distillery he could use them there. Then there was the extra Northern sergeant and constable driver he'd been gifted for the day, along with their patrol car.

'Sergeant – ah—'

'Wishart,' murmured Moss. 'First name Fred.'

'Sergeant Wishart, you and your driver are going exploring – every house, every cottage, where our two bodies with the Nissan might have hidden up as a stop-over.'

'No problem, sir.' The black bearded Wishart was happy enough. He could have drawn worse, like being condemned to be along with DC Harron.

'Detective Inspector Moss will act as overall controller from the Ardshona storeroom.' Thane felt the glare from Moss, but ignored it. 'Let him know what's happening, let him know often. I'll be out and about. Talk to anyone you can, then listen to them – whatever they say.'

The group broke up, and Moss sourly followed Thane back

into the inn and through to their storeroom headquarters. Sandra Craig was there, studying the map pinned to one wall and being guided around it by Maggie Donald.

'You two.' Thane thumbed both policewomen towards the door. 'Shift. Sandra, you're with me. Maggie, give her your car keys – and I want you to take a hike over to Broch Castle. You're a poor little female constable who has lost her way.'

'Yes sir,' Maggie chuckled. 'Saying ba-ba-ba. Looking for what, sir?'

'Gossip. Chat with the housekeeper or whatever they've got,' Thane told her. 'Find out how the Rankin family usually get along together, any recent rows – whatever you can get.'

'Like do they have anyone who lurks around with a rifle?' Maggie Donald's dark eyes sparkled. 'Yes, sir.'

Once she and Sandra had gone, Phil Moss spent a few acid moments checking through the communications equipment, which had gained a small computer screen and keyboard, then settled himself beside one of the trestle tables and gave a small, disgusted belch.

'Have fun,' he grunted, then picked up a discarded magazine and began reading.

Thane grinned and left him. Sandra Craig had the Northern force's blue Range Rover outside and was in the driving seat with the engine quietly ticking over. As he got aboard he noted that someone – Maggie Donald, he presumed – had given the Range Rover an overnight wash. It wouldn't have been any of the Crime Squad team. Squad vehicles were deliberately left dirty most of the time, the theory being that a dirty car drew less attention. In too many locations a clean car shrieked police.

'Cameron's place first?' queried Sandra.

Thane nodded. The dead night-watchman had been almost overlooked with so much else happening, and that could have been a mistake. He sat back in his seat as the Range Rover began moving.

'Know where we're going?' he asked mildly.

Sandra Craig nodded. As usual, she had her small transistor radio propped on the dashboard and, despite the mountain interference, it was managing a crackling reception of one of her country and western programmes. Immaculately turned out, that red hair brushed like burnished gold, his sergeant was wearing denim trousers with dark-blue trainers, a knitted blue sweater, and a faded white jacket. A colourful shoulder patch on the jacket was the crest of a crack RAF Harrier squadron, and how that squared with a certain naval lieutenant commander, currently overseas, was something he didn't want to know.

'Cameron had wheels, didn't he?' he queried as they headed out of the village and the road took them past Broch Castle.

'An old van, sir – Post Office surplus.' She steered carefully round some small children playing football in the roadway. 'It's lying in the distillery parking lot, already checked. Nothing there.'

The road wound north along Glen Laggan, empty apart from a farm tractor that stopped to let them squeeze past. After a couple of miles they left it for a narrow, winding hill track. The track climbed steadily through a mix of bare rock and scrub. Occasional drystone walls surrounding patches of coarse grass where sheep were grazing.

Thane pointed to their right. A line of almost a dozen red deer, only their heads visible above the heather, were watching the Range Rover from higher up the hillside. A single stag with a regal spread of antlers stood guard in the open above them.

'Beautiful,' murmured Sandra Craig.

'Tomorrow's venison,' said Thane cruelly.

The Range Rover kept moving. Another few hundred yards on, past a long outcrop of rock and beyond a straggling line of stunted fir trees, they pulled in at the tumbledown cottage which Iain Cameron had called home. It had stone walls, a battered corrugated iron roof, and narrow windows. Sandra switched off, they left the vehicle, and they walked over towards the cottage door. Weather had stripped off most of the paint from its wood, empty tins and rubbish littered the ground. There was empty hill land all around, with the snake-like track they'd travelled heading on towards the distant dark mass of the Dorsair Ridge.

Sandra Craig produced a rusted key and used it in a lock which squeaked, the door swung open to more squeaks, and they went in. The air smelled stale, almost rancid, and something small and black scuttled across the stone floor as they looked around.

The cottage had a large kitchen and a single bedroom. The bedroom had an army-style cot, a chest of drawers, and a chipped china washbasin on a stand. The grubby bedclothes were a crumpled heap, probably tossed back that way when Cameron last got up. Discarded clothes littered the floor.

The kitchen had even less to recommend it. One window pane had been broken and a torn piece of blanket had been stuffed into the gap. A sink with a hand-pump for water was almost filled with dirty dishes. There was an ancient, unlit wood-burning stove, a large and grubby food cupboard with one door missing, a small bottled gas cooker, a filthy table and a couple of greasy, dilapidated armchairs.

'Let's get on with it,' said Thane wryly.

A Northern car had paid a brief visit on the Sunday, following Cameron's death. But that had been routine, with no reason it should have been more. This time, there was a purpose.

The search didn't take long. There were a few scraps of food in the kitchen cupboard beside the remains of a six-pack of beer and an unopened bottle of whisky. Back numbers of a West Highland freesheet newspaper were stacked under one of the chairs with some dog-eared magazines. An old shoebox under the second chair held a few old letters and photographs, a couple of paid bills, and an ignored tax demand.

They moved on into the bedroom. While Thane checked around the army cot and under its mattress, Sandra quickly examined a coat and some jackets hanging on pegs behind the room door then switched to the chest of drawers. The first two drawers held a few crumpled shirts and some underwear, but the third was where she struck gold.

'Got it!'

He joined her and gave a satisfied nod. The bottle of five star Remy Martin brandy, lying on its side and wrapped in a grey shirt which had once been white, had been hidden under a sweater and some socks. Iain Cameron's faith in the Highland neighbourly code had not been absolute. Using a pen, Thane checked the bottle. It was still almost half full and a price sticker over the label said Fraser Stores, Inverness, with a bar-code price.

So now they knew why the autopsy on the dead night-watchman said he had been drinking his special treat. Expensive brandy. Probably supplied by new friends told about his weakness – new friends maybe checking on night security at Broch Distillery.

They took the brandy bottle, still wrapped in its shirt. Just in case, they also took the shoe-box file of papers from the kitchen. Then they were glad to leave the cottage to its beetles and its staleness. Back aboard the Range Rover, Thane stowed their haul behind his seat and Sandra started the vehicle again. But almost as soon as it began moving she knocked the gear lever into neutral and braked to a halt.

Still not much more than a patch of dust cloud, another car was coming up the track from the direction of Ardshona township. It disappeared as the track took a dip, reappeared again, and came on steadily.

'Sir?' Sandra looked at Thane, a question in her green eyes.

'Behind the trees,' he decided. 'We'll wait and see.'

The next time the other car disappeared into a dip she moved the Range Rover, drove it in deep behind the straggle of trees, then switched off. They watched through the screen of firs until the approaching vehicle was near enough to become a grey Volvo station wagon.

Thane had seen the car before, parked outside Broch Castle. He waited, hoping they might be in good enough cover.

It seemed that way. The grey Volvo rumbled past on the stony track, reached the cottage, and stopped. The car's horn sounded twice, there was a silence, then it sounded twice again. This time the driver's door opened and they had a clear view as Finn Rankin got out. The white-haired whisky firm chairman stood beside his car, lit a cigarette, then waited, smoking, for a full couple of minutes. Finally, he tossed the cigarette away, got back into his car, closed the door, and the Volvo station wagon drove off, heading further out along the track.

'So what the hell was that about, sir?' asked Sandra in a puzzled voice.

'How the equal hell should I know?' countered Thane bleakly. He nodded in the direction the Volvo had disappeared. 'What's along there?'

'Just more like this, says the map.' His sergeant reached into a pocket, produced a chocolate bar, and bit off a chunk to help her thought processes. 'This track goes on north along this side of Glen Laggan, all the way to the Dorsair Ridge.'

'But it crosses plenty of others?' Thane sighed when she nodded. 'Then forget him for now. Back we go. Next call, Donny Adams – or wife. And are you going to eat all of that damned chocolate?'

81

'No sir.' She grinned and tucked the bar away.

They drove back down into Ardshona township, reached its far edge, then took a side road which led into a cluster of small houses with TV aerials, gardens where washing fluttered on drying ropes, and a scatter of parked cars. The Adams home was half-way along, and they parked outside it. A flickering curtain showed they were being watched as they walked up a narrow gravel path, and then the front door opened as he reached for its bell button.

'Police again?' The woman who stood on the doorway was a timeworn blonde of uncertain middle age and with a bitter hatchet face. She was wearing a button-front floral pattern mail-order dress.

'Again, Mrs Adams,' agreed Sandra sympathetically, showing her warrant card.

'Donny still hasn't shown up,' snapped Jess Adams. She stepped back and they followed her in through a tiny hall into a comfortably furnished front room where polished brass ornaments gleamed and a mist grey cat looked up from its basket beside the brick fireplace.

'You'd better sit, I suppose,' she said reluctantly.

'We still want to talk with your husband, Mrs Adams.' Thane settled in a chair near the cat while the woman chose another beside the window. Sandra stayed on her feet, content to lean against a heavy oak sideboard.

'So you're wasting your time—'

'No.' Thane smiled at her. 'You see, we also want to talk to your son.'

'Willie?' The woman's manner changed and she stiffened. 'Why?'

'To ask him a few questions,' said Thane easily.

'You're staying at the Inn, right?' The woman's eyes hardened at the thought. 'That bitch Belle Campbell has been talking to you, hasn't she?'

Thane shrugged.

'Belle Campbell!' Jess Adams rose angrily. 'Damn her, the woman is nothing but a whore, a prostitute, a trollop and a slut!'

'She doesn't seem to like you either,' said Sandra mildly. 'But she put it differently.'

The middle-aged blonde stared, her mouth twitching. Then,

82

suddenly, she gave a loud laugh. 'Now there's a surprise! What has Belle Campbell been saying?'

'Not a lot.' Thane grinned to match her mood. 'You've known her a long time?'

'We were in the same class at school. Sometimes we went around together – up here you haven't much choice.' Her mouth tightened. 'She doesn't matter. What's Willie supposed to have done?'

Thane shrugged. There was a photograph in a brass frame on the fireplace. He reached over the cat and lifted the frame. The photograph showed a proud-faced clear-eyed young infantry soldier in dress uniform.

'Your son?' asked Thane.'

She nodded proudly. 'Six years with the colours, then wounded and invalided out.'

'Does he live with you?'

'No.' Jess Adams took the photograph and carefully repositioned it. 'Him and Donny – well, they don't get on. Willie moves about, wherever there's work. Usually forestry work.'

'When did you see him last?' asked Sandra crisply.

'A few days ago.' Despite Belle Campbell's lurid assessment, her one-time schoolmate wasn't a good liar. 'I – uh – I don't know when he'll be back.'

'Does he have transport?' Thane took over. 'A car?'

'No.' She walked into it. 'Just what he calls his trail bike.'

'Fine.' Thane got to his feet. 'Thank you, Mrs Adams. When either of them show up, we want to know. It could cut down on hassle.'

She looked surprised it was over, but saw them out.

Sandra stayed silent until they were back in the Range Rover and she had set it moving.

'So he's got a trail bike,' she said slowly. 'And he's ex-infantry. That means good with a rifle.'

'Better than good,' said Thane. He had recognized the tunic badges in that photograph. The Black Watch regiment had always rated high at marksmanship, and there had been another partially shown badge to underline it in Willie Adams' case.

He sat silent as they headed back through the township. Then, as they passed the same group of children at the roadside still playing their game of football, Sandra Craig gave a near yelp.

'What's wrong?' he asked.

'Something just clicked, sir.' She drew the Range Rover to a halt a little way along and turned to face him. 'Remember when we flew up here, remember how we had a bunch of football fans on the plane, left over from Saturday's game in Glasgow?'

'So?'

'They missed their Saturday flight back north, they tried to change their tickets to the Sunday.' She was suitably patient. 'They couldn't. Sunday's flight had already been booked solid, every seat taken.'

Thane frowned. 'Well?'

'Morris Currie,' said his sergeant. 'Broch's sales director, sir. The distillery fire is late on Saturday night. He hears about it early Sunday morning. How does he still manage to get a seat on the Sunday flight?'

'Dear God!' Colin Thane knew he should have thought of it. first. 'Find out.'

4

Priorities had altered. Colin Thane gave Sandra Craig a further list of things to be done, then they parted outside the Ardshona Inn. While his sergeant headed for the makeshift incident room inside the building, Thane slid over behind the wheel of the borrowed Northern force Range Rover, set the fat-tyred four by four moving again, and drove south out of the township. Feeling like a schoolboy playing truant, he booted the accelerator hard as soon as he reached open road, and delighted in the responsive rasp of the exhaust note.

Traffic was light. Thane's goal was Broch Distillery, and when the Range Rover reached there he left the vehicle in the visitor's parking lot. He found a lone special constable dozing at the security hut, but there was activity outside the fire-damaged warehouse. A small squad of workers were doing more clearing up, shovelling debris from the building into a line of rusty metal skips.

'Back again, superintendent!' Alex Korski marched over and

gave him a reasonably friendly handshake. 'Solved any of our problems yet?'

'Still trying,' Thane smiled at the distillery manager, who wore overalls, and green rubber boots, then nodded towards the activity. 'You've enough work there to keep everybody going.'

'They aren't long started. We had to wait on your people giving us the All Clear to move in.' Korski stopped to shield a flaring match in his cupped hands as he lit one of his small cigars. 'Well, what new excitements today?'

'None I know about,' lied Thane. 'I don't need any more. How are things with you?'

'The same.' Korski carefully extinguished the match he'd used then tucked the blackened remains in a pocket. He saw Thane notice what he'd done. 'It pays to be careful, Mr Thane. If the wind had veered round a few points or been any stronger on Saturday night then the fire could have spread to the heather. Ever seen heather catch fire after a dry spell?'

Thane shook his head.

'It doesn't burn, it explodes,' said Korksi grimly. 'And our nearest fire brigade is stationed at Ullapool, more than an hour away.' He drew on his cigar until the tip glowed red, then thumbed at the almost cloudless sky. 'We need rain. The only reason production at Broch hasn't been cut back is that we use a hill stream which starts a long way from here, on the snow line.'

'Something else for you to worry about,' mused Thane. 'But, as long as you keep distilling and Morris Currie keeps selling—'

'Currie?' Korksi rose to the bait with a snort. 'I'd ditch him tomorrow. Finn Rankin has the real drive, the real contacts!'

'Currie didn't waste any time getting up here after the fire,' reminded Thane innocently.

'God knows why.' Korski scowled. 'Even the girls pitched in, trying to help. Not Currie. Maybe he got brownie points for coming north so quickly, but he made damned sure he didn't get his hands dirty.' The distillery manager glanced at his watch, then broke off to yell at the work squad shifting debris. 'Right, you lot! Lunch break, be back in forty minutes!' As shovels clattered down, he returned his attention to Thane. 'Are you here for anything special? Like I said, we had some of your people along earlier – they said you still haven't picked up Donny Adams.'

'We'll find him,' promised Thane. 'What about his son? Do you know Willie Adams?'

Korski shook his head. 'I've a vague memory that he did summer work for us years ago. Nothing more.'

'Are Finn Rankin or Lisa around?'

Korski shook his head. 'The boss is out. He had a couple of things to do around Ardshona, but I'm expecting him back about now. You won't find Lisa. She left with Anna to drive to Inverness this morning. They've a meeting scheduled with Customs and Excise.'

'Trouble?'

'Only for Customs.' Korski chuckled. 'Lisa and Anna are two tough ladies – the same goes for Gina, the other sister. They're used to getting their own way, except when father is around!' He drew on his cigar again. 'Believe me, Finn Rankin is always top boss.'

'No exceptions?' asked Thane.

'Maybe one, superintendent.' The distillery managery gave a soft laugh. 'A lady. You can probably guess who I mean.'

'Probably,' agreed Thane, and left it at that.

Leaving the man, he walked across to the main distillery building and went in at the General Office. Joan Kerr was there and alone, at a desk near a window, fingers busy at a computer keyboard. She sat back and smiled up at him.

'Looking for me, superintendent?' she asked. 'Everyone else has gone to the moon – or at least for lunch. Including Jazz.'

'You'll do for now.' Thane propped himself on the edge of her desk. 'Joan, why didn't you tell me that Donny Adams had a son?'

The dark-haired woman blinked. 'Should I have?'

'You're a special constable, you're supposed to think that way,' said Thane stonily.

'What way?' Joan Kerr sighed. 'Look, Mr Thane, I've never met this son, never seen him, barely know he exists.' Her mouth tightened a little. 'Now I know you're interested, when I hear anything, if I hear anything, you'll know.'

'I'll settle for that.' Thane made it an apology. 'We've a few problems, Joan, and Willie Adams is maybe one of them. Do you know his mother?'

'Everybody knows Jess Adams.' Joan Kerr's smile returned. She wasn't in her Broch hostess outfit of the previous day.

Instead, she wore a white long-sleeved blouse and a lightweight blue-grey tweed skirt which stopped a little below knee length. The blouse was decorated with a large grouse claw mounted on a silver brooch. 'Mr Thane, I've had to lock up Jess Adams a few Saturday nights as drunk and disorderly. When she drinks too much, she beats hell out of her husband. Then he goes out and beats hell out of someone else – so my Andy arrests him. We keep it in the family.' She chuckled. 'Did she give you a hard time?'

'She could have made it easier,' said Thane woodenly, and changed the subject. 'What's been happening here?'

'Not a lot.' She gave a slight grimace. 'Except that suddenly a lot of people seem to remember Andy and I are specials. They stop talking when we appear.'

Thane nodded his understanding. If you're involved with policing in any shape or form then sooner or later that kind of reaction came your way. Or your family's way. Young cops had a war chant party howl that underlined it all with a bellowed chorus that they were cops, nobody liked them – and they didn't care.

Except they did, but that was the way things were.

'How's Jazz after yesterday?'

'Fine,' said Joan Kerr dryly. 'Very interested in your fair-haired Detective Dougie from Glasgow.' She read his mind. 'No, don't warn him off. Jazz wouldn't thank you and that young woman knows how to handle men.'

'If she changes her mind, tell me.' Thane grinned. It would do no harm if Dougie Lennox came up against a surprise. 'But did Jazz get anywhere sorting out Lisa Rankin's office?'

Joan Kerr shook her head. 'A charity box had gone. It usually held a few pounds. An antique silver sgean dhu knife has vanished. Nothing else.'

'No missing paperwork?'

'Not that we know about.' Glancing towards the window, she paused. 'But there's someone else you could ask.'

Thane looked. Finn Rankin's Volvo station wagon was driving into the distillery parking lot. The vehicle stopped and Rankin got out from the driver's side then paused for a moment to talk to someone in the front passenger seat. Then Rankin had closed the driver's door and was walking briskly towards the main distillery building.

'Who has he got with him?' he asked Joan Kerr.

'The beloved Jonesy, who else? He said he'd collect her.' Joan Kerr gave a pleased smile. 'That usually means he takes a quick look in, then is gone – and that's always good. I like to get home and feed my kids early now and again.'

Thane nodded, remembering only that Rankin had been along when he had driven out to Iain Cameron's hillside cottage.

Another couple of moments passed, then the distillery owner threw open the general office door and strode in. He greeted Joan Kerr with a brisk nod – then switched to a tetchy frown as he saw Thane.

'Any chance you're bringing good news, Thane?' he asked caustically. 'We're due some.'

'A few things are coming together.' Thane pushed himself up from the desk. 'We've identified the dead men in the car – both from Glasgow, both known criminals. Outside of that,' he shrugged – 'you know that Donny Adams seems to have done a runner?'

'Donny the Shovel?' Finn Rankin gave a dismissive grunt. 'Whatever he's done, he'll turn up eventually.' He paused and pursed his thin lips. 'But I want a word with you, Thane. Alone.'

Thane followed the man out of the general office and through to the Broch visitor centre room and its display of the firm's products and successes. Rankin glanced up at the security TV camera, then led the way over to the far corner of the room, where a trio of whisky casks, each a different size, sat together. They were empty examples, wooden staves scrubbed clean then varnished, glinting under the spotlights.

'Now.' Rankin raised one hand and slapped it down hard and emphatically on the lid of the largest cask. 'Let's sort something out. After I saw you yesterday, I heard you'd given some of my people a hard time about security. Including my daughter Lisa and Alex Korski. Is that true?'

'I won't deny it.' Thane shrugged. 'You're sitting on top of a whisky mine. I've seen better protected corner shops.'

Rankin snorted hard through his beak of a nose. 'What you didn't know, because you didn't ask, is that Lisa and Korski have both asked me more than once to improve our security systems. I turned down their ideas. Why? Because what they wanted would cost a fortune – and because our insurance company has been perfectly happy with what we've got.' He saw Thane's raised eyebrow. 'You want to know why? Simple. All Broch single malt whisky goes into wooden casks like these. Do you know any thief who is going to grab one and run away with it under his arm?'

'None I can think about,' admitted Thane.

'This size is called a butt.' Rankin tapped the largest cask again. 'It's our biggest. Facts? It holds 500 bulk litres at sixty per cent alcohol and forty per cent water. Add customs duty and it's worth around £6,000 cash. Weight, around 550 kilos – that's damned nearly half a ton in the real weights I learned at school.' Rankin moved to the next cask. 'Now this one is what we call a hogshead – an uglier name, but it holds 250 litres.' He indicated the third in line, the smallest. 'That leaves baby – a standard barrel, holds 200 litres. That's still damned heavy. You follow me?'

'I think so,' said Thane wryly.

'Your average thief setting up a whisky raid always waits until the stuff is in bottles. That's unless he knows how to get hernia repair operations at wholesale cost,' said Rankin sarcastically. 'The bottom line is that our security may have been low-key by city standards, but it was approved. How was anyone to know some moron would try to burn me out?'

'But you know now, Mr Rankin. There's always something to learn.' Thane saw the distillery chairman flush, but gave him no chance to reply. 'There's another thing that worries me. Somebody was firing a rifle not far from your broch yesterday. He was shooting too close to me for comfort.'

'I suppose he just didn't see you.' Rankin made it a a minimal apology, then made a small attempt at a smile. 'It was probably a poacher trying for a rabbit. We've some big rabbits, superintendent.'

'Do many of your rabbits carry warrant cards?' Thane didn't hide his sarcasm. He rested a hand on the lid of the hogshead cask beside him, matched Finn Rankin's steady gaze, then moved things on. 'About Donny Adams. Do you know he has a son?'

'Yes.' For a moment an odd flicker showed in Rankin's hazel eyes then had gone. 'The boy's name is Willie. I've met him a couple of times. Why?'

Thane shrugged. 'Willie might know where his father has gone. It might help if we could find Willie to ask him.'

'That sounds practical. If I can help, I'll let you know.' Rankin gave a glance at his watch. 'I have to head back to Mrs Kerr, superintendent. I'm still trying to run a business.'

'I'm finished for now. Thanks for your help.' Thane made as if to leave, then stopped. 'I'm going out to look around Iain Cameron's cottage. I was given some directions, but maybe you could help—'

'Sorry.' Rankin shook his head apologetically. 'I'm not very sure where it is, susperintendent. Cameron wasn't exactly on my visiting list.'

'I suppose I'll find it.' Thane smiled, accepted the lie, and left.

He was heading back across the parking lot towards the Range Rover when he heard a car horn give a brief peep. A hand beckoned from Finn Rankin's Volvo. He walked over, and Jonesy wound down her window.

'Hello, superintendent.' The woman looked up at him and gave a cautious smile. 'We didn't exactly meet yesterday, but—'

'But' – Thane returned the smile – 'do I call you Jonesy?'

'Everybody else does.' That expensively cut iron grey hair went with looks which were still eye-catching, only enhanced by the first crop of tiny crows feet crinkles at the corners of her mouth. Her eyes were dark brown, she was wearing a pastel green dress, and she had a large diamond cluster ring on her engagement finger. 'The formal version is Natalie Jones. You know about me?'

Thane nodded. 'Jonesy rules, okay.'

'Thank you.' The woman gave a small, quick laugh. Then she spoke quietly and earnestly. 'I had to speak with you, Mr Thane. I would have sneaked round to the Ardshona Inn last night, if I'd had the chance. It's about Finn – things are happening to him, things he won't talk about – not even to me.'

'But you think I can help?' frowned Thane. 'How?'

'Try to give him some breathing space, whatever way things may look.' The woman bit lightly on her lower lip. 'He needs help, your kind of help, but he's too damned stubborn to admit it. That's his nature. Whatever happens, will you remember that?'

'I can't promise, but I'll try,' agreed Thane.

'Thank you.' She gave a grateful nod. 'Try – that's all I ask. Try, and when he asks you, listen.'

'I could use some kind of a hint, Jonesy,' said Thane quietly.

She hesitated, then glanced past him. Her expression changed. 'Not now. I – I'm sorry.'

He looked back. Rankin was walking towards them from the distillery building, his long-legged gait eating the distance. Colin Thane gave Jonesy a smile, raised a hand in a vague, casual salute towards the approaching, white-haired figure, then went over to the Range Rover. Once he was aboard the Northern vehicle, he looked back. Finn Rankin was standing motionless beside the Volvo, watching him.

Starting his engine, Thane made an unhurried business of driving out of the parking lot. He exited in a wide turn which took him past the Volvo and Finn Rankin was still standing, still watching.

He encountered Jazz Gupatra as he drove in towards Ardshona. The young student was cycling her way back towards the distillery, pedalling fast on a downward stretch of the narrow road, pigtails flying behind her. She saw him, waved cheerfully, and he flashed his headlights to return the greeting.

For a moment Colin Thane smiled as she pedalled past. Then he cursed the way most other things seemed to be shaping up.

Everyone else had returned by the time Colin Thane reached the Ardshona Inn. He parked the Range Rover immediately behind Jock Dawson's dog van, then, conscious of two pairs of eager eyes watching him from its rear window, he went past it and into the inn. On his way through the building he exchanged a smile with the elderly couple who seemed to have dug a corner for themselves at the bar. Harron and the Northern force Scenes of Crime man, Nikki Neilson, were eating in the restaurant, but he didn't stop until he reached the storeroom incident room.

Phil Moss was there, using one of the telephones but ending the conversation and hanging up as he saw Thane enter. Frowning in concentration, shirt collar loosened and tie unfastened, uniform jacket hanging over the back of her chair, Maggie Donald was clicking away at a computer keyboard. The solid bulk of Ernie Vass filled another chair, his feet up on a table top while he ate a sandwich and read yesterday's newspaper. Thane's mouth tightened as Vass acknowledged his arrival by swinging his feet down to the floor. Ernie Vass was efficient. But he was still a constant reminder of the traumatic death of the Squad detective constable he replaced.

'Thank you for looking in – sir.' Phil Moss's sour greeting went with the scrawny detective inspector hauling himself to his feet and making a performance out of stretching his back muscles. 'How's the scenery out there?'

'Hasn't moved much since yesterday.' Thane glanced at the scatter of fax messages and report sheets in front of Moss. 'Have things been happening?'

'In some directions.' Moss allowed himself the luxury of a gargantuan belch, one loud enough to put Maggie Donald off her key-stroke and to bring a startled blink of respect from Vass. 'Will we get rid of the small stuff first?'

Thane nodded. It was the way they always worked when teamed.

'Still no trace of Donny Adams, his pick-up truck, or his son. But Jock's dogs earned their keep again – they located two used .22 long-nose cartridge cases roughly where you thought they'd be. There were some traces of footprints around, and Neilson made a Scenes of Crime check. He says none are good enough for identification purposes. But things were better when he took a first look at that brandy bottle from the cottage. It shows umpteen fingerprints. Now Inverness are checking where the brandy was purchased, in case anyone has a good memory.'

They moved on down Moss's list: Harron was plodding away at trail bikes and their owners with little to show for it, and was also working his way through a print-out of local firearms certificate holders who owned rifles, meeting bland innocence when he asked about unlicensed weapons.

Next on the list were the bearded Sergeant Wishart and his driver, the crew of the Northern car assigned to find where the two men in the Nissan had slept or eaten. There was a service station near Lochinver where they'd bought fuel and a tiny cottage-fare restaurant on the Ullapool road where the men had eaten twice. The Glasgow twosome appeared to have spent three days in the area around Glen Laggan. But where they'd spent most of the time remained a mystery.

'What about local door-to-door?' asked Thane.

'Zilch, boss. That was mine with Dougie Lennox.' Ernie Vass abandoned his newspaper and sniffed the disdain of a died-in-the-wool Aberdonian faced with culture shock. 'God, you practically need an interpreter to understand some of these Highlanders.' Which was how Thane sometimes felt about Vass when the one-time traffic cop unleashed his North-East dialect. Vass wasn't finished. 'No sightings – or none anyone wanted to tell us about. But Dougie met up with one local ancient who says there are plenty of caves in the hills around here. Places the Bonnie Prince Charlie mob used in the old days.'

'Now there's a happy thought,' murmured Phil Moss.

Vass nodded in earnest agreement. 'Some of these caves were big enough to hide a whole damned clan, boss. Even their cattle – which they'd probably stolen anyway.'

'And all best Aberdeen Angus,' agreed Thane wryly, then switched back to Moss. 'So where's Sandra?'

'She can wait.' Moss showed his yellowed teeth in a slight grin. 'Maggie, it's your turn.'

'I tried Broch Castle first like I was asked, superintendent.' Maggie Donald's plump young face reddened at being the new centre of interest. 'They've no live-in staff, a couple of women come daily from the village and there's a handyman. I talked my way into the kitchen for a cup of tea.'

'Tea and gossip, the feminine way,' prompted Moss with a touch of impatience. 'And you were told that Finn Rankin and his daughters don't always play happy families. When they fight, they take no prisoners. Correct?'

She nodded.

'Tell the bit that matters, girl.' Moss made it a growl, then spoiled the effect with a half-strangled burp. 'Colin, she nailed your rubber gloves bandit!'

'May have, sir,' corrected Constable Maggie Donald anxiously, the Highland lilt in her voice gaining in strength. 'When I was walking back from the castle, past the general store, I checked the window display then went in. They sell domestic rubber gloves. But you see, they only had blue gloves left—'

'Get to it,' snarled Moss. 'Forget the bagpipe bits.'

Maggie Donald blinked indignantly. 'The woman in the store said she sold her last pair of yellow gloves yesterday morning to Jess Adams – Donny's wife. She always buys yellow.' She saw the frown shaping on Thane's face and hurried on. 'Jess Adams wasn't happy about buying new gloves. She reckons either her husband or her son took her old pair over the weekend. She said they've done it before – but this time she'd make damned sure they paid for the new ones.'

'How to kit up for a break-in.' Thane sucked hard on his teeth. 'Steal mum's kitchen gloves.' He considered Maggie Donald for a moment, then nodded. 'Nicely done. Keep it up, and I'll maybe even come to love your Loch Ness Monster.'

'Sir—' she started a protest, then a flicker of warning from Moss changed her mind. 'Yes, sir.'

'So where's Sandra?' asked Thane again.

'Being busy.' Moss spelled out the redhead's actions since Thane had dropped her off earlier. First there had been fax messages and telephone calls on a list which included Crime Squad headquarters in Glasgow and Black Watch regimental records in Perth. As she'd finished, a police car had arrived from Inverness to deliver several sets of enlarged still prints of John Rogers and Peter Marsh, reproduced from the Broch Distillery security video. For the first time, officers now had head and shoulders likenesses of the two dead fire-raisers to show around.

'So then she demolished what she had the nerve to call a snack lunch, borrowed Dougie Lennox, and headed out with a set of the video stills to see if they sparked any new memories.' Moss made it plain he didn't particularly believe in that kind of miracle. 'We're waiting on most other things.'

The courier car had already returned home, taking various Scenes of Crime items back to Inverness. More of Thane's borrowed Northern officers would soon be past their 'sell-by' date as far as being on loan was concerned and would have to head off in the same direction. He was at the mercy of time, yet most of the things he needed to know were already being rushed and couldn't be done faster. He felt hungry, he heard his stomach rumble, and that made up his mind on priorities.

'Keep everybody at it, Phil,' he ordered. 'My turn to eat.'

He ordered a beer in the bar then took it through to the dining room. It was empty when he arrived, but Belle Campbell appeared and bustled over as soon as he sat at a table. The landlord's massively built wife slapped a handwritten menu in front of him. She had been working hard over the lunch period and her dress was dark with perspiration under the armpits.

'I heard you went round to see Jess Adams,' she said, a sweetly

94

malicious grin on her lips. 'The stupid bitch didn't like it. As soon as you'd left her place she was on the phone to me, spitting poison!'

Thane avoided being drawn. He ordered soup, and chose wild salmon steaks in preference to a venison stew, but then he stopped Belle Campbell as she made to leave with his order.

'When you and Jess Adams were at school, was Donny Adams in the same class?'

'No, Donny was a couple of years ahead.' Belle Campbell rested her hands on her massive hips for a moment. 'He was in the same class as my husband Leckie.' A memory showed in her eyes. 'There was a year or two when we ran around as a foursome – at that age, you keep daft company.'

Thane nodded. 'Was Finn Rankin around at that time?'

'Finn Rankin?' Belle Campbell gave a surprised frown. 'He was older than us, the boy who lived in the Big House, his folk sent him to boarding school in Inverness. We only saw him around here at holiday times.'

Thane thanked her and she left. A girl from the kitchen brought his food. The soup was a vegetable broth almost thick enough to support the spoon, while the salmon was magnificent in taste and texture with a creamy sauce and side salad which included tiny new potatoes.

Phil Moss joined him purely as a spectator as he finished the salmon. Then Belle Campbell reappeared with a sweet course choice of homemade blackberry pie or a chocolate gateau.

'Coffee only,' decided Thane.

The landlord's wife fussed around Moss for a moment, asking him if he wanted anything, then brought Thane's coffee and left them alone.

'God, I thought you'd never get rid of her.' Moss scowled, reached into his jacket pocket, and brought out a fax sheet. 'Read, enjoy. We were due a break.'

Thane took a sip of the coffee, took the message, read it, then read it again more slowly, savouring every word. Checked back through a travel agent and the airline, it gave the lie to Morris Currie's story of his dash north to help.

Sandra Craig had wondered how Currie had obtained a seat when the weekend flights to Inverness had been so busy. The answer was simple enough. He had booked his flight on the Friday, a full thirty-six hours before the arson attack.

95

'Damned fool,' said Moss acidly. 'Didn't he think we'd check?' Then he belched loudly, painfully. 'Would we have?'

Thane didn't answer. He watched as Moss brought out a small tin tobacco box from one pocket and opened it. Inside was a fine white powder and he watched Moss take a generous pinch, swallow it, and carefully close and put away the box again. The powder was industrial strength magnesium oxide, used as mineral insulation in mainly old-fashioned fire resistant electrical cables. Leaning forward, Moss borrowed Thane's cup and took a mouthful of coffee to wash the powder down.

As a treatment for a duodenal ulcer, it would have terrified most medics. But Sandra Craig had had a grandfather who had been an electrician, who had sworn by the stuff, and she had salvaged some old scrap cable and scraped out the powder. A raging feud between Sandra and Moss had ended the day that Moss first tried it.

'So what do we do about Currie?' asked Moss, returning the borrowed cup.

'We don't rush him.' That much, Thane was certain about. 'We're not ready yet, Phil.'

'That's a reasonable understatement.' Moss opened a shirt button and scratched at his thin chest through the gap. 'But we're getting a damned stupid pro-am mix of leads, Colin. I'd rather stick with the out-and-out pros, thank you.' He stopped scratching. 'I almost forgot. Jock Dawson wants a word with you.'

'About what?' asked Thane.

'I didn't ask, he didn't tell me.' Moss shoved back his chair and rose. 'I don't do dogspeak – it's in your pay grade, not mine. Take some dog biscuits.' He left, and Thane drained another half cup of coffee from the pot into his cup. Except part of the edge of his cup now had a white ring of magnesium oxide. He pushed it aside and was rising when Belle Campbell returned.

'Enjoy your lunch?' she asked.

'Yes, I did.' Thane started to edge towards the door.

'Your friend Inspector Moss is a pleasant wee man,' she said, neatly blocking his escape. 'Needing a tidying, but pleasant.'

He smiled and nodded. Pleasant was not a word used too often about Moss.

'Yet still a bachelor, I heard.' She was puzzled. 'He's not – um – gay, is he?'

'Nobody would ever call him that,' said Thane solemnly.

'Good,' said Belle Campbell, and ambled off.

Leaving Colin Thane with the distinct impression that whatever strange kind of magic attracted middle-aged women to his tramp-like second-in-command had just struck again. They were a regiment, from landladies who might see him as a future police widow's pension to church-goers who could consider salvaging Moss as being part of their religious duty.

With women, there was no accounting for taste.

He left the dining room, went through to the bar again, and found it empty except for the landlord washing and drying glasses at the sink behind the bar. Leckie Campbell was using a grubby dishtowel which gave hygiene a whole new definition.

'Spare me a moment, Leckie.' He waited while Campbell laid down the dishtowel. 'I was talking with your wife—'

'Then you're a brave man, superintendent,' said Campbell dryly.

'She said you were at school with Donny Adams, that you were friends.'

'On and off, and back then.' Campbell gave a cautious nod. 'But you grow away from people. We were in our teens.' He leaned his elbows on the damp surface of the bar counter and lowered his voice. 'There was even a spell when Donny fancied my Belle, and I thought I had a thing going with his Jess. Thank God we grew out of that!'

'Donny is in trouble. It could get a lot worse if we don't find him soon.' Thane paused a moment to let his words sink home. 'Suppose he's hiding somewhere near here. Some place he's known about since he was a teenager. Some place you maybe know about too. It might be an old hut, a ruin, even a cave, a hideaway place you used years ago. Think about it, Leckie.'

Campbell frowned, straightened behind the bar counter, gnawed his lower lip for a moment, then drew a deep, doubtful breath. 'There might be a place or two, I suppose.'

'How about somewhere south of Broch Distillery,' suggested Thane. 'A place where someone who knew about it could hide a vehicle?'

'His pick-up truck?' Slowly, Campbell made up his mind. 'I'd put my money on Ben Nathair – Serpent Rock. It's near enough, there's the remains of a road that hasn't been used since Lord knows when, and there's a cave.' A small smile flickered across his face. 'It's big and it's dry. It started off as a cave, then some dam' fools in Victorian times tried tunnelling for gold or something.' His smile widened. 'We spent a few nights up there – and let's just say we were not always alone! This – well, it wouldn't get Donny into any more trouble than there is already?'

'It wouldn't.'

'I'll believe you, superintendent.' Reaching under the bar counter, Campbell produced an old invoice form and a pencil stub. 'I'll draw a map – the road you want goes off on your left, just beyond a rock slide. Just remember, it's a hell of a long time since I was there.' The reminiscent smile became a sly chuckle. 'We gave the cave a name. We called it the Honey Trap, but don't mention that to Belle. She might not understand!'

He drew the map in a few scrawled pencil lines and handed it over. Thane briefly checked the details, thanked him, left, and found Phil Moss slouching in the corridor outside.

'I think I heard most of it,' said Moss, unabashed. 'When are we going?'

'We?'

'Who else?' demanded Moss. 'I've been stuck at a desk since I got here.' He took the roughly drawn sketch map, considered it, and grimaced. 'And would I let you loose with this on your own?'

Thane sighed, and accepted the inevitable. On their way out, they found Harry Harron standing in the inn's lobby. The Northern officer's long, horse-like face shaped a hopeful beam and he trotted over as Thane beckoned.

'We're going to Ben Nathair,' said Thane. 'Do you know it?'

'Serpent Rock?' Harron nodded. 'Where it is, yes. But—'

'Get hold of Jock Dawson. I want him and his dogs as back-up.' Thane saw Harron's expression. 'You can ride shotgun with him, but don't annoy the dogs. Tell Jock to stay well back, and to watch for a turn-off at a rock slide. Get word to Sergeant Craig. Tell her she's minding the shop. Now move!'

'We've a radio link,' said Moss while Harron hurried off. 'Dougie Lennox waved a magic screwdriver and we can patch into the Northern frequency.'

'Nobody told me,' complained Thane.

'You're a superintendent.' Moss gave a modest belch. 'I'm a

humble inspector. There's a lot that superintendents don't get told – sir.'

Thane driving, they took the Range Rover out of the township and headed south without waiting for Dawson. A band of high cloud had come in from the west and was passing over the long, hill-lined glen, but still with no promise of rain.

'What the hell has gone wrong up here?' demanded Moss. He looked around with apocalyptic gloom. 'This is Scotland at tourist time – so it should be raining, right? The TV weather charts say that's the way it is everywhere else. What they've got in this patch isn't natural.'

'Don't complain too much,' warned Thane. A fat, mottled pheasant half-flew, half-scurried across the road, too fast for him to even think of braking, reached safety, and vanished. 'When it rains up here, it probably floods.'

Moss's shaping growl of a reply ended as their radio came to life. Jock Dawson reported his dog van was under way, with Harron also aboard. There was barking in the background and Thane smiled maliciously, wondering how Harron would enjoy his trip. Then, just beyond the Broch Distillery road end, he gave a mild, warning tap on the Range Rover's horn as they overtook an immaculate old Volkswagen. The occupants, the elderly couple who were still stubbornly remaining as guests at the Ardshona Inn, waved a greeting as they were passed.

'They're loving being in the middle of this,' reported Moss stonily. 'And they're getting a twenty per cent room-rate reduction for having us around.'

'Lucky them.' Thane kept his eyes on the road ahead. 'Phil, I'm trying to make up my mind about something.'

'Like what?'

'How soon I tell Finn Rankin that I know he is lying.'

'He's a fairly big fish.' Moss paused, and Thane could hear his stomach rumble above the low growl of the Range Rover's engine. 'What does a fisherman do when he hooks a respectable size fish, Colin? He plays the thing until it tires, and that way he don't lose him. Hold off until you've got even more, then land him. But maybe you could have another try at his daughters once they get back from Inverness – really go for them.'

'Maybe.' Thane pursed his lips.

He drove on, eyes narrowed against the bright sunlight, barely noticing when they passed the scarred roadside verge which marked where the blue Nissan had crashed. One way or another, he had to locate the way which would lead through to the truth of what was really happening around Broch whisky.

'Hey!' Moss suddenly brought him back with a dig in the ribs and pointed ahead. 'There's your rock fall!'

The Range Rover had just come to a slow bend in the road where it curved round the base of a steep rise of ground. On the far side, the whole face of the rise had come away at some time in a long, wide jumble of naked boulders and earth which time had interlaced with thin patches of scrub. A little beyond where it ended, the overgrown remains of a vehicle track started on a winding upwards climb across a long steep rise that seemed mostly composed of raw, sun-baked stone.

They had reached Ben Nathair, Serpent Rock.

Slowing the Range Rover, steering it off the road and onto the start of the track, Thane flicked the gear-change into four-wheel drive and the transmission whined briefly as it settled into its new mode. Then, as they started the climb, his wing mirrors showed him the dust cloud being thrown up in their wake.

'Tell Dawson we're here,' he told Moss. 'Tell him to ease his speed right back and keep his dust down.'

Moss used the radio handset and Dawson acknowledged. By then, Thane had already reduced his own speed. They lurched and they climbed, and very quickly the main road was left far below, a mere ribbon of tarmac winding through the dramatic high hills that surrounded the stark bulk of Serpent Rock. Further on, an inquisitive brown hare watched as they approached, then scurried off.

'And Campbell's bunch genuinely used to cycle up here when they were kids?' Moss's voice was one stage short of disbelief as the track took another upward wind and they bounced on over the pot-holed, broken surface. 'What were they fed on? Magic porridge?'

'Porridge wasn't the attraction,' murmured Thane.

'I know that,' snarled Moss. 'But who would have any energy left for it?' He checked the pencilled map in his hands, then pointed. 'There's our fork. Take left.'

The track divided a short distance ahead. The main branch wound on and upwards, the other, lesser branch dipped down a shallow slope where the exposed grey rock was heavily veined with black. Slowing again, speed reduced to a crawl, the Range Rover headed left while its suspension suffered on the dried out, badly broken surface.

'Phil.' Thane flicked his gear lever into neutral, nodded ahead, then brought the Range Rover to a halt.

The track ran another hundred yards or so towards a high wall of that grey, black-veined rock, then disappeared into the tunnel-like mouth of a large cave. A light wind stirred an old rag of canvas which hung to one side, but nothing else moved. Anywhere.

'What do you think?' asked Moss. His fingers were already resting on the door handle. 'Straight in, or a look-see first?'

'Look-see,' decided Thane.

Engaging bottom gear, he let the Range Rover trundle slowly towards the cave mouth, then halted it again a short stone's throw away from the start of the black darkness ahead. He flicked the headlamps on at high beam. and heard Moss grunt as they came to life in the sunlight but still lanced deep into the cave. They lit up the vehicle which lay hidden some distance back. It was an old pick-up truck, green in colour. The pick-up which had disappeared with Donny Adams.

'Wait.' Thane stopped Moss as he made to get out. For another long moment he studied all he could see. The pick-up seemed empty and lay in deep shadow, but there were a few vague shapes scattered on the rock floor beside it which could be food or fuel containers. Deeper in, the cave faded into dark emptiness again. He tried a blast of the Range Rover's horn, waited, then glanced at Moss. 'Phil?'

'Looks clear,' agreed Moss. 'Let's do it.'

Thane switched off the engine, opened his door and was aware of Moss doing the same. He climbed out, took a half-dozen steps away from their vehicle, heard a sharp, distant whipcrack of a shot, and made a dive behind the shelter of the Range Rover as a bullet slammed into its bodywork. A moment later Moss came rolling in beside him in a cursing tangle of arms and legs as a second shot punched a neat, star-shaped hole in their windscreen.

'Maybe I was wrong,' said Moss apologetically, crouched down beside him.

'What do you mean maybe?' snarled Thane.

He rose up on his knees, then to a crouch, keeping the reassuring bulk of the big four by four between him and the area where the shot might have come from. They were in the kind of situation where some genius of an army commander might order a regroup to try something different. How were two men, on their own and pinned down, expected to regroup or do anything else?

But time passed and there were no more shots. Stiff from crouching, Thane waited another two full minutes by the second hand of his wrist-watch then deliberately rose to his feet. When nothing happened, Moss also made a cautious appearance.

'Have you lost a screw?' demanded Moss 'You could have got your damned fool head blown off.' His indignation boiled over. 'Then who gets the lousy job of going back to tell Mary she's a new member of the widow's union? Me, right?'

'I think that was Willie Adams leaving his calling card,' said Thane soberly, his mouth feeling strangely dry. 'If he misses, it means he didn't mean to hit.'

'Do we thank him then?' Moss's thin nostrils flared. 'Sorry, but I'm not exactly up on sniping etiquette!'

'Give it a rest, Phil.' Thane opened the driver's door. Reaching across, he grabbed the radio handset and used it to call Jock Dawson's dog van. When Dawson acknowledged, Thane ordered him up to join them. 'But with care, Jock. Someone tried to use us for target practice.'

Dawson acknowledged and Thane tossed the handset back on its shelf. Like most police vehicles, the Range Rover had a powerful hand torch clipped under the facia and he yanked it loose and glanced at Moss.

'Ready?'

'You know I get frightened when I'm left alone,' said Moss sarcastically.

They moved out of the Range Rover's cover and set off, feet crunching across the broken stone and pebbles of the the sun-baked track. What before had been a very short distance to the mouth of the cave suddenly seemed much longer and the hill wind much colder. Both men walked with every sense ready for the sound of another shot.

It didn't happen. They reached the mouth of the cave, walked a few paces inside, their shadows thrown ahead of them by the headlight beams, then Thane paused and shone the torch around.

It flickered over the pick-up truck and a scatter of other items including two old boxes obviously used as seats, and a folding table which held a few pieces of dirty crockery.

'We've found home base.' Thane fanned the torch beam back along the side of the pick-up truck then swore under his breath and steadied the beam. The body of a man lay on the cave floor, close beside the pick-up's cab. Sprawled face down, he wore denim trousers and a khaki shirt with grubby white trainer shoes.

'Now who the hell might we have here?' His lined face suddenly impassive, Phil Moss went over, stooped, and reached out a hand to touch their find.

'No! Don't, Phil!' Horror-struck, Thane yelled a warning as he caught a glimpse of the thin line of wire running out from under the man's body and vanishing beneath the truck. In the next unthinking instant, as a startled Moss looked round, Thane catapulted forward and his solid six-foot build crashed hard into his second-in-command's slight frame. Sheer momentum carried both men skidding across the floor of the cave, hurtling them away from the dead man and the green pick-up.

Two seconds later the world seemed to explode inside the cave. A searing flash blended with a flat, compressing blast which numbed the senses, slammed into lungs and chests, subjected their eardrums to an instant of agony. Sharp flakes of metal and pieces of debris raked the air around them. Something heavier crashed against the cave wall behind them, flames were suddenly licking around the pick-up's underside.

But they were alive. Somehow, they helped one another to their feet then staggered out through the flames and choking smoke, reached the mouth of the cave, and kept going until they reached the Range Rover then collapsed behind it.

'Thanks,' wheezed Moss while they lay side-by-side. Smoke had blackened his face, except where small rivulets of blood from tiny stone-flake lacerations had oozed their paths. Licking his lips, systematically checking that every part of his body still seemed to work, he gave a massively thankful burp and stared at an equally blackened and lacerated Thane. 'What the hell happened?'

'The body was booby-trapped,' said Thane simply. 'Northern Ireland style.'

'But it was Donny Adams?'

'I think so.' Thane looked back at the cave as more fire and smoke came billowing out from its hell-like mouth. He didn't know for sure. Any more than he knew whether Willie Adams had ever served as a soldier in Northern Ireland. Or whether the two shots fired at them had been a simple warning ... or even who had fired them.

'Well, I can tell you one thing for real.' Moss managed a grin, then winced as he raised himself up om his elbows. 'When you decked me, it was like being hit by a flying brick privy. Next time, I'll take my chance with the bomb. All right?'

Two minutes later, Jock Dawson's dog van raced in and screamed to a halt. Back-up had arrived. High overhead, a black buzzard lazily rode a thermal and watched for prey on the hillsides below.

Buzzards always got their priorities right.

5

They let the new arrivals take over.

First, Jock Dawson brought out his dogs, stationed them like sentries, then radioed back to Ardshona township. A tight-lipped Harry Harron fetched water from a clear trickle of a burn which ran nearby, and made a surprisingly gentle business of ministering to their cuts and bruises. As the Northern man finished, Dawson produced a flask of coffee from his van. The coffee was strong, steaming, and liberally laced with the brandy which Dawson listed as a priority in a dog handler's travelling emergency kit.

'Priority is right.' Thane emptied his cup in a long gulp, and took some of the taste of smoke and dirt out of his mouth. He accepted a refill while he wondered if he could look as bad as Moss, whose face and hands were peppered with small cuts from the results of the blast. By the time he'd finished sipping a way through the second cupful, the worst of the trembling had left his body. Setting down the cup, he nodded to Harron. 'Give me a hand up.'

Harron helped him upright. Propped against the Range Rover,

Thane considered the borrowed Northern vehicle and sighed. The windscreen had a hole punched by a flying rock, one headlamp had ceased to exist, and the paintwork showed a multitude of chips and dents. In the background, the fire inside the cave seemed to have gone out. He heard a grunt, and Moss arrived beside him.

'Do you reckon our rifleman has gone?' asked Moss sourly. 'Or do I walk around and tell you if I get shot?'

'By now, he's probably far away.'

'On his trail bike?'

'If we're guessing, yes. Even though we didn't hear it.' Thane sucked hard on his teeth. 'Whoever he was, my other guess is he was expecting someone else to come to the cave, and the boobytrap was to be the welcome. When we turned up instead, maybe he tried to warn us off.'

'So we should thank him?' Moss sighed. 'Who gets to tell Mick Farrell we need the rest of his people back again?'

'Who gets to tell him about his car?' Thane could imagine the Northern CID chief's reaction. He looked around, then had the answer. 'Harry—'

'Sir?' Detective Constable Harron responded eagerly.

'Harry, I want you along while we take another look in that cave. Then it's your turn to radio back to Sergeant Craig. Give her another update. After that, if she can patch you through to Inverness, you can – uh – do the same for Chief Superintendent Farrell.'

Harron blanched at the thought. 'Me, sir?'

'You,' said Thane firmly. 'You're one of his officers, aren't you?'

Sadly, Harry Harron joined the other three men as they walked over to the blackened entrance to the cave. Jock Dawson brought a large battery lantern from his dog van and they used it, going in behind the beam of light.

All around them the shadowed walls of the cave had been blackened by fire. Tendrils of smoke still hung lazily in the air, and there was the strong stench of burning. They found the green pick-up truck had been reduced to a burnt out wreck. The steering wheel had melted into a misshapen curve, the cab seats had been reduced to bare frames and some pathetic metal springs.

'Hard luck, mate,' muttered Jock Dawson as he played the beam of the battery lamp over the body at their feet. 'Looks like you had it rough!'

The dead man's clothes and shoes had been charred by the flames, but his body had been partly protected by the pick-up's metalwork. His hair had gone and one side of his face had been burned away. Adding to the horror, the entire blackened body had twisted and stiffened into that crouching, pugilistic shape which even after death was the usual result of intense heat and coagulated muscles.

Harry Harron made a gagging noise and blundered away. They heard him retching somewhere outside.

'I think I'll take a wee breath of fresh air too,' said Jock Dawson soberly, laying down the battery lantern, and following him out.

'Lucky them.' Taking the battery lantern, trying to ignore the sickly sweet odour of burned flesh and the way his own stomach was twitching, Thane squatted beside the blackened body and considered the thin, smoke-dulled wiring of the boobytrap. Someone had known exactly what to do and how to do it.

'Really set things up, didn't he?' Moss pointed to the half-exposed length of a shotgun. The rest of the weapon lay under the dead man. Another thin wire trace showed how the shotgun had also been a back-up part of the boobytrap mechanism.

'He had the bait, he used it.' Thane got to his feet, picking up the battery lantern. There was nothing more they could do until the specialists arrived. 'Seen enough?'

'Enough,' agreed Moss grimly.

They were on their way out of the cave when they heard the dogs begin a fierce barking, then the blast of a police whistle. Running, they got out into the open and stared. Neither dog had moved from its post, although their barking continued. Jock Dawson was the whistle-blower, watched by an open-mouthed Harron. The cause was about two hundred yards away, on the narrow path that led down to the cave from the main track.

'I don't believe it!' Moss gulped.

The elderly couple from the Ardshona Inn had arrived, their beautifully polished Volkswagen's paintwork glinting in the sunlight. They had parked on a patch of level ground where a few low clumps of yellow flowering gorse clung to the thin mix of gravel and pale brown soil. The man was setting up folding chairs and his wife was spreading out a small tablecloth. Looking over towards the cave, both gave a cheerful wave.

'Sir—' Dawson gave up. 'They're having a bloody picnic!'

'Not here they're not!' Thane drew a deep breath and tried to keep a grip on his sanity. 'Get rid of them, Jock. Now. Send them right back where they came from! Now!'

Shaking his head, the lanky dog-handler galloped over with the massive tan and black Rajah and the sleek yellow Goldie bounding at his heels. While Dawson spoke to the man, Thane swore in near disbelief as he saw the woman calmly feed sandwiches to both animals. But an amicable agreement was reached, the picnic equipment was packed away again, and within a couple of minutes the Volkswagen had bounced round in a tight turn and was heading back the way it had come.

'Tell me that wasn't real,' pleaded Moss to the world in general.

'It's about as real as anything else around here.' Thane walked over to Harron, who still looked pale around the gills. 'All right now?'

'More or less, sir.' The man showed his chipped teeth in a forced grimace of a smile. 'I'm sorry. I should have remembered Proverbs 12, 16 – "a prudent man covereth shame".'

'I've a better idea,' snapped Phil Moss. 'Next time, try the gospel according to Saint Moss. A prudent cop doesn't throw up over the only reasonable tyre tracks I've seen.'

Thane silenced Moss with a scowl, 'Harry, if you don't turn down this spur then where else does the track lead?'

'Through a gap in the hills, then it joins an old forestry road, sir. From there you've a choice – either head back for Ardshona or work towards the west.'

Thane sighed in resignation. It was the way the maps suggested. The hills might be empty and lonely, but they were still threaded from end to end by a network of tracks.

'Who was he?' he asked grimly.

'That one?' Instinctively, Harron gave a sick glance towards the cave.

'That one.' Thane stayed patient. 'I only saw Donny Adams on that video clip. You met him.'

'In the flesh,' said Moss cruelly. 'Walking. Uncooked.'

Harron winced and closed his eyes.

107

'Well?' demanded Thane. 'Was that Donny the Shovel?'

'Yes,' said Harron wearily.

They left him. With Moss following, Thane walked a few paces to where the ground was heavily laced with old, broken mine spoil. Strange weeds clung to life around the base of a piece of rotted timber which had once been a roof prop.

'You know what we're looking at?' said Moss, disgust in his voice. 'It could be son kills father, then son uses father's body as dead bait.'

'I'm maybe thinking it, Phil,' admitted Thane. 'But I'm not saying it – not yet.'

There were things to do. While Harry Harron used the radio in an extended conversation with his force headquarters at Inverness, Moss went back into the cave again. While that was happening, Jock Dawson took his dogs on a circling patrol around the immediate area. By then, Colin Thane had perched himself on a boulder, viewing the entire crime scene.

'Sir – got a moment?' asked Dawson, coming over.

'Be my guest.' Thane thumbed at the space beside him on the boulder.

Dawson lowered himself thankfully. He was wearing his usual faded blue overalls and short rubber boots, and his dogs sat at his feet, waiting, no longer barking. Their tails wagged frantically as he reached into an overall pocket and brought out two squeaky rubber toys. The yellow duck belonged to Rajah, the blue fish was Goldie's property. Either dog happily tackled armed gunmen as part of their working week. But even police dogs needed time to relax, a chance to play. All hell could break loose if the wrong dog got the wrong toy on a rest-break.

'Well, sir—' Dawson tossed the yellow duck to the massive German shepherd, who began chewing happily, then repeated the process for the yellow Labrador bitch ' – I'm not sure. Maybe this matters, maybe it doesn't—'

'Jock.' Thane made it a warning. 'Get to it. I'm not having a good day.'

'Sorry.' Dawson grinned, brought out a battered metal cigarette tin, opened it, took out a cigarette, lit it with a match, and took a long, deep draw. 'Remember how you sent me out to work the dogs around the bushes near that broch place. They found cartridge cases, sniffed some tracks—'

'I remember.' Thane nodded.

'There was something else. It was Goldie.' Dawson glanced towards the Labrador, now rolled over on her back. 'You know how it goes – Goldie is the brains, her big pal is the brawn.' He took another long pull on his cigarette and let the smoke out slowly. 'Goldie was working this one scent, your rifleman, right? She kept picking it up here and there, and almost every time, wherever it went, that scent led back to the same spot – right to the door of that broch place. Like – well, like the scent came that way regular enough to have a season ticket.'

'You're sure?' Thane stared.

'No, but she is.' Dawson crinkled a grin. 'So I thought you'd want to know.'

'You're right,' said Thane softly. 'You're very right.'

It wasn't long afterwards that more dust plumes began to show on the track leading up Serpent Rock. The first car to arrive brought Lennox and Vass, and the two Crime Squad men were hardly out of their vehicle before Andy Kerr arrived aboard his telephone linesman's van, followed by his wife driving their old Peugot.

'We've been mobilized as Specials,' said Kerr happily.

'Says who?' asked Thane.

'Your sergeant,' Kerr beamed. 'She told us to get out here, fast.'

'Who authorized it?'

'We've no idea,' said Joan Kerr impatiently. 'How can we help?'

Two more dust plumes were toiling up the hill road towards them. When they arrived, one contained Nikki Neilson, the flat-nosed Northern scenes of crime officer. Diverted with his driver just as he finished at Iain Cameron's cottage, he had been ready to leave for Inverness. The other was a trio of Northern uniform officers scraped together and grabbed by Sandra Craig. They were led by the bearded Patrol Sergeant Wishart. With him came his driver and Fergus Gordon, the young Fadda constable.

'I've a message for you from that red-haired terror of a sergeant of yours, sir,' said Wishart, a reluctant admiration in his voice. 'She's using Maggie Donald as her back-up and the lid is on everything at her end. No problems.' He grimaced. 'But I've also to tell you that Chief Superintendent Farrell is on his way, red alert style!'

For a change, Thane had the luxury of troops to spare. He sent Andy Kerr into the cave to view the burned body, with Joan Kerr insisting on going with her husband. When they emerged, the linesman looked green – but they agreed on the dead man's identity. They had Donny the Shovel. That done, he teamed the two specials with Fergus Gordon and Wishart's driver then sent them off in pairs to seal both ends of the Serpent Rock track.

One set of visitors who wanted a picnic was more than enough.

Neilson and his driver rigged battery lights inside the cave then carried in the scenes of crime man's glinting aluminium boxes of equipment. The others spread out behind the dogs and began a steadily widening circular sweep which used the cave mouth as its base point. The afternoon seemed to become steadily hotter under the sun in that vast cloudless sky and swarms of flying insects of various shapes, sizes and biting potential came buzzing out of nowhere. An electronic camera flash began spitting at regular intervals inside the cave.

'It's too damned hot,' complained Phil Moss. He had knotted the corners of his grubby handkerchief and was using it as a crude sunhat. Sweat was running down the cuts on his face. 'So we've a murder – but what else brings Pat Farrell galloping up from Inverness?'

'I've a feeling we'll find out.' Thane looked over to where Harry Harron was awkwardly picking his long-legged way over a stretch of stunted heather, part of the line in the latest sweep search. Whatever had been said in the radio exchange between the Northern detective constable and his chief superintendent, Harron had avoided talking about it afterwards. 'Don't expect any prizes.'

Moss's acid chuckle came to a halt as there was a shout and an urgent waving from one of the Northern men further along the hillside, then Jock Dawson was crashing across with both his dogs. A few more moments was enough for both dogs to be circling around a tight area of ground, then Dawson was signalling. Thane waved back, then set off to join him. Moss close at his heels, he covered the distance of rough hillside at a fast trot.

'This boy knows what he's doing, sir.' Dawson said it with a loud, grudging admiration as Thane arrived. Then he aimed a bellow at his dogs. 'You two stupid devils stay out o' it – right out, you hear me?'

As the German shepherd and Labrador reluctantly backed off, Thane looked down at a crushed depression among the thin mix of heather and semi-Alpine plants. They'd found the sniper's nest, big enough to hold a man in comfort, right down to a pillow of bracken leaves with a flattened area where his head had rested. Squatting down, careful not to disturb the scene, Thane sighted an imaginary rifle towards the cave mouth. The range was ideal, the field of fire was ideal.

'Well done,' he told the Northern man who had made the find. Then he turned to Dawson again. 'Work your dogs from here, Jock, see what they get.'

'Here's a start.' Phil Moss had stopped a short distance away. 'One of the cartridge cases. Looks like the last ones.'

Moss bent down beside the glinting brass and pushed a pencil into the ground beside it to mark the spot for later. Almost immediately, Harron gave a pleased grunt as he located another.

'Any luck with vehicle tracks?' Thane asked.

The group around him shook their heads. There were traces of tyre tracks and suspicions of tyre tracks, probably from more than one vehicle – but on the Serpent Rock's harsh mix of scree and mine spill there was very little that would stand up as any kind of evidence. In court, they were traces which would have been thrown out as a waste of time.

'We've got something,' announced Jock Dawson suddenly. After sniffing around in an apparently aimless fashion, both dogs had settled on following a definite route. The scent led away from the cave then headed up a slope covered in scrub and gorse.

'Stay with it,' ordered Thane. He sent a man off with Dawson, left Moss to keep the others searching the more immediate vicinity, and walked back towards the cave. He got there as Nikki Neilson re-emerged into daylight.

'It must have been like amateur night barbecue in there,' grimaced the Northern Scenes of Crime man. 'This part of the world is great on burning people, sir.' He drew a deep, thankful breath of clean air. 'Do we know who he is?'

Thane nodded. 'We're pretty certain.'

'Well, it was neat, but it was still a DIY job, superintendent.' Neilson pulled out his cigarettes and offered the pack.

Thane almost reached for one, then shook his head. He'd been stopped for a long time, even if the instinct was still there, liable to surface when other pressures were on. 'What do you mean, DIY?'

'Somebody used leftovers from the the Broch warehouse fire.' Neilson lit his cigarette with a gun metal lighter which bore the Northern Constabulary crest. 'Same kind of explosive charge, designed to start a fire. The same kind of el cheapo fuse device, but cut down to a three-second delay.' He drew on his cigarette, reasonably pleased with what he'd done. 'The same with the booby-trap wire. There's a whole reel of the stuff lying in there, the same gauge they used to make up the warehouse firebombs.'

The double-barrelled shotgun wired into the booby-trap had been loaded. It looked as thought both shotgun shells had exploded in the heat of the blaze. Nikki Neilson had taken scrapings and samples everywhere for forensics to look at later.

But he had nothing else that was new.

Thane thanked him, told him about the flattened hollow in the heather and the cartridge cases, then left him and went over to the Range Rover. Phil Moss had decided to put one of the Crime Squad team on radio watch, and Dougie Lennox peeped out at him from the opened driver's door. A soft crackle of static was coming from the monitor speaker on the facia.

'Anything?' asked Thane.

'All quiet, sir.' Lennox shook his head. 'Sergeant Craig made a routine check a couple of minutes ago. Nothing else.'

'Out.' Thane thumbed Lennox down, took the vacated seat, and used the radio's handset. He grinned at the speed with which Sandra Craig answered the call.

'Everything okay your end?' he asked.

'That's supposed to be my line, sir,' she said grimly. 'According to Dougie, you and Inspector Moss both have faces like grated carrots.'

'Scraped, not grated. Our DC Lennox exaggerates a little,' said Thane dryly.

'When should we expect Mick Farrell?'

'The Chief Superintendent said as soon as he could make it. Wait, sir.' She broke off, and he could hear Maggie Donald's voice for a moment in the microphone's background, querying something, a swift agreement from Sandra, then she was with him again. 'Commander Hart called from Glasgow.'

'That makes my day.' As Crime Squad commander, Jack Hart made sure nothing that mattered slipped past him. 'How did he sound?'

'I've heard him happier,' the redhead admitted.

Thane allowed himself a small chuckle, though it made his face nip. It sounded a reasonable understatement.

'What else should I know about?'

'I'd reckon the rest can keep till you get back.' She had a question of her own. 'Is it a positive ID on Donny Adams, sir?'

'Near enough. But sit on that for now.' Thane paused, hearing a new throbbing noise which was rapidly growing. He saw a helicopter had appeared round the shoulder of Serpent Rock and was heading towards them. 'Visitors, sergeant. I'll get back to you.'

He signed off, then glanced at his watch as the helicopter, a yellow Sea King with Royal Navy markings, lost height and looked for a landing place. It was hard to believe. Two full hours had passed since he and Moss had driven up that track to the cave mouth. Even so, Mick Farrell hadn't wasted time.

The Sea King landed in a noisy thrash of rotor blades and a storm of dust less than the length of a football pitch from the cave. Thane started towards it as the rotors slowed and the dust settled and got there as a door opened and a naval crewman helped out three people. Chief Superintendent Farrell was first, next came the bald-headed Detective Inspector Mack, then Linton, the plump, bushy-haired police surgeon. They hurried out from under the still churning rotors and came towards him.

'Making a habit of this, aren't you?' Mick Farrell gave him a grudging handshake, then indicated his companions. 'They're staying, Thane. I'm just looking, on my way to somewhere else. The rest of the back-up team are on their way by road.' He looked around. Dougie Lennox had whisked himself over to the mouth of the cave and was giving a reasonable imitation of being on guard. 'That's the place?'

Thane nodded and the Northern Force's CID chief sent Mack and Linton off towards it with a gesture. Then he faced Thane again, gave a long sigh, and shook his head. 'Colin, what the hell is going on up here? Do we know?'

'Not yet,' admitted Thane wryly.

'Well, you're honest about it.' Farrell saw the Range Rover, strode towards it, and his mouth tightened as he saw its state.

113

'My God, do you know how much form-fillling it will take before we can get that thing looking respectable again? Not that you're much better.'

'Thanks,' said Thane woodenly. 'It matters when people care, sir.'

Farrell grinned a little, then slapped away a large, buzzing insect hovering near his mouth. 'Still the same bottom line here? Your body has a probable ID as Donny Adams, and you want to find his son?'

'Yes. With reasons.' Thane took about a minute to give the Northern chief superintendent a brief update.

'All right.' Farrell didn't look impressed. 'I've heard you, I'll wait, although this time we're talking murder. There's also the media to worry about' – he pronounced media as if it had a bad smell – 'we've kept them out of things so far, and I'll do my damnedest to keep it that way.'

'For everybody's sake?' murmured Thane.

'Yes.' Farrell fell silent for a long moment, looking out at the harsh shadows on the sun-baked hills. Briefly, the personal strain he was under showed on his face, then disappeared. 'Right now, I need the media sniffing up here like I need a hole in the head. Luckily, on this side of the Highland Line we're remote enough to lose them most of the time. We've also taken on a new PR woman. She's good, she's ex-Strathclyde Force Information, and she acts wonderfully thick when it suits her. I'll make sure she does her smokescreen act.' He frowned at his feet. 'Now, how about Finn Rankin?'

Thane shrugged. 'He tells me what he wants me to know. Which isn't a lot.'

'I'm friendly with Rankin. I like him.' Farrell pursed his lips. 'But don't let that stand in your way. The same goes for anyone else at Broch – man or woman. Understood?'

'Understood,' agreed Thane unemotionally.

'Good.' Farrell stole a glance at his wrist-watch. 'One thing more, Colin. I've a Chief Constable who now thinks calling your mob in wasn't such a good idea. He'd like us to take over again, send you packing. Except we can't, we need you. At least until the end of the month.'

'The end of the month.' Thane raised an eyebrow. 'Is that when . . . ?'

'When our special operation ends.' Farrell nodded. 'Hell, I hate

114

this cloak-and-dagger nonsense. Be glad you're not involved.' He took a deep breath, then let it out like a sigh. 'The last thing I need is for this Broch business to go nuclear on me. But if it does . . .'

Thane nodded his understanding.

'Right.' Farrell gave a wry grin. 'Now I want a quick look at your cave and your body, then I'm gone. That's a promise.'

They went over. There were extra lights now in the cave. Andy Mack and David Linton were hunched over the crisped body on the floor and Mack made to rise as he saw his chief superintendent. Pat Farrell waved him down again, looked around for a couple of minutes, then glanced at Linton.

'Any revelations yet, doctor?'

'He's certainly dead,' murmured Linton.

'We always rely on your judgement, doctor.' Farrell gave a dry nod. 'Thank you.' He barely paused. 'Any immediate problems, Andy?'

'No, sir.' Andy Mack shook his head.

Farrell glanced at Thane, nodded, and they went together back out into the open. The helicopter was there as before, rotors still turning slowly.

'Good luck,' said Farrell.

'I could use it,' said Thane as they shook hands. 'Uh – have you far to go?'

'From here? Maybe about—' Farrell stopped himself in time and twisted a grin. 'Mind your own damned business!' Then he hurried over to the Sea King, and the rotors began quickening as he got aboard.

Seconds later, the big yellow helicopter took off. Flying low, it vanished behind the peak of Serpent Rock and didn't reappear. Mick Farrell didn't invite guesswork.

The evening shadows were beginning to lengthen before Colin Thane finally got back to Ardshona township. He returned as a passenger in the damaged Range Rover with Dougie Lennox driving, the baby-faced detective constable intended as a relief for Sandra Craig at the incident centre.

Thane sat quietly while the Range Rover lurched and swayed down the long hillside track to where it joined the metalled surface of the road for Ardshona. He tried to ignore the constant draught coming in through the hole in the windshield, glad of a chance to think. Over three hours had passed since Farrell's helicopter had departed. The next arrivals had come some time later, a three-vehicle convoy from Inverness – a police car with a crew of two uniformed men, a Scenes of Crime station wagon driven by a civilian forensic aide bringing equipment for Nikki Neilson, and a mortuary van crewed by a driver and attendant. As soon as they arrived, Thane had released the Kerrs from their respective ends of the Serpent Rock track.

The husband and wife special constables drove in to see him before they went home. Andy Kerr had turned back two forestry trucks. Joan Kerr, stationed where the hill track branched with the Ardshona road, had been busier. She'd turned away several tourist cars bent on exploring, then two trail-bike riders who claimed to be out testing their machines. Except that both were notorious poachers.

Once the Kerrs had gone homeward, with hungry children waiting there to be fed, Thane had talked with Jock Dawson, who had returned with his dogs. The scent first picked up by the dogs at the sniper's nest in the heather had led over the best part of a mile of rough, broken hillside, crossing several burns and a stretch of dried-up bog. Where it ended there were clear signs that a motor cycle had been hidden among the bracken then had headed off cross-country towards the forestry roads.

'Scenes of Crime may be able to do something with what they're getting,' Phil Moss had reported a little later. 'They also want to make another full forensic check of the cave again. But they'll leave it until tomorrow.'

Jock Dawson had withdrawn his dogs, saying they were due a break – which usually meant that Dawson wanted a rest. Dr Linton was stubbornly refusing to say anything about how Donny Adams had died until after an autopsy. The mortuary van, carrying Adams in a black zip-front body bag, had already left. Things were quietening down again.

Thane had left Moss to close down the rest of the operation for the night and Andy Mack was arranging an overnight watch rota by his own Northern men. But although they might be dealing with murder inside Serpent Rock cave, Thane knew he was heading back once more to the real heart of the matter – the brooding menace that hung over Broch Distillery and the family who owned it.

Heading for Ardshona, the Range Rover encountered at least a dozen trail bikes coming out from the township. Some puttering, some snarling, a few pouring out smoky exhaust, they outnumbered any other traffic. Some riders were women with shopping bags lashed to their panniers, part of the Ardshona equivalent of homeward rush-hour traffic. Most of the time, Dougie Lennox tried to keep up some kind of a conversation. But Lennox's main topic seemed to be all computer speak – kilobytes and gigabytes mixed with strange noises about multi-tasking and networking. Thane was glad when the young DC gave up.

They drove in through the centre of the township, conscious of people stopping and watching in a way that hadn't happened before. When the Range Rover parked at the Ardshona Inn, Thane went through on his own to their storeroom incident room at the rear. Sandra Craig was slouched in a chair, reading some report sheets and eating an apple. Maggie Donald was in her shirt-sleeves again, combing her hair in front of a small mirror they'd fastened to a wall.

'Superintendent—' Maggie Donald saw him first in the mirror, turned, then stared, her mouth falling open.

'Sir—' Sandra Craig swung round, looked hard at his face, then winced. 'You look rough.'

'Thank you, sergeant.' Thane propped himself against her table and scowled. 'Kind words always help.' There were more apples in a paper bag beside her, and he helped himself to one, taking a first bite. 'Constable Donald . . .'

'Sir?' Maggie Donald finished wriggling back into her uniform jacket.

'Your Range Rover is outside, with DC Lennox. Better take a look. At the car, I mean – you may not be too happy.'

'Yes, sir.' She gave a quick blush and left them.

'Lennox?' asked Thane wearily. 'Another one?'

'He's like a baby-faced sex virus,' said Sandra Craig. The redhead abandoned her apple, set down the report sheets, and her mood became suddenly serious. 'Sir, I wanted to come out when I heard what happened—'

'But you didn't.' Thane cut her short. 'And you called it right. Keeping this incident room open mattered most.' He saw the doubt still lingering on her attractive, fine-boned face, and laid a hand lightly on her shoulder. 'Look, Sandra, you're still learning.

Part of being a sergeant is that you can miss out on some of the action.' His mind recoiled from a vision of a burned, partly melted face. 'You did what you should have done. You did it well.'

She shrugged. 'There's something you don't know about . . .'

'It can wait.' Thane used a foot to hook a chair over towards the table. 'Our next priority isn't pretty. We've got to go round to tell Jess Adams that she has become a widow.'

'She knows already.' Sandra said it flatly. 'That's what you didn't know, sir.'

Thane stared. 'How?'

'Joan Kerr. But some of it was maybe my fault.' His sergeant gave an unhappy shrug. 'She looked in here when she got back from Serpent Rock. Up till then, people only knew that there had been some kind of fatal accident out there.' She sighed. 'I didn't warn her enough, she talked – and after that it was jungle drums time. Jess Adams was here half an hour ago, wanting to know if her husband was dead.'

'And you told her what?'

'That I didn't know for sure.'

Thane drew a breath and let it out slowly. 'Have we had anything back from Army Records about her son?'

'Willie Adams got his medical discharge, like she told you. He was a corporal – and a proficiency badge as the best marksman in his unit.'

Thane swore softly. 'We'll go round and see her. But only to tell her about her husband – for now.'

'There's something else.' Sandra Craig picked up her half-eaten apple and tossed it viciously into a waste basket. 'The Rankins are back at Broch Castle – all of them. Lisa and Anna got back from Inverness a couple of hours ago. The other sister, Gina, was with them.'

'You saw them?'

'Maggie heard and checked. Gina and her husband arrived on the afternoon flight from Glasgow. Morris Currie, the sales director, came up with them.' She showed her strong white teeth in a bitter, humourless smile. 'Maybe they're having a council of war.'

'Maybe they need one.' Thane shoved away the unused chair and beckoned. 'Jess Adams.'

They left the inn without meeting anyone. Outside, Dougie

Lennox was lurking cautiously near the Range Rover while a tight-lipped Maggie Donald considered the damage to her charge.

'A respray will fix most of it,' soothed Thane. He glanced at Lennox. 'Take over in the incident room – Maggie will bring you up to date. We've something to do that can't wait.'

Thane saw Sandra aboard. Then he took the wheel and set the Range Rover moving on the short journey round to Jess Adams' home. Although it was barely dusk, the window curtains were closed when he parked outside the house. But there were lights behind the windows. He glanced at Sandra Craig, nodded, and they got out, then crunched up the pathway towards the front door. The door swung open as they reached it – and Belle Campbell looked out at them.

'Superintendent.' She nodded a greeting.

'Belle?' Thane didn't hide his surprise. 'I didn't expect you to be here.'

'It's my place.' The big woman who had traded so many insults with Jess Adams brushed all that aside. 'She needs someone. We go back a long time.'

She beckoned them in, closed the door again, then led the way through to the living room. Jess Adams was sitting in an armchair. Swollen eyes showed that she had been crying.

'Thank you for coming, superintendent,' she said with a strange, formal dignity. 'You're here to tell me about Donny?'

'Yes. I'm sorry, Mrs Adams.' Thane gave her a small, sympathetic nod. 'And sorry we weren't certain enough to tell you earlier.'

Belle Campbell had taken up position behind her schoolfriend and gave a derisive snort. 'Why not?'

'We had to be sure first.' Thane took a step nearer the woman and compounded one lie with another. 'There was an accident with his pick-up truck, then a fire. We still aren't sure of details.' He anticipated her next question. 'His body has been taken to Inverness. We'll need a post-mortem.'

She gave a silent nod.

'Is there anything we can do to help?' asked Sandra.

'Belle's here.' Jess Adams raised a hand, and Belle Campbell gave it a gentle squeeze. 'She's all I need.'

'What about your son, Mrs Adams?' asked Thane. 'Has he been in touch yet?'

'No.' Something that had to be caution showed in her eyes.

'When did you last see Willie?' asked Sandra quietly.

'Sunday afternoon – he only stayed about an hour.' The woman avoided their gaze. 'He had heard about the warehouse. He rode over on his trail bike to make sure Donny was all right.'

Thane tackled what mattered head on. 'Have you any idea where he was heading after he left here?'

Jess Adams shook her head.

'We'll try to find him, Mrs Adams.' As she spoke, Sandra reached for the framed picture of the young soldier in uniform. 'We need his photograph. I'll make sure you get it back tomorrow.'

'Belle . . .' Uncertain, the woman looked at her companion for help.

'Better do what they ask.' Belle Campbell gave a suspicious frown, but nodded. She looked firmly at Thane. 'I think the woman has had enough for tonight.'

'We're finished for now,' soothed Thane. He nodded to Sandra Craig, she tucked the photograph under one arm. They had turned to leave when Jess Adams spoke again.

'I didn't like Donny very much, superintendent.' Her voice was strained but determined. 'But he was still my husband. He never did me any harm.'

'We'll remember,' said Thane quietly. 'Get some rest, Mrs Adams.' He glanced at Belle Campbell. 'You'll stay with her?'

She nodded.

'We'll see ourselves out,' said Thane.

They did. Relieved it was over for the moment, knowing that sooner or later they would have to be back, Thane sat silent in the car for a long minute with his hands resting on the steering wheel. Then he drew a deep breath, keyed the ignition, and set the vehicle moving.

Dusk was greying into night when they returned to the Ardshona Inn and the scent of woodsmoke was in the air as Thane parked the Range Rover and led the way into the building.

Phil Moss was waiting in the incident room.

He nodded to Sandra Craig, then looked at Thane. 'How was it?'

'Not good.' Thane dumped his jacket over the back of a chair.

The one-time storeroom was beginning to acquire an established air with numerous notices stuck to its walls, files and paperwork starting to accumulate on the trestle-table desks, and a steady clicking and buzzing from its electronic hardware. Moss – it had to be Moss – had acquired a coffee perculator, now bubbling in a corner. But Dougie Lennox was more likely to blame for a police radio which looked like it had gone through major surgery and now murmuring a background programme of static-free combo jazz.

'You've had a telephone call – an invitation.' Moss scratched absently at a scab of dried blood on his face. 'Finn Rankin wants you to call round at his place tonight. Have a drink, meet the assembled family.' He saw Thane's blink of almost angry disbelief. 'Relax. He knows about Donny Adams . . .'

'Doesn't everybody?' muttered Sandra Craig.

Moss gave a slight twist of a grin, but otherwise ignored her. 'Rankin made apologetic noises, Colin. But he said there were things it was important you knew about – particularly now.'

'All right.' Reluctantly, Thane nodded. 'When?'

'They'll expect you around nine-thirty.' Moss treated himself to the luxury of an alarming belch. 'While you're socializing with a glass in your hand, I'll be trying to make sure a certain twice-damned detective sergeant gets her team's reports up to date.'

Behind his back, Sandra Craig shaped a silent snarl.

'That goes equally for her similarly damned boss when he has the time,' added Moss. 'And I'm only doing my job. Message received?'

Thane nodded sadly. More and more, policing seemed to rely on forms and computer disks, less on handcuffs and hunches. The photograph they'd collected of Willie Adams was in front of him, and he tapped it with a finger.

'I want this out of its frame, photocopied, then sent out as an all-forces fax. Let's find out if it rings bells anywhere.' He glanced across at Sandra Craig. 'Where's the Army Records stuff that came in?'

'Here, sir.' His red-headed sergeant placed a message form on top of the photograph.

Thane skimmed through the army wordage. Willie Adams seemed to have been a more than competent soldier. He had twice been a corporal and twice had lost his stripes – each time for brawling. As a trained marksman he had been an instructor,

121

had won proficiency badges, and would probably have made sergeant if he hadn't been invalided out. His mother was listed as his next of kin.

But there was something else there, something Thane had more or less expected. Willie Adams had instructed in something more than musketry. He had taken a full course to qualify in teaching how to combat terrorist street-fighting techniques – which had to mean knowing about booby-trapping a corpse.

'There's also this, sir.' Sandra handed him a second sheet then went back to unwrapping a thick bar of nut chocolate produced from one of her secret stores.

The new sheet was an initial Northern Constabulary ballistics report on the two ejected cartridge cases found near the Pictish broch.

'Seen this, Phil?' asked Thane.

Moss gave a slight nod and Thane silently read through the precise wordage.

'The cartridges, long reach rifle ammunition, showed marking consistency with being fired from an imported Mossberg .22 rimfire model, probably a Model 480S autoloader, which may use a seven-shot clip. The weapon, which has a distinctive walnut stock and which has mountings for a telescopic sight, is a frequent professional choice of small bore rifle being extremely accurate and capable of bringing down deer in the right hands.

'An aspect which should be emphasized is that both cartridge cases show additional markings consistent with having been hand-loaded. This further sign of professional usage can be interpreted as meaning ammunition likely to possess a greater accuracy, range, and stopping power than equivalent commercial ammunition.'

Thane laid the report down with a vaguely sick feeling in his stomach as he remembered the two occasions he'd been fired at.

'Reads like we've got ourselves an updated Billy the Kid,' declared Phil Moss almost cheerfully. 'You know what it means? If he shoots you, it won't be an accident.'

Thane nodded. In a strange way, he was clinging to that hope.

There were other reports to sort through before he got to the one he knew could matter most. He checked through them while the radio switched to a piano virtuoso who could only be Art Tatum.

First, the opened brandy bottle found in Iain Cameron's

cottage had still to reach Inverness for final forensic examination. But checking on the price tag from the Inverness store where it had been purchased had yielded a minor lucky break. The store didn't sell too many bottles of five-star brandy and had a video security camera which recorded each transaction. The brandy had been purchased by the older of the two men killed in the crashed Nissan car. Nikki Neilson had been scenes of crime officer when the bodies had been recovered from the car. He had fingerprinted the dead men as a matter of routine. Going by experience and a judgement call, Neilson was certain the same fingerprints were on Cameron's brandy bottle.

Meaning the two arsonists, already linked with Donny Adams, had also set up some degree of a relationship with the night-watchman. And now all four were dead.

There was a brief telex from the Scottish Crime Squad in Glasgow, a simple report stating that 'inquiries continued into the Nissan's purchase at the Glasgow car auction and a screening of known associates of the two who died in it was being carried out.' When the Squad knew more, he'd hear more.

Another small clutch of negative reports were for filing. That left only one lengthy Crime Squad fax message, several pages long – the report Thane had asked for on Broch Distillery and its directors. He brought a chair over to the trestle table, sat down, shoved a used coffee mug aside to clear a space on the table, then spread the fax pages in front of him.

The first few sentences told him it was a typical Crime Squad research job by the two named honours graduate detective sergeants. They always operated on the same principles – soak up every possible piece of information they could collect, analyse the results, then condense down to outline the basic and import-ant along with any aspects that might be trivial but intrigued them.

The story began at the beginning. In the late nineteenth century a small backyard distilling plant gave a modest extra income to Thomas Rankin, a young gamekeeper employed by the local laird who owned Broch Castle. Rankin had been a merchant seaman, and his young Norwegian bride came with him when he settled in Ardshona. Their distillery prospered and grew at a time when malt whisky was taking over from brandy in the Victorian world. Long before he died the same Thomas Rankin had made enough money to buy Broch Castle from its bankrupt owner. The laird had lost everything by investing in South American railway stock.

The name Broch Distilleries had been born that way. But the business that Finn Rankin had inherited four generations later had lost direction. It was a time when small independent whisky distilleries were dying like flies all over the Scottish Highlands, when big had become beautiful, when wise firms like Broch gave up.

Except nobody told Finn Rankin, then in his early thirties. He prepared a vigorous fight-back advertising and marketing plan. He talked two banks who didn't know about each other into loaning him money, he modernized, he expanded. Single-handed, Rankin dragged Broch Distilleries out of the doldrums and made it grow again.

The next paragraph made Thane raise an eyebrow. His wife was killed when the car she had been driving crashed. All three daughters had been travelling with her, but Finn Rankin had also been aboard. Lisa had been scarred for life, her two small sisters had escaped uninjured, Rankin had suffered only a broken shoulder.

The original police incident report had said, 'The cause of the accident was dangerous driving. When the car left the road and crashed, no other vehicles were involved. If Mrs Rankin had survived, she would have faced charges.'

The next fax page switched to Broch Distillery in straight business terms. City commentators regarded the firm as healthy, debt-free and respected. Because it remained family-owned with Finn Rankin as the sole majority shareholder, and because it was coy about turnover figures, the exact financial state couldn't be accurately gauged for possible future investment analysis. But tax figures available showed a reasonably prosperous turnover at the main Broch single-malt distillery, its local satellites, and in particular at the rapidly expanding Broch Highland blended whisky production plant near Prestwick, in lowland Ayrshire.

The same city commentators saw Highland Blend as the main growth factor in Broch's future.

'City commentators,' scoffed Moss reading over Thane's shoulder, 'if they're so damned clever, why don't they make their own fortunes?' He snorted. 'Getting anything out of it so far?'

'That maybe someone could see Broch as ripe for a takeover.'

Thane moved to the remaining sheets of the Crime Squad report. They amounted to thumbnail sketches on the people who ran Broch.

Finn Rankin was 'stubborn, clever, and self-opinionated'.

Lisa Rankin was rated as almost a mirror image of her father but with an even worse temper. A series of romantic links to wealthy, usually older men were said to have always foundered for that reason. Her chestnut-haired lawyer sister Anna, had parted from her husband, a London accountant, at the end of an angry marriage and a messy tussle through the courts. Sister number three, the happily pregnant Gina, ran the expanding Broch Highland Blend operation at Prestwick with the help of her husband, Robert Martin. They had been married for four years.

Next in line came Morris Currie, given some in-depth treatment with relatively little success. The round-faced, thick-lipped sales director had been taken on, apparently as part of the deal, when Broch Distilleries took over a Canadian-owned whisky broking firm he had operated. That had been two years back and the whisky trade still regarded it as a small mystery that Currie hung onto his job.

Morris Currie had a wife somewhere who had walked out on him years before. Something else buried in his past was a conviction for fraud. It had involved a faked insurance claim and he had been sentenced to six months imprisonment.

'Finished.' Thane pushed aside the fax sheets. They amounted to another mixed trawl of facts to add to what they had already gathered. He glanced at his watch and looked around. Sandra Craig had already gone out. 'I'll clean up, have something to eat, then head over to Rankinland.'

'Do that,' said Moss stoically. 'I'll look after things. Don't expect to be missed by your loyal troops.'

Thane grinned, threw a scratchpad in his second-in-command's direction, then went through to the main building and up to his room. He took a shower, then used some aftershave on the raw areas of his face, coming close to yelping at the stinging results. But a clean shirt left him feeling better and he went down to the Ardshona's restaurant. It had several tables occupied, but he was surprised to be greeted by Belle Campbell.

'I thought you were staying over with Jess Adams?' said Thane, as the large woman showed him to a corner table.

'So did I, superintendent,' she shrugged. 'But in the state she's in, Jess changed her mind about wanting company – almost threw me out.' She bent nearer as Thane sat down. 'Have you seen Inspector Moss's face? Yet he's the kind who doesn't complain!'

'No, he doesn't.' Thane asked himself what was so special about Moss's face that his own was ignored. He glanced around. 'You're busy tonight, Belle.'

'Busy enough that it's just as well I'm back, I suppose.' The woman laid the handwritten menu in front of him. 'We've lost one of our girls – that's the second we've lost in a week.' She sniffed angrily. 'But they won't find it so easy when they want their jobs back, I promise you!'

Thane nodded, studying the menu. He ordered the vegetable broth soup, followed it with broiled trout with a lemon sauce dressing, then allowed himself a glass of the house white wine. But as soon as Belle had gone he rose from his table and went through to the incident room. Sandra Craig was there, scowling over a report.

'Find Lennox and Vass,' he ordered. 'Get them on surveillance outside Jess Adams' house – I'm interested in why she waited until we were gone, then said goodbye to Belle Campbell.'

His sergeant gave a small, interested nod. 'Like maybe she was expecting her son to show up, sir?'

'Like maybe,' agreed Thane. 'If he does show, tell them to call for back-up. I don't like dead heroes.'

Then he left her, and was back in the restaurant long before Belle Campbell brought in his soup, ladling it out into his plate from a large, dented silver tureen. He was hungry, he quickly finished the soup, then the trout was in front of him and he tackled it with relish. When he'd finished the trout, he drank the last of his wine then made a deliberate way through to the bar. As he'd expected, Leckie Campbell was behind the counter. The Ardshona's landlord was in an obviously good mood.

'You'll have a drink, superintendent?' Campbell already had an empty glass positioned under the whiskies gantry. 'On the house, of course.'

'Thank you. Your choice, landlord.' Thane watched Campbell pour a measure from a blend that wasn't local.

'A wee change,' said Campbell, passing it over. 'Slainte, superintendent!'

126

'Slainte.' Thane returned the Gaelic toast and sipped his glass. 'Leckie, I've a couple of small puzzles. Will you help?'

'I always support the law, superintendent,' said Campbell with a humorous edge. 'Try me.'

'You told me about how you and Belle used to run around as a foursome with Donny Adams and Jess.' Thane nursed his glass gently.' Was there anyone else then that you hung around with?'

'Different people, no one in particular.' Campbell shook his head.

'Did Donny and Jess ever have any real fall-outs because of anyone?'

'You mean apart from me?' Campbell grinned. 'Donny would chase anything in a skirt. Jess felt the same way about trousers – and they had some battles, believe me. But no, there was never any other big romance thing, if that's what you mean.' He noted Thane's disappointment and polished another glass with the bar towel. 'You said a couple of puzzles, right?'

Thane nodded. 'What do you know about Jonesy?'

'Finn Rankin's woman?' Campbell set down the towel. 'I like her, Mr Thane. Most people do. Before she arrived on the scene, you just kept out of Rankin's way. It had been like that ever since his wife died – even his kids had a rough time.'

'Where did she come from?'

'You mean how did they meet?' Campbell chuckled. 'Jonesy was some kind of advertising executive with a London agency. She came up from London to help him plan a new sales campaign, they had one hell of a fight after the first day and she took the first train back south. Two days later, he follows her down to London. Another two days, and they come back together. End of story, superintendent.'

Thane thanked him, finished his drink, and went back to the incident room. Maggie Donald had taken over from Sandra, she confirmed that Lennox and Vass were watching Jess Adams' home. For once, only a standby hum was coming from the room's electronics.

He settled in a corner, picked up a telephone, called home, found the number wasn't engaged and talked for a few minutes with Mary. Then Clyde the dog began barking in the background and Tommy and Kate and some friends made a noisy invasion from somewhere. Mary gave up first, reminded Thane that she wouldn't be at home until late the next night, and ended the call.

Moss's latest incident room acquisition was a clock on the wall. Thane saw it was time he went round to Broch Castle, and decided to walk. He told Maggie Donald where he'd be, and left.

It was a dark night walk through the township, where street lamps were rare. There was a light wind from the north west but the weather was still dry. Television screens glowed behind some windows and a dog barked for a spell as Thane passed one cottage, but that was about it.

When he reached Broch Castle there were lights burning behind several of its windows. He could hear voices and a clatter of dishes as he reached the front door and pressed the doorbell. After a moment a light came on above his head, then the door opened and Lisa Rankin looked out.

'Superintendent.' She smiled in a way which faded the scar on her face. 'We're expecting you.' She beckoned. 'Come in. You haven't met my brother-in-law.'

'Robert Martin, superintendent.' The man who had been standing behind her came forward and shook his hand. 'We're glad you came.'

Lisa Rankin closed the door once Thane was in the castle hallway. She was wearing a long, loose dress with a multi-coloured pattern, held at the waist by a plaited leather cord. At her side, was Robert Martin, a sandy-haired, stockily built man in his late thirties, casually dressed in a white rollneck sweater and moleskin trousers. He had a broad-boned face and alert brown eyes.

'We heard you had new problems,' he said soberly. 'The whole thing is going crazy, superintendent. What else can happen?'

'Give him a chance, Bob,' frowned his sister-in-law. She made an apologetic gesture. 'I'm going to leave you. We've just finished our meal – I'm helping Jonesy dishwash in the kitchen.'

Lisa departed, and Martin gave a small, friendly headshake. 'This place is run by women, superintendent. Interfere at your peril.'

'I heard you and your wife got here this afternoon,' said Thane as he followed Robert Martin along the broad softly lit hallway. 'Will you be staying for long?'

'No.' Martin shook his head. 'It's a straight business trip – we're flying back tomorrow afternoon.'

'And the same with Morris Currie?' queried Thane.

'The same.' Martin grimaced. 'Finn decided he wanted an urgent meeting of directors. When he says jump the way he did, everybody jumps.' He paused at a door, reaching for its handle. 'I knew I'd have to come anyway. Some of the whisky we lost in the warehouse blaze was intended for the Highland Blend operation – now I'll need to rearrange what's to be shipped.'

He opened the door and waved Thane through into a large, well-furnished living room. Finn Rankin was standing with his back to the logs blazing in a large fireplace, a drink in one hand. The other people in the room parted to let him through as he saw Thane and came over.

'Thanks for coming, Thane.' He frowned at the cuts on Thane's face. 'I heard most of what happened – I reckon you were lucky. Give it a few days, and they'll heal.'

'Not like what happened to Donny Adams,' said Anna Rankin. His middle daughter came forward. She was wearing a white lace blouse and black trousers, her long chestnut hair held back by a silver clasp, and her eyes were serious. 'Is it true you're trying to find his son?'

'You're a lawyer, Anna. You're supposed to know better than to ask,' said Rankin curtly. He paused. 'Right, you've met Currie, our sales director . . .'

Morris Currie was sprawled in an armchair. The fleshy-faced man rose reluctantly to his feet then nodded.

'Which leaves this young lady.' Proudly, Rankin reached out and brought forward the other person in the fireside group. 'My daughter Gina, who is going to make me a grandfather before very long!'

Early pregnancy gave an extra glow to Gina Martin. Smaller than her sisters, her reddish brown hair cut elfin short, she wore a loose-fitting pale blue linen suit with a small, dark blue bow on each lapel. She gave a mildly embarrassed grin, sharing it between Thane and her father.

'Any day now, me and my bump are going to be entered in some dairy show,' she complained. 'Either that, or I'll be advertised on TV!'

Thane smiled. 'Congratulations anyway.'

'Offer the man a drink,' commanded Rankin. 'Anna – whisky for our visitor.'

Anna Rankin nodded, went over to a side table, poured a

generous measure from a decanter into a glass, then brought it over. That left Martin as the only one without a drink. He saw Thane's glance and shook his head.

'I don't drink, superintendent. I can't.' He saw Thane's surprise. 'I'm a master blender. That means I earn my living from this,' – he tapped his nose – 'my sense of smell. Get the bouquet the way it should be and you've got the blend the way it should be.'

'So you don't—'

'Daren't,' corrected Martin. 'Not when I'm maybe juggling up to a score of malts we've bought in from different distilleries and the result has to match what went before.'

'Don't bore everybody,' grumbled Morris Currie.

'His sense of smell is still insured for more than your whole damned hide,' snapped Finn Rankin. 'Remember that.'

There was an uneasy pause, finally broken by Martin. 'If you'd like to know more about it, see if you can make half an hour's free time tomorrow morning, superintendent. Meet me here, if you can make it around ten a.m.'

'I'll try,' agreed Thane.

As he spoke, the door opened and Lisa Rankin came in arm-in-arm with Jonesy. The older woman wore a black and silver linen dress which looked as though it would probably have cost a month of Thane's pay.

'Finished,' declared Lisa. She nudged her companion. 'Who broke what this time?'

They grinned at each other in a conspiratorial way.

'Nothing for a change,' declared Jonesy. Her mood sobered as she nodded to Thane. 'Sorry, superintendent. You can't be in the mood for family jokes.'

'I break lots of the dishes at home,' mused Thane. He turned to Morris Currie. 'Last time I saw you, you were rushing to make a plane south to a fairly important meeting. Did it go well?'

'All his meetings are important,' said Anna Rankin tartly. 'You can tell by his expense sheet.'

'It was important, it went well,' said Currie stiffly. 'You can't rush these deals. And I have to travel a lot. Usually at short notice.'

'Like last weekend.' Thane nodded. 'You always manage a seat?'

For just an instant, Currie's fat face flushed. Then he gave a quick, emphatic nod. 'Depends who you know, superintendent. I've no problems.'

'Right.' Finn Rankin raised his voice. 'Superintendent, you and I have some talking to do.' He looked at the others. 'In private. Some of it you know about, the rest, I'll explain later. He's a busy man – he'll probably leave afterwards.'

Amid murmured farewells Thane found himself neatly extracted from the room still clutching his glass. Rankin steered him back down the hallway to the stair that led up to his turret office.

'Finish your drink,' he invited.

Thane obeyed, set down the empty glass on a side table, then followed him up the stairway. When they reached Rankin's office, the distillery chairman switched on the overhead light, closed the door, and waved Thane towards a seat.

'I'm going to start with something you probably know already,' he said bluntly. 'I haven't been totally honest with you, Thane.'

Thane nodded. 'I had that feeling.'

Rankin sighed. 'Remember I was supposed to be at the distillery all afternoon yesterday, but I wasn't around when you came looking for me?' He didn't wait for a reply. 'I'll tell you why. I had a telephone call – a man's voice. He said there was a package lying inside the broch, told me exactly where, and that I'd better see what was in it. I came back, I saw, I felt sick. Then late last night there was another phone call. Another voice.'

The man rose, went over to his desk, unlocked a drawer, and brought out a cardboard box. Wordlessly, he handed it over and waited while Thane opened the box. Inside a small girl doll rested on a layer of cotton wool. The doll was smartly dressed and her hair had been cut short and coloured grey.

'Jonesy,' said Rankin simply.

Thane nodded. 'Who are they and what do they want?'

'I don't know – I just don't know,' said Rankin wearily. 'Jonesy hasn't seen that doll, nobody has. They said no police, so you haven't seen it either, right?

'It doesn't work that way.' Thane shook his head. 'Not when there are four men dead.'

'Listen,' pleaded Rankin. 'They said next time I'd be told what they want. Are you willing to help me that far?'.

'How?' asked Thane.

'Make sure nothing happens to Jonesy,' said Rankin simply.

131

'That's all you're going to tell me?' pressed Thane.

'It's all you need.' Rankin's expression was suddenly stubborn.

'I'll think about it.' Thane closed the lid on the doll then put the box into his jacket pocket. 'And you think about it too.' He got to his feet. 'Be real, Mr Rankin.'

Finn Rankin saw him down the stairway again then to the door.

'Superintendent . . .' he hesitated.

'Goodnight,' said Thane neutrally and walked away.

He heard the door close behind him.

More than once, retracing his path back to the Ardshona, he could have sworn he was being followed. But each time he looked round he saw nothing. Though by that time he was almost too tired to care.

6

The air temperature had dropped, and Colin Thane wakened to Wednesday wishing that he had packed a sweater when he came north. He showered, dressed, made a painful job of shaving around the cuts to his face, then went down and looked in at the makeshift incident room in the Ardshona Inn's storeroom.

Maggie Donald was on duty, looking too fresh and bright-eyed to be true. Thane nodded when she said good morning, then silently checked through the overnight log book. Lennox and Vass had maintained their watch at Jess Adams's cottage until dawn, but without a result. Beyond that, there were only a few overnight fax messages, all of them routine, and a bundle of photocopies of the borrowed picture of Willie Adams in army uniform. Thane initialled the log book, told the young police-woman he needed Sandra Craig and Phil Moss for a meeting in twenty minutes time, then went through to the Inn's dining room.

It was almost empty, and a young, freckle-faced girl he hadn't seen before made a clumsy job of serving him a coffee and rolls breakfast. Neither Belle Campbell nor her husband were in sight, but Jock Dawson and Harry Harron were demolishing bacon and eggs at another table – or were, until a howl of rage came from the Northern officer as the freckle-faced girl spilled coffee on his lap. The girl went scarlet and fled while Harron departed to mop up his dignity. Dawson simply grinned from ear to ear then stole some bacon the horse-faced Northern man had left on his plate.

Finished and feeling more awake, Thane had got up from his chair and was leaving as Lennox and Vass yawned their way in. Overnight duty had left the two Crime Squad detective constables red-eyed and unshaven.

'Nothing happened, boss,' reported Ernie Vass gloomily. 'And the whole damned population had us spotted.'

'We were a joke.' Dougie Lennox scowled his disgust. 'One old dear even brought us out mugs of tea.'

Thane gave them a dry grin of sympathy, then headed back to the incident room. Phil Moss and Sandra were already there, and so was Andy Mack. The Northern Constabulary detective inspector gave a mildly cautious smile of greeting and stayed where he was, while Moss and Sandra abandoned studying one of the large-scale maps pinned around the room.

'You're usually bad news,' Thane considered Mack suspiciously. 'What is it this time, Andy?'

'Nothing that will surprise you, superintendent.' The baldheaded veteran shaped a slight shrug of apology. 'Our Scenes of Crime team are heading back up to Serpent Rock for another look around, as agreed. But once that's done, they're being pulled out. I'm staying on for today, but Headquarters also need to pull out some of their uniformed men. Sorry.'

'Sweet Jesus.' Thane made it a mixture of a prayer for patience and a snarl. 'Your damned Special Operation strikes again?'

'That's part of it.' Mack glanced towards Moss and Sandra, saw their faces carefully blanked, and turned to Thane again. 'Look, I can't say what's going on, because I don't know a hell of a lot more than you do. But my bosses are having their strings pulled from a lot higher up. Mick Farrell has been hand-picking cops from all over Northern force. They've been briefed, then more or less held in quarantine, just waiting. Meantime, the rest of us are supposed to get on with pretending to the great wide world that everything is normal.'

Thane stayed silent until the Northern man had departed and the door had closed again, then he cursed, dropped down into a seat and considered his companions. Sandra Craig was wearing

133

faded blue jeans and a matching waistcoat with a white rollneck sweater. She had combed her red hair back, fastening it with a deerskin thong. Phil Moss had made an even less successful business of shaving than Thane. The result was that what had been a clean shirt front looked like a blood-stained battle zone.

'Have we any good news?' asked Thane bitterly. 'From anywhere?'

'Maybe this, sir.' Sandra Craig warily handed him a telex message.

From Northern's Identification Bureau at Inverness, the telex reported on three sets of fingerprints found on the empty brandy bottle recovered from Iain Cameron's cottage. They were a positive match for the dead watchman's prints and of the men who had died in the crashed Renault car. There were other prints on the bottle, but they were smudged, most likely going back to when the brandy was purchased in Inverness.

'It helps,' agreed Thane softly.

It more than helped. It supported a scenario of John Rogers and Peter Marsh, using Donny Adams as local help, getting to know Iain Cameron well enough to ease their way into the Broch Distillery compound after dark.

Meaning that Iain Cameron, bought with a bottle of brandy, had probably helped set the wheels in motion which led to his own death.

Thane laid the telex aside. 'Anything from the post-mortem on Adams?'

'I phoned.' Moss scowled and shook his head. 'All I got was a snarl from some pathology bod who wouldn't say who he was – they'll get back to us when they're ready.'

'What about our own people in Glasgow?'

'My turn, sir.' Sandra Craig flicked back a loose strand of that copper-red hair from across her forehead and took over from Moss. 'Francey – uh – Inspector Dunbar phoned with an update. They're still working on Broch background inquiries, including an extra sniff around their sales director's history. Customs and Excise are interested enough to be co-operating.' She glanced at a notebook in front of her. 'Francey is still hopeful of getting more on known associates of our two dead arsonists. Including a small surprise.'

'What kind of a surprise?'

She grinned 'Banjo Kingsley, sir.'

Thane shaped a soft whistle through his teeth. There was nothing small about Banjo Kingsley – either in size or reputation. He was a fixer for anything illegal, his nickname in no way related to musical talent, but a Glasgow label for a willing ability to hand out beatings.

Inspector Dunbar – Thane knew he could leave it to Francey to keep digging. He still had to get used to his former sergeant's promotion. Like Francey was having to get used to a smashed leg and walking with a stick.

He glanced at his watch, thinking. The macabre doll he'd been given by Finn Rankin was already on its way to Inverness. In about an hour he was due to meet Robert Martin, the outsider who had married into the Rankin clan. Thane corrected himself. The second outsider to do that.

'Do we know Anna Rankin's married name before she was divorced?' he asked.

Sandra checked a notebook and shook her head.

'Ask Francey to find out, if he doesn't know already,' ordered Thane.

It was a sideline, something they should know, and low priority. More immediately, he had other things to organize. He was working through that list with Moss and Sandra when there was a brisk double-tap on the storeroom door, then it swung open.

'Just me, folks' said Jazz Gupatra, ambling in. Her wide-mouthed smile and her flawless dark skin made the young assignment student's white teeth glint like pearls. The jeans and pigtails of the previous day were gone. This new Jazz wore a tailored grey linen jacket and skirt. Combed out, her raven black hair brushed her shoulders. She turned to Sandra Craig. 'Okay, sergeant. What's needing done?'

'My idea, sir.' Sandra Craig gave a hopeful glance at Thane. 'I thought if we had Jazz keeping her eyes open for us inside the Broch offices again . . .'

'That's sense.' Thane nodded.

'Except I won't be around all the time, superintendent.' The girl frowned. 'I've to drive the sales director into Inverness and put him on a plane. Then I've to run some business errands around the town for Finn Rankin.' She indicated her suit. 'That's why I'm dressed like this. Chairman boss likes a female up-market image.'

'All you need to do is keep your eyes open,' suggested Thane. 'Stay out of trouble, tells us anything unusual that happens . . .'

'Keep my nose clean.' Jazz nodded her understanding. 'I know about yesterday. So believe me, I will!' She took a casual step forward, looking down at the bundle of photographs on the tabletop beside her. 'Hey, that picture wasn't taken yesterday, but it's a good likeness. Poor old . . .' Then her voice died away and she frowned, puzzled. 'Except it isn't him, is it?'

'Isn't who?' asked Moss sharply.

'I thought it was a young days' picture of Iain Cameron.' Jazz moistened her lips. 'Except that's army uniform. Iain Cameron gossiped enough about how he stayed out of the forces because he was merchant navy.' She gave a vague gesture. 'You know – places he'd been, things he'd seen, how he hadn't always been a night-watchman.'

'Take another look,' invited Thane. 'It's no one else you know?'

Jazz took her time then slowly, seriously, shook her head.

'I'm going to ask you a question,' said Thane. 'Then, whatever you answer, you forget ever seeing that photograph. Right?'

She nodded.

'You knew Donny Adams. Have you ever met his son Willie?'

'No.' A startled expression on her face, shook her head. 'You mean that's . . .'

'You forget that I asked,' reminded Thane grimly. 'You don't even mention it to anyone. Just get on with what you're supposed to do.'

'So I forget,' agreed the girl. She gave another puzzled look at the photograph, then went out, clicking the door behind her.

'Sir—' began Sandra.

'Sergeant, shut up,' said Moss curtly. He looked at Thane, waiting.

'Don't go near Belle Campbell,' said Thane. 'But find Leckie, Phil. You know what to ask.'

Moss nodded, stalked towards the door and went out.

'Can I ask what the hell is going on, sir?' asked Sandra Craig icily.

'No. Wait until he gets back,' snapped Thane.

A full three minutes passed, then Moss returned and closed the door carefully behind him.

'The way you probably expected, Colin.' His lined, thin face was impassive. 'Iain Campbell grew up in Ardshona. He was older than the rest of the Honey Trap bunch, but he, well, joined in most things.'

'Then went away to be a sailor.' Thane said it softly and saw a slow understanding dawning on his sergeant's face. 'We've been chasing in the wrong direction, Sandra. Donny Adams and his son never got along. I thought that could be because Donny guessed that the boy's real father might be Finn Rankin. Not Cameron – someone none of us ever met.'

'But Jazz saw the likeness the moment she saw the photograph—'

'So why didn't other people?' Thane shrugged. 'Maybe some did.'

'But kept their mouths shut?' grunted Moss. 'Most probably just watched a child grow up and didn't see beyond that?'

Sandra Craig took a deep breath of understanding. 'Except a total outsider like Jazz just sees what she sees. Dear God.' She faced Thane. 'So what do we do?'

'Mainly, we wait.' Thane went over to the wall map and scowled at its mountain contours. 'Or do you expect me to tell Jess Adams that we think her son murdered her husband?'

'Except, of course, we have to know if Willie's father was really Iain Cameron,' mused Moss. 'Then if she admits it and that Willie knew it . . .'

They didn't have to put the rest in words. But they shared the same thought. If that was true, if Willie Adams had come round to realizing that Donny had played any part in the way Iain Cameron, his natural father, had died, that was a major motive for murder.

'I could use a sandwich,' said Sandra wearily.

Thane looked at Moss. Being hungry usually meant that Detective Sergeant Sandra Craig's thought processes were firing up.

The best part of the next hour crawled past, partly filled by catching up on the inevitable flurry of incident reports and tasks like approving overtime schedules. Thane initialled an apparently unending flow of paper that Moss and Sandra Craig placed in front of him. Now and again a telephone rang or the fax machine came to life, but never with anything of importance.

Until Sandra Craig answered one call, raised an eyebrow, looked at Thane, and put her hand over the telephone mouthpiece.

'It's Maggie Fyffe. Commander Hart wants you. But she needs a word first.'

Thane nodded and took the telephone from her. As the Commander's personal secretary, Maggie Fyffe also acted as den mother to the Squad and vigorously denied running its bush telegraph.

'Something wrong, Maggie?' he asked.

'You tell me.' Her voice came frostily over the line from Glasgow. 'I'm looking at a fax report which says your face looks like it hit a blender. Does Mary know?'

'No. It's not so bad, so I—'

'So you left it for your wife to hear some other way?' The frost became ice. 'Great. Then she maybe hears a version that you need a remould job.' Being a cop's widow gave Maggie Fyffe an inside track on possibilities. 'Well, I'll tell her. As of now, you owe me half a salmon or whatever those Highlanders use for money. If that is settled – hold on—'

There was a double click, then Jack Hart's voice took over.

'Good morning,' said Hart slyly. 'What's it going to be, Colin? Another day, another body?'

'We aim to please,' countered Thane, grimacing at the mouthpiece.

'If you want to please me, just wrap things up so you can get back,' grumbled Hart. 'I've enough case files on my desk to choke a horse. Plenty are coming your way.' He paused. Thane heard papers rustle. 'No cause of death yet on your latest body?'

'They're working on it,' said Thane stonily.

Hart grunted. 'Well, you know what they say. North of the Highland Line, there's no word so urgent as *mañana*.' The squad commander sighed. 'And you still can't find your local sniper?'

'No, sir.' Thane's voice was bleak.

'Don't get so damned uptight,' soothed Hart. 'We're trying to help. The moment we get anything, we'll let you know. And I heard something that might please you about Mick Farrell's big secret.'

'Do I get to know?' asked Thane frostily.

'This, yes. But I didn't tell you.' Hart chuckled. 'Whatever it is, maybe it's all off! If it is, then believe me – there's going to be a shortage of happy faces among Northern's top brass.'

Then Hart hung up and the line went dead. Thane looked across at Moss and shook his head. Moss shrugged and belched.

It was almost ten a.m. when Thane formally handed over to Moss then left the inn. Outside, the same chill wind had its occasional gusting edge and the same grey clouds continued to refuse to produce rain. The Northern force Range Rover was parked outside, some plastic sheeting taped over the hole in its smashed windscreen. Maggie Donald was there, working determinedly at cleaning the vehicle's damaged bodywork. She saw Thane, and moved to get behind the wheel, but he shook his head.

'Stay around,' he told her. 'Inspector Moss might need you.'

Thane walked on, passed Jock Dawson exercising his dogs, and kept walking until he reached Broch Castle and strode up the driveway. The usual small cluster of vehicles was parked outside the main door, but one of them, the white Ford Escort, started up as he arrived. Reversing out, then turning and coming forward, it went past him in a spatter of gravel. A grinning Jazz gave a wave from the driver's side, a sour-faced Morris Currie contented himself with a nod from the passenger seat.

'You're punctual, superintendent.' Anna Rankin had emerged from the castle doorway. As the white Ford disappeared down the driveway she came over and greeted him with a slight smile. 'Punctual as well as house-trained!'

'That's modern policing. They send us on courses,' explained Thane dryly. The chestnut-haired Rankin sister had teamed a tailored grey shirt and a black leather waistcoat with black corduroy trousers and black ankle-length boots. She looked good, and he had the distinct feeling she knew it. He gestured in the direction the Ford had vanished. 'I thought Currie planned to stay, then leave with your sister and her husband, in the afternoon.'

'Morris Currie had a small disagreement with my father after you left last night,' said Anna Rankin with a lingering amusement. 'He hasn't been formally thrown out – but it became a good idea he caught an earlier flight. Gina and Robert will still go later, the way they arranged.'

'Is your father around?' asked Thane. 'I want a quick word with him.'

'No, sorry.' Anna Rankin shook her head and thumbed to the space where the oldest Rankin sister usually parked her red Lancia coupé. 'Lisa drove father over to the distillery this morning. They've some production schedules to iron out with Alex Korski.' She gave a resigned grimace. 'Speaking as the company lawyer, I'd say my beloved father had a drink too many last night. At least he still had sense enough to know he couldn't risk driving this morning – not while so many police are prowling around.'

Thane chuckled. 'Have you been left on your own?'

'Hardly. Gina is indoors, talking baby things with Jonesy.' Anna Rankin showed a mild irritation. 'Her damned pregnancy is shaping to take over everybody's life. Have you children, superintendent?'

He nodded. 'Two. Large, as in teenage.'

'Two.' She slid her hands into the side pockets of her black trousers and looked away. For a moment there was something in her expression that might have been regret, might have been envy. 'I wanted children when I married. Except by the time I got my divorce I was damned glad it hadn't happened.' Then, as if a switch had been thrown, she brightened again. 'Now you'd better meet up with Robert. He's waiting round at the old broch. I buzzed him on the internal line when I saw you coming.'

Thane thanked her and followed the path that led round to the rear of the Victorian mansion. Behind it, the great beehive shape of the ancient Pictish structure and its honey-coloured sandstone seemed to almost brood in the grey midday light. The solitary entrance door was lying open, and Robert Martin lounged against the stonework. He was wearing a white laboratory jacket over a shirt, grey corduroy trousers, and black loafer shoes.

'Glad to see you, Thane.' A mild grin touched his broad-boned face, and he beckoned. 'Welcome to my private kingdom – at least, that's what Jonesy calls it.' He stepped back inside the broch. 'Come on in – but watch your head. These Picts came small in size – either that, or they didn't like high ceilings.'

Thane followed him into the broch, cautiously keeping his head low as instructed, still brushing the low roof, occasionally stubbing a toe on an unseen rock ledge in the floor. The air was cold and damp, light either came from cracks in the beehive shell or from a few small lamps slung on wires. As they went on, he was conscious of passing through a minor labyrinth of narrow passages. The dull light showed shadowed, small, cell-like openings and occasional larger chambers coated in spiders' webs.

'Almost there.' Martin paused, opened a modern, close-fitting door, and light poured out from the area beyond. 'Come in.' He winced as Thane promptly cracked his skull against the door lintel. 'I said watch your head, didn't I?'

Still dazed, Thane looked around. This part of the broch, which had to be close to its heart, had been converted into a modern room with neon tube lighting, brick walls, and a concrete floor. It was furnished midway between office and laboratory, complete with chairs, a table, and filing cabinets. A work bench was topped by a miniature array of bottles, each with a hand-written label. A line of small wine glasses sat in front of the bottles, some used, others still sparkling clean.

'I need a place of my own for testing and sampling whiskies. Private and secure. After I moaned long enough, Finn agreed I could have this. It's ideal.' Resting his hands on the work bench, Martin grinned sympathetically at his visitor. 'How's the head now?'

I'll live.' Thane could still feel a hammer throbbing in his skull.

'Good. I'm almost finishing here. I'll explain a couple of things, then we'll move on.' Expertly, the sandy-haired master blender poured modest amounts from a few of the line of bottles into separate, clean glasses. Taking one glass, he gently swirled its liquid around. 'First, an important part of my job is to keep an eye on the general quality of Broch Single Malt.' He tapped a finger against the side of his nose. 'I sample by scent, by aroma. Your serious whisky drinker would start a war if each bottle of Broch Single Malt didn't match the last one he'd bought. Then we have our own blended whisky. You know about that?'

'Broch Highland.' Thane nodded.

'Good.' Robert Martin was relieved. 'Blended whisky is just that. Created from – well, individual whiskies from maybe a score of different distilleries. Whiskies that are considerably less expensive. Unknown—'

'Cheap?'

'Let's say each with different characteristics,' grinned Martin. 'We buy where we like what's available and the price. We can get some that are smooth, some that are – well, rough at the edges. Whiskies like these, from all kinds of distilleries. Some who overproduced, others too small to do their own marketing, some moving old stock from firms that have shut down.' He shrugged. 'My job is simple enough. I sniff, I decide which whiskies will blend to create the match that we want. I try it, I sniff again—'

'And if you got it wrong?'

'Then several million whisky drinkers would want to burn me at the stake.' Martin chuckled. 'Look, my father-in-law can lecture you on the merits of his Broch Single Malt – fine. Except that Single Malt whisky is a rich man's drink. The blended stuff we produce at Prestwick costs a lot less and totally outsells his single-malt – and he knows it.'

'But he doesn't like it?' asked Thane.

'No, he doesn't.' The sandy-haired master blender brushed that aside. Reaching for one of the whisky glasses, he offered it to Thane. 'Sniff it. Long and deep. Don't taste. Tell me what you think.'

Thane sniffed at the anonymous whisky. The aroma was strong and distinct.

'Almost like seaweed?' he suggested cautiously.

'Well done!' Martin grinned at him. 'That's a Skye malt – all seaweed and spice. Hellish to hide, which makes it one of the easiest to spot.' He offered another glass. 'How about this one?'

Thane tried and got it wrong. He missed a hint of smoke-like odour from an Islay malt. Three more came his way and again he failed each time. A delicately aromatic sample was West Coast. A background trace of heather honey meant another was from the north coast, and the last, a deliberate set-up, was from Broch Distillery with a spice-like finish as its main nosing element. As a small revenge for getting it wrong, he drank it.

'I'd say you earned that,' said Martin, turning away and pulling off his white laboratory jacket. 'All right superintendent, let's continue your education.'

They left the testing room, Martin putting out the light and closing the door behind him. Then they retraced their way out of the broch and back out into daylight, the man carefully locked the outer door.

'How many people can get into this place?' asked Thane very casually.

'Only family, I suppose.' Martin checked the door. 'There's

142

always a key hanging up in the kitchen, and most of us probably have our own. Why?'

'I wondered, that's all,' shrugged Thane.

As they walked round to the front of the castle, Jonesy and Gina Martin appeared at an upper window. Both women waved.

'Gina and I are in countdown mode.' Robert Martin cheerfully returned the greetings. 'A lot to do, and not too much time to do it in before we leave.'

He led Thane to the travel-scarred jeep among the remaining vehicles at the front driveway, thumbed him into the passenger seat, got behind the wheel, and set the little workhorse moving. Thane had expected they would head south through Ardshona, towards the distillery, but when they reached the road they turned north then almost immediately west on a small, partly overgrown side-road.

Suddenly, they were approaching a large single-storey brick warehouse building, windowless, painted black, with heavy metal vehicle doors at one end. It was surrounded by a spike-topped iron fence crowned with barbed wire and Robert Martin stopped the jeep beside a locked vehicle-width gate.

'This is our number-one bonded warehouse.' Martin rested his hands on the steering wheel. 'Somebody takes a look at it every day, goes inside maybe once a week. Superintendent, you're look-ing at about five thousand barrels of bulk whisky' – he saw Thane's raised eyebrows and nodded – 'worth a lot of money. Except it doesn't belong to us. You've heard of whisky investors?'

Thane frowned. 'They buy young whisky, maybe just a barrel or two. They leave it to mature—'

'You've done your homework.' Martin nodded approvingly. 'They leave their investment maybe ten, fifteen years, they don't have to pay customs duty while it's in bond. Then when they bring it out, they hope to make a damned good profit.'

'Do they?' asked Thane.

'Enough to keep them very happy.' Martin leaned more of his weight against the jeep's steering wheel and grinned. 'Liquid assets, superintendent! We sell them the whisky, we charge for storage and insurance – they decide when to put it on the market.' Martin glanced at his watch, slid the jeep back into gear, and set it moving again. He made a turn and began driving back the way they'd come. 'Broch sold them that whisky, a dribble at a time, over a lot of years. Whatever we got for it was spent a long time ago.'

On the main road again, Martin turned south and the jeep drove back almost to the outskirts of Ardshona township. There was a fork in the road and they turned left, steering away from the township, splashing across a ford at a shallow stream then skirting around a low hill.

'Next stop.' Martin pointed ahead to another long, low warehouse block lying half-hidden in a patch of trees. 'This is our B Warehouse – B for blending stock. I'm meeting Alex Korski and some of his people here.' He kept explanations until he'd stopped the jeep again at the sturdy perimeter fence. 'One of Alex's roles is to travel around buying any bulk whisky he hears is on offer – maybe just a couple of casks in one place, maybe a bulk lot somewhere else. We ship them along to here and Alex takes samples for me.'

'So you can assess them as blending stock?'

'Got it in one.' Martin nodded like a schoolteacher pleased with his pupil. 'Some of the whisky we lost in the warehouse fire had already been moved from here, to be shipped on south for me. That's one of the reasons I came up, to choose replacements.'

'I see.' Thane let the thought perculate for a moment. 'Why didn't the Black Hats burn this warehouse?'

Martin shrugged. 'No idea, superintendent. Except again a fire here wouldn't hurt Finn as much as a fire at Broch Distillery.'

'This time because we're talking blend.' Thane digested the fact slowly. 'I heard Morris Currie had a rough time from your father-in-law last night. Any idea what that was about?'

Martin sighed. 'Let's put it this way. Currie may be our sales director. But there are times when he doesn't give the impression he even made the queue when they were handing out brains. Finn hauled him up to his office, alone. Finn did some shouting, then they both came back down and Currie more or less went into hiding.'

'Who appointed Currie?'

'Finn did. Years ago – God knows why.' Martin ended it there and thumbed at a truck approaching from behind them. 'Here's Alex.'

The truck stopped beside them. The dapper little distillery manager emerged from its cab while at least a dozen of his men climbed down from the back of the vehicle. Thane and Martin got out of the jeep, there was a brief exchange of greetings, then Korski opened up the gate in the fence and had the warehouse doors swung open.

Overhead lights blazed to life and Thane stared. Row upon row of whisky casks were stacked in tiers on their sides down the whole length of the building. They were grouped according to size – butts, hogsheads, barrels in the kind of numbers he didn't even try to count. Some were dark, some were light in colour. Some had lettering painted on their sides, others were similarly marked on their exposed lids.

'You're looking at a lot of whisky, Mr Thane,' said Robert Martin soberly. 'Maybe another six thousand casks. Not anything like as valuable as single-malt stock, but still worth a hell of a lot of money. No watchman – but we took care of security our way. Here and at the investment warehouse. Despite Finn.'

He pointed towards the roof. Looking up, Thane understood. He could see the network of sensors and security lights, CCTV units strategically placed to cover every aspect of the warehouse from ground level up.

'I'm impressed,' said Thane.

'With what it costs, you should be,' said Martin dryly. 'Finn rules at Broch Distillery. But out here we won because we had the insurance people on our side.' Just inside the warehouse doors, some of Korski's men were starting up two forklift trucks. As their electric motors began to purr, Martin produced a thick piece of yellow chalk from one pocket, strode into the warehouse then began walking down the stacked wooden casks. The master blender knew what he wanted, stopping every so often to chalk symbols on casks at near ground level or climbing on staging to reach others.

'What happens now is simple,' said Alex Korski, stopping beside Thane. 'My boys use the forklifts to bring out the casks he marks, then tomorrow we start trucking them down to the Prestwick blending plant.' He broke off to shout an order to one of the forklift drivers then turned to Thane again. 'It's a damn dangerous job – nobody fools around. Pull the wrong cask out the wrong way, a lot more could come rolling down like an avalanche. Maybe drink can kill people, but who the hell wants to be flattened out of existence by it?'

Thane nodded. He could see Robert Martin clambering across a high wooden gangway further along and chalking more casks.

At the nearer end of the warehouse, the whining forklifts and their attendant crews were starting work. Using chains and pulleys, blocks and levers, the Broch men worked with the smooth precision of people who had carried out the same tasks hundreds of times before. As each chalk-marked cask was extracted it meant others around it had to be moved to compensate. Then the extracted cask was quickly rolled away towards a loading bay area near the doors. By the time it got there, the rest of the Broch men had moved on to another.

'However it looks, they know exactly what they're doing,' mused Korski, clamping one of his small, black cheroots between his lips. 'How about you, Mr Thane? How are things?'

Thane shrugged. 'Win some, lose some – for now.'

'I know the feeling.' Korski spoke around his cheroot, which he left unlit. 'Life can be a complete bitch, can't it?'

'At times.' Thane watched another chalk-marked cask extracted from half-way up a stack. Hands in his pockets, he turned back to the distillery manager. 'Does Morris Currie ever come here?'

'Sometimes.' Korski gave a derisive grunt. 'He says he likes to keep an eye on things.'

'What about the investment warehouse? Does Currie visit there?'

'No chance.' Korski's plump little face showed a grin. 'The investment warehouse is special, the boss doesn't let Currie go near it.'

Thane blinked. 'Why not?'

'That's the way it is.' Korski shrugged sardonically. 'There's a memo from Finn Rankin that goes back years – it says polite things about areas of responsibility but what it means is simple enough.'

'God has spoken, Currie is banned?' suggested Thane.

Korksi nodded, and one of the electric forklifts whined to full power. Another cask was being extracted from an almost roof-high stack.

Time passed, the work tempo seemed to slow and Korski

began to look vaguely puzzled. Then Robert Martin returned and came over to Thane.

'I've problems,' he admitted. 'Some of these casks don't match what they're supposed to be, so I'm doing a rethink. I'll get one of Korski's boys to drive you in. Then I'll get word to Gina – she can drive over and pick me up here, then we'll head straight to the airport.' He made an apologetic gesture. 'If you want to see our blending operation come down to Prestwick at any time. That's an open invitation.'

Martin went back into the warehouse and Alex Korski produced the promised driver, a gloomy man in overalls who was toothless, badly needed a shave and whose fingers were stained brown with nicotine.

They took the jeep, and his new companion drove in silence for a spell then began half crooning, half howling some Gaelic tune which didn't seem to have words. As the man sang, saliva sprayed from his mouth at any alarming rate. But he drove quickly. He dropped Thane outside the Ardshona Inn, grinned, spat over one shoulder and the jeep roared away again.

There was only one police car parked across from the inn, and Thane felt a couple of spots of damp on his face that might almost have been rain. Then, as he reached the Ardshona's porch, the Inn door opened and the angular shape of Detective Constable Harron lumbered out.

'Sir.' The Northern officer straightened.

'Going somewhere, Harry?' asked Thane mildly.

'Ending my meal break, sir.' Harron showed his chipped teeth in a token smile. 'I'm still on observation watch at the Adams house. DC Lennox is covering until I get back.'

Thane nodded. 'Anything yet?'

'Nothing, sir. But his widow is moving about inside.'

'You've seen her?'

'Aye.' The Northern man frowned. 'Isaiah talks about "a woman of sorrow and aquainted with grief" – it says a man, to be accurate. But this Adams woman has her TV on, and isn't missing any of her soaps.'

'And her son can't have got to her?'

'No chance, sir.' Harron dismissed the possibility and strode off.

Thane shrugged, went into the Inn, then walked through to the incident room. Sandra Craig was there, holding the fort on her own using the main blade of a Swiss army knife to peel an apple.

'Where's everybody?' demanded Thane.

'Working, sir.' She finished removing the apple skin in one piece with one final triumphant twist. 'There was a report of a man seen near Serpent Rock and carrying a rifle. It's probably a false alarm, but Inspector Moss has gone with one of the local specials to check it out. Harry Harron—'

'I've seen.'

'I used Dougie Lennox to cover his meal break.' His sergeant ran through the rest of her mental checklist. 'The Northern team has been cut back again – it's down to Inspector Mack and two uniforms. He took them off on another door-to-door check around where Iain Cameron lived.'

Which left Jock Dawson – out on another prowl with his dogs out beyond Broch Castle – Ernie Vass, who was interviewing a couple of workmate friends of Donny Adams at the distillery, and—

'What about Maggie Donald?' frowned Thane.

'Taking her meal break. She's waiting Juliet style until Dougie Lennox gets here.' Sandra Craig stretched like a cat and used both hands to smooth back her copper-red hair. 'Maybe we should have him neutered.'

Thane sighed, partly for Lennox. There were some new fax messages and other notes lying in a pile for him and he thumbed through them. There was still nothing from Inverness about the post-mortem on Donny Adams, nothing else that excited interest.

'I'm going to eat,' he announced. 'Send a fax to Crime Squad in Glasgow. I want them to start from the beginning again on Morris Currie before he joined Broch.'

'Early stuff.' She nodded then took a first crunching bite from her apple. 'What are they looking for, sir?'

'That somebody like him maybe did something naughty and was baled out of trouble,' said Thane grimly. 'Maybe not the the kind of trouble that could have ended in front of a judge. But still trouble.' He scowled. 'Then you can wring someone's neck at Inverness. What the hell is taking them so long to write that post-mortem report? Are they trying for a Booker Prize?'

He went through to the main inn, and saw that Leckie Campbell was on duty at the bar. A foursome of tourists were keeping the Ardshona's landlord busy, but Thane managed to order a beer.

'Where's your wife, Leckie?' he asked as the drink was placed in front of him.

'In the kitchen, working her tail off – and she won't let me forget it. Why?'

'I need some help again.' Thane sipped his beer. 'How's your memory?'

'It comes and it goes.' Campbell took the money for the beer, then came back with change.

'Think back to when Iain Cameron was one of the local heroes around Serpent Rock,' said Thane quietly. 'Did he have a steady girlfriend?'

Campbell gave him a quizzical look. 'You're asking about him and Jess Adams?'

Thane nodded.

'They played around now and then.' The landlord began polishing a whisky glass. 'They – uh – weren't the only ones. Of course, it had to end when she married Donny the Shovel.'

'How did people react to that?'

'Surprised!' Campbell grinned. 'But Jess was nobody's fool. Iain Cameron never had more than two pennies to rub together, and Donny had a good, steady job.'

Thane thanked him then took his beer through to the restaurant area. It had non-police customers at three of its tables, all being served by the waitress who had appeared that morning. As he settled at a corner table, Belle Campbell bustled through from the kitchen with a laden tray, thrust it at the flustered waitress, then disappeared again with time for only a quick nod in Thane's direction.

He ordered an Aberdeen Angus steak, said he wanted it the next stage beyond well done, and asked for a side salad. Dougie Lennox and Maggie Donald came in while he waited. The young Northern policewoman had changed out of uniform and was wearing a tweed skirt and a knitted red jumper and joined Lennox in a courtesy smile in Thane's direction before they headed for another table as far away from his as possible.

The steak arrived, charred round the edges, and was laid in front of him. As the side salad followed, the restaurant door opened again and Sandra Craig looked in. She caught his eye and beckoned.

'Keep my meal for me,' Thane told the waitress sadly, rose, and joined his sergeant. They went out in the corridor.

'Things happening, sir,' she reported briskly. 'There's a phone call from Inverness about the Donny Adams post-mortem. You've got Dr Linton waiting on the line for you.' She kept talking as Thane began striding towards the incident room. 'I took a call from Joan Kerr at Broch Distillery. The grapevine says Iain Cameron's cousin has got ashore from his oil rig and is heading this way with a gang of friends, looking for trouble. She'll let us know if she hears more.'

Thane swore vehemently and kept on going. When he reached the incident room he grabbed a notepad and pen then dropped into a chair and lifted the telephone receiver.

'I've been twiddling my thumbs waiting for this, doctor,' he said curtly. 'What's been going on?'

'We've had a multi-vehicle pile-up on the Inverness–Perth road. Six dead,' David Linton's voice snapped back in his ear. 'Now are you going to growl or listen? Your choice, superintendent.'

Thane glared at the receiver, picturing the plump, bushy-haired David Linton, with the edges of his deerskin jacket rammed down his throat. 'I'll listen.'

'Good.' Dr Linton made it a sigh. 'You're not going to like this. You know what we had. A fire-damaged body and all the rest.' There was a pause on the line then Thane heard a sound of crockery before Linton was back again. 'I'm having lunch, superintendent. Lunch is a cold, greasy sausage of uncertain parentage, a slice of yesterday's bread, and a glass of milk. For this, I starved through medical school? For this, I cope with idiot lawyers and temperamental police?'

'Dr Linton . . .' Thane made it a warning rumble.

'Here's what we did,' said Linton, suddenly in gear. 'Your body got the full treatment, like we were peeling an onion. More like a fried onion, and layer by layer.' He allowed himself a sigh. 'The bottom line on proximate causes of death is delightfully simple. Every student has it drummed into him at forensic medicine lectures. All deaths may be attributed to either coma, syncope or asphyxia. Your man died from syncope – sudden cessation of the action of the heart.'

'Go on.' Thane sensed trouble coming.

'It was straightforward degenerative heart disease, superin-

150

tendent,' said Linton flatly. 'No room for argument. His heart was a timebomb, nothing to indicate he was on medication. Something happened – a shock, emotion, panic – take your pick. And your man dropped dead.'

'Just like that?' Thane was left bewildered. 'Nothing else at all?'

'Like I told you, we went in layer by layer,' said Linton soberly. 'I checked my findings with two Regius professors of forensic medicine – one in Edinburgh, the other in London. They both say they reckon I've got it right. There are small signs he may have been in a struggle – but look at the same signs another way, and maybe he wasn't. It doesn't alter anything, but one thing you might do is check whether his widow knew of any history of heart disease.'

'I will.' Thane moistened his lips. 'Thank you.'

'I'm faxing you the formal report.' Linton paused, there was another clink of crockery, and he was chewing when he came back on. 'And I nearly forgot – I promised that I'd pass on something to you. Scenes of Crime say the shotgun that was lying beside your man had one barrel fired. At first they thought that was caused by the heat of the fire. It wasn't. The shotgun had been triggered, and they found where rock in the cave had been hit by shot. They think he probably aimed at someone also in the cave but missed.'

The police surgeon dealt in facts and occasional, reluctant medical opinions. He had nothing more to contribute. Thane thanked him, ended the call, and put down the receiver.

'You heard?' he asked the watchful redhead opposite him.

'Most of it, sir.' Detective Sergeant Sandra Craig knew when it was best to say little. Another of the telephones began ringing and she answered it, listened, murmured a quick thank you, then swiftly hung up. 'DI Mack, sir. He's heard about Cameron's cousin. He says to tell you that it's Northern business and his people will see them off. I thanked him.'

'I owe him for that,' said Thane fervently. That kind of worry he could do without. 'Anything else?' When she shook her head, he gave his verdict. 'I'm going back to my steak.'

When he got back to the restaurant, both Dougie Lennox and Maggie Donald looked towards him expectantly. He shook his head, and they went back to eating. They left some time before he finished, and when he finally returned to the incident room

151

he found that Harron was back. Maggie Donald was talking earnestly to Sandra.

'I'm going over to see Jess Adams,' he told them.

'You'll tell her about the autopsy?' asked Sandra.

He nodded. 'It might even help, sergeant.' He beckoned. 'You're driving.'

When they got there, Dougie Lennox was once more on duty outside the Adams house and reported everything was peaceful. Thane left Sandra Craig with their car, walked up the small garden path, and knocked on the front door. Long seconds passed and then the door opened and Jess Adams looked out. She wore a white blouse and a black skirt, her face was pale, and her eyes were still swollen from crying.

'You'd better come in,' she said resignedly, and led the way through to the living room. Thane noticed that the photograph of Willie Adams in army uniform was back in its place and silently thanked someone for doing that.

'Sit down, superintendent.' She waited until he was seated, then took a chair opposite. 'What is it now?'

'There's something you should know.' He chose his words carefully. 'It's about how your husband died.'

Her mouth trembled a little, then she moistened her lips. 'Does it make any difference to me?'

'It may.' Thane nodded slowly. 'Jess, we've got the post-mortem results. Donny died from natural causes – simple heart disease. He may have been in a struggle at the time, but that didn't kill him.'

'Heart disease?' she stared at him. 'They're sure?'

'Positive.'

'Thank God,' she said in little more than a whisper. Then, suddenly, she raised her voice. 'Tell me I've got it right, super-intendent. Donny died from heart disease? Natural causes?'

'Natural causes.' Colin Thane heard a soft rustle somewhere near. It could have been the wind, but he had the sudden, strange feeling that they weren't alone in the house, and there was only one way to play the situation. 'Did you know he had a heart condition?'

'He saw a doctor in Inverness a year ago, about pains in his chest. When he came back, he told me it was nothing to worry

152

about.' Dragging her chair nearer, Jess Adams grasped Thane by the hand. Her voice rose again. 'You're saying nobody killed him?'

'Nobody.'

'Thank you.' There were fresh tears in her eyes. 'Can I tell folk?'

'Anybody,' confirmed Thane. He glanced towards the photograph. 'Including your son. Particularly your son. When you see him, that is.'

Suddenly, the rustling noise was there again, louder, positively from the next room. Thane heard a door open softly, then click shut again. He knew Jess Adams was also listening. A full two minutes passed, then a small engine started up at a gentle tick-over somewhere behind the house. Then the trail bike purred away.

'How did he get in?' asked Thane simply.

'There's an old coal cellar at the back. When he was a wee boy and in trouble, he often sneaked in and out that way.' Jess Adams smiled through her tears. 'What will happen to him now?'

'Not too much. I think I can promise that.' Thane rose and gently gripped her shoulders. 'Straight question, Jess – and I need a straight answer. Was Willie's natural father Iain Cameron?'

She looked up and nodded.

'Did Donny know?'

'No. Sometimes I think he guessed that that was why they didn't get on. But he didn't say anything.' She bit her lip. 'Willie found out by accident about the same time he joined the army. I made him promise to keep it secret. Even from Iain Cameron.'

'Cameron didn't know?'

'That he had a son? Never.' She forced a weak smile. 'Yet, you know, Willie always liked Iain. Blood is thicker than water, isn't it?'

Jess Adams was fragile witness material and Thane treated her that way. She admitted that her son had sneaked into her house three times in the previous twenty-four hours, but she wouldn't discuss what they'd talked about. A nightmare worry, that her son had killed her husband, had gone. She could live with the rest.

153

'Tell Willie that if he has any sense he'll come in now,' said Thane. 'The sooner he talks with us, the better.'

'I'll try,' she agreed.

'Good.' Thane moved things on. 'Tell me, how deep was Donny involved in the distillery troubles?' asked Thane.

'As deep as he could get,' she said bitterly. 'As long as I knew that man, he loved stirring trouble. What made this time special was he was getting paid for it.'

How much or who by, she didn't know. Exactly what her husband had done for the money, she wasn't sure. When Thane gave up and decided to leave, she went to the door to see him out.

'One thing,' she said suddenly, opening the door. 'There was a woman in it somewhere.'

Thane stared in surprise. 'How do you know?'

'She met him a few times. Maybe in a car – I'm not sure. I asked him about it, and he told me to mind my own damned business.' She gave a twist of a smile. 'You're a man, so you won't understand. But sometimes he'd maybe make the effort and shave, or even put on a clean shirt. I've even smelled her perfume when he came in – expensive perfume, not a kind I've ever owned. And at least with Donny, I knew it wouldn't be sex. It had to be trouble-making.'

The door closed. Thane swallowed hard and walked down to where Dougie Lennox was waiting. The young DC greeted him with a cheerful nod.

'You didn't hear a trail bike drive away from somewhere near here?' asked Thane.

'I thought I maybe did, sir.' Lennox saw Thane's expression and changed his mind. 'But I suppose I had it wrong.'

'I suppose you did,' agreed Thane woodenly. 'Hang about until you hear for sure those idiots we had earlier are totally clear of the area. Then pack it in. Don't wait for a relief.' He saw the immediate glint in Lennox's eyes. 'And keep away from local females, whatever their age. Particularly females in uniform. Or I'm calling a vet. Understand?'

'Sir,' said Lennox sadly.

And Thane felt better.

*

154

Sandra Craig drove him back to the Ardshona Inn. When he left the vehicle, Thane saw Phil Moss leaning on the porch rail looking out at the world in general and watching Jock Dawson's dogs being fed behind their van.

'They look like they're enjoying their food,' said Thane, joining him.

'They should,' said Moss sourly. 'They're better fed than I am.'

Maggie Donald was still running the storeroom incident room when they went through. A handful of faxed messages and sight of some scribbled notes brought Thane up to date. Andy Mack was making quite sure that Cameron's cousin and his supporters didn't cause further trouble. Their four carloads had been intercepted and the Northern detective inspector was now leading the police escort which would stay with them all the way back to Inverness then see them disperse. From Inverness itself there was a fax on the laboratory examination of the boxed doll with grey hair delivered to Finn Rankin. It amounted to a series of negatives – no fingerprints, no way of sourcing the box or doll, no markings of any kind on the wrappings. The doll's hair had been greyed using watercolour of the kind that could be found in any child's paintbox.

Another fax, received because it was being sent out by Northern's traffic department to all units, advised that several roads in the Brora–Dornoch area, along the coast north of Inverness, would be controlled by police road blocks for up to an hour at a time during that afternoon and evening. This would allow 'special census work' to be carried out. As an excuse, it smelled. It was probably part of Mick Farrell's magic roundabout scenario – and he was welcome to it.

The latest Crime Squad message, from Francey Dunbar in Glasgow, reeked of Dunbar's disgust at being so far removed from the action. Morris Currie had created enough fuss about his need to fly back to Edinburgh for a business dinner with important clients on the Monday. The trouble was finding where it had taken place. Every high-grade expense-account watering hole in the capital had been checked. Plenty of them knew Currie, none had seen him that night.

Sandra disappeared in the direction of the Ardshona's kitchen and returned with sandwiches, sweet biscuits and coffee. While

Thane ate and she nibbled, with Moss giving the occasional background mutter, Thane told them what Jess Adams had said.

'Every time you stir this pot a woman surfaces,' grumbled Moss. 'And the people who were watching that house and who didn't spot Willie the Kid sneaking in and out will get their backsides kicked.' He scowled. 'Do we believe her?'

'Let's say we go along with it.' Thane took another bite of sandwich, wishing that Belle Campbell hadn't been so generous with the mustard. 'I'm sold on it because of what Jess Adams wouldn't tell me.'

'Like how much Willie told her.' Sandra Craig frowned. 'I feel sorry for her.'

'She still has a son who used her husband's body as a boobytrap bomb,' grunted Moss. 'It's Happy Families with dynamite.'

'That bit where she said a man wouldn't understand' – Thane turned to Sandra – 'all right, you're a woman.'

'Thank you for noticing, sir.' His sergeant flushed to the roots of her red hair.

Thane sighed. 'You know what I mean. Would you believe her?'

Slowly, Sandra Craig nodded.

'Hell and damnation,' said Phil Moss softly. 'If that part is right, you realize where that could end up leading us?'

Thane nodded. He was trying not to think about it.

Time dragged. If the pot was starting to bubble, Thane knew he was moving into a period when he had to be ready for when that pot might boil over. One by one, he had every officer involved brought in and their statements checked. As a task, he hated every minute of it. He would have dumped the lot on the laps of Moss and Sandra Craig, but it was his job, it went with the rank.

There was also a fax update to be sent to Jack Hart at Crime Squad headquarters – and Thane could imagine the squad commander's reaction when he learned that even their fourth death hadn't turned out to be what could be termed a 'proper' murder. A shorter, follow-up fax to Inverness kept Mick Farrell informed.

Finally, after eight p.m. and with Andy Mack returned, Thane called a halt. They left Ernie Vass on watch in the incident room, went through to the restaurant, ate, then went their different ways. Sandra vanished and Moss got himself involved in a game of darts with Jock Dawson in the bar. Colin Thane looked in at the incident room, found everything still quiet, and was about to telephone home then remembered that Mary would be out.

He headed back towards the bar. Before he got there, he was intercepted by Belle Campbell. The landlord's wife had obviously been out and was still wearing her coat.

'Jess asked me to visit,' the big woman said without preliminaries. 'I'm just back.' She went on before Thane could say anything. 'And there's someone outside who needs to see you, superintendent. She's waiting, she won't come in.'

'She?' asked Thane

'Try across the road.' Without another word, Belle Campbell walked away.

Puzzled, suddenly cautious, Thane looked in at the bar. Moss and Dawson were totally involved in their darts match, and had a small audience. He hesitated, then made up his mind, went along the corridor, and stepped out into the night.

The clouds had gone, and with them the wind. In their place there was moonlight, stars, a crisp edge of frost in the air, and the inevitable smell of woodsmoke. Thane looked around, then looked again at the vehicles across the road. He heard one of Dawson's dogs moving restlessly inside their van. But there was nothing else as he walked over.

'Mr Thane.' Small, bandbox smart in a belted Burberry coat and fashion boots, wearing a neat little peaked leather hat, the woman everyone called Jonesy stepped out of a patch of shadow and came towards him. She gave a small, tight smile. 'Thank you for coming. It matters.'

He looked at her, seeing tension and worry in her face. 'How long have you been waiting out here, Jonesy? You look frozen.'

'Not too long. I didn't want to be seen asking for you. I thought I'd see someone I could trust.' She shaped a small grimace. 'Belle was the first.'

'Over here.' Thane moved her over into the token shelter of the dog van.

Inside, its occupants made inquisitive, snuffling noises. 'What's this about?'

'Finn needs to see you,' she said simply. 'Just you.'

'So he sent you?'

'He doesn't want anyone else to know.' Jonesy eyed him

earnestly. 'He's asking for help, Mr Thane. Finn doesn't often ask that from anyone.'

Thane knew he couldn't refuse, not the way things were. 'Where is he?'

She gave a low sigh of relief. 'At the Broch, waiting. You've to come back with me – we'll walk. All right?'

The wind was chill. But Thane nodded. As they set off, she surprised him by taking his arm.

'What's it about, Jonesy?' he asked as they began walking.

She shook her head. 'Something happened a couple of hours ago. I don't know what and I don't know why. But it—' the woman's grip on his arm tightened a little ' – well, I think it left him afraid.'

'Family or business?'

Jonesy glanced at him sharply, seemed on the brink of saying something, then changed her mind and shook her head. 'Ask him – he won't tell me.'

They walked on along the empty main street of the little township. A truck rumbled past, then an inevitable motor cycle. Both times, Jonesy briefly turned her head away as if to avoid being recognized. The usual TV screens glowed behind some of the cottage windows, they heard a couple arguing, but Ardshona's inhabitants were staying snugly indoors. Then they reached the driveway leading up to Broch Castle.

'I'll leave you now.' Jonesy released his arm. 'I'll go in – I told Anna and Lisa I was going for a walk, that I needed the exercise.' She paused. 'Whatever it is, listen to him – please.'

Thane watched her walk away, her feet crunching on the gravel approach to the main door. She reached the door, went in, then as the door closed again he avoided the gravel and took to the grass verge. From there, Thane cautiously worked his way round to the rear of the building and soon he was looking over to the moonlit shape of the Pictish broch. Somehow, the giant stone beehive seemed to be able to project an immovable, brooding, menace.

Thane suddenly came to a halt, aware of movement somewhere near, straining his eyes and ears against the night. A dog fox gave a hoarse, high bark from the nearby trees, and something large and swift crashed through the bushes. He swore, thought wistfully of Glasgow's more predictable tenement canyons, then set off again. As he came nearer, he gradually became aware of tiny, isolated cracks of artificial light showing here and there between the broch's stonework.

'So you came, Thane.' Without warning, Finn Rankin stepped out of a patch of shadow. His white hair glinted in the moonlight, his thin face was hard to read. He waited until Thane reached him then added, 'Thank you.'

'Thank your messenger,' said Thane.

'Her too.' For a moment the distillery owner paused, looked past Thane into the night, then gave a soft, two-note whistle.

'Willie Adams?' queried Thane.

'Standing him down.' Rankin frowned. 'A quick word, super-intendent. It – well, let's say it might be that the same young man tells a story about getting into an argument with someone. Except that the someone lost his temper, fired a shotgun at him, and then there was a struggle and – ah – the other party dropped dead.' He considered Thane carefully. 'Wouldn't you call it self-defence?'

'A good lawyer would.' Thane nodded. 'And more than a possibility.'

'A possibility. That's fair.' Rankin beckoned, led the way, and a dull light spilled out as he swung open the door of the broch. 'Come in. Watch your head.' Once they were both through, the man closed the door again.

Thane followed him through the same dimly lit maze of passageways and rough stone chambers. They passed the door to Robert Martin's whisky sampling office, then Finn Rankin opened another door a few paces on. He flicked a switch, and twin overhead tube lights spat to life, lighting a similar room but furnished with only a desk, a selection of chairs round a large polished oak table, and two metal filing cabinets.

'The nearest we've got to a boardroom. Sit down, superintend-ent.' Finn Rankin gestured towards two of the chairs already placed beside the table.

Thane took the nearest of the chairs. As he settled, he watched Rankin. The man wore a knitted grey polo-neck sweater with Lovat pattern trousers and blue suede shoes. It didn't matter, but he wondered if Rankin knew that inmates at two of HM Prisons were currently turning out that style of footwear to meet commercial contracts.

'I'm not going to offer you a drink,' said Rankin in a voice empty of emotion. 'I don't think you'll want one.'

He went over to one of the filing cabinets, opened a drawer, brought out a full, unopened bottle of Broch Single Malt, and laid it on the table under the glare of the tube lights. Thane looked, frowned, looked more closely, and winced. A human forefinger, complete with fingernail and crudely amputated at the top joint, was floating inside the bottle.

'It's real.' Rankin gave the bottle a small twirl. The finger bobbed and stirred obscenely in the whisky, sank down, then gradually floated up again to just above the half-way mark.

'So tell me about it,' said Thane softly.

'There was a telephone call to my home about eight this evening, while we were still eating.' Rankin remained standing, his face grim at the memory. 'I don't know who he is, but he'd called before. He said I was to look in the broch.' He paused, his voice bitter with anger. 'Then he asked me how much I thought a grandchild was worth.'

'So you went, and you found this.' Thane considered the bottle. 'Someone opened it, someone resealed it.'

'Easy enough done if you've a spare bottle cap.' Rankin went back to the filing cabinet and came back with a slip of paper and laid it down. The note amounted to a typewritten set of six numbers, prefixed by two code letters. 'The bottle was on this table – our board table. The note was wrapped around its neck.'

Thane made a physical effort to stop looking at that bobbing finger. 'And these numbers translate into something?'

Rankin nodded, and slumped into the chair opposite Thane. 'The bastard is telling me exactly where the bottle could have come from. We've a shipment of Broch Single Malt due out of Prestwick on a Boeing freighter, heading for Tokyo. This is the lead number for the cartons in the shipment.' He saw Thane's raised eyebrow. 'The prefix letters tell me that on their own.'

'What do they want?' asked Thane bluntly. 'You know, don't you?'

Finn Rankin hesitated, then drew a deep, reluctant breath. 'Control of Broch Distilleries, and my resignation. Right from the start, that's what it has been about. In a nutshell. First, I'm told the trouble stops if they get two million dollars cash – dollars, not pounds sterling.' He gave a bitter laugh. 'We're already heavily into the banks, Thane. These people had to know I couldn't raise even half that amount. Except, wonders never cease, suddenly in comes an offer from a Swiss-based company.

They'll give five million dollars if I sell them a controlling interest. Like the coincidence?'

Thane nodded grimly, understanding. Finn Rankin could take the offer, pay off the blackmail bid, and still be three million dollars in pocket. But he would have lost Broch in the process – and the blackmail money, or most of it, could probably go round in a circle back to the Swiss company.

'Who are they?'

'The Swiss? Some off-the-shelf nominee company named Ophelia Holdings – probably set up just for this. Impossible to know who runs it.' Rankin went back to the filing cabinet and returned with an envelope. 'You'll want this – it's a photocopy of their offer.'

Thane nodded and tucked the envelope in an inside pocket. Nominee companies, shell companies, could launder their real ownership through God alone knew how many hands. But that wasn't his immediate puzzle.

'Why haven't you told me any of this before? And why now?'

'Why?' Rankin looked away for a moment, gnawing his upper lip. 'Because at first I thought I could deal with it, maybe just use your people to keep things tidy – I've got myself out of tight corners often enough. Except the threats about what could happen kept growing. Until we got to the warehouse fire, people dying, that doll threat to Jonesy – and now this.' He glared his fierce anger at the whisky bottle with its floating finger. 'What kind of people threaten an unborn child, Thane?'

Thane shook his head. 'Do your daughters know any of this?'

'No. I want to keep them out of it as much as I can.' Rankin made it a plea. 'You can try, can't you?'

'Maybe for a spell. No promises.' Thane leaned forward in his chair, considering Rankin, wondering how much of the truth he was being told. 'How much would it hurt if a bottle with a human finger turned up on some supermarket shelf?'

'It would be a disaster.' Rankin paled at the thought. 'The repercussions could cost us a fortune. But they're hinting at worse – what could happen to our export trade. A bottle like this turns up in somewhere like Tokyo or New York, and we could kiss a whole damned country goodbye.' He raised an eyebrow. 'Next?'

'Now we get personal,' warned Thane. 'You've had Willie Adams working undercover for you?'

Rankin nodded. 'As a sort of family bodyguard.'

'And he ransacked Lisa's office?' Thane sighed as the white-haired man nodded again. 'Why?'

'Lisa is production director, she has a confidential file which covers production, sales, and market projections. I wanted to see it.'

'You're the chairman,' frowned Thane. 'Couldn't you—'

'Ask her for it?' Finn Rankin shook his head. 'She'd want to know why. I thought there could be something in that file on market projections which could explain a lot. But Willie blew it – end.'

'Do you trust your family?'

'Most of the time.'

'Do you trust Morris Currie?' Thane saw the grin fade as Rankin didn't answer. 'He's your sales director. He'd handle market projections—'

'Some of them.'

'You quarrelled with him last night, you more or less threw him out this morning.' Thane built a steeple with his finger-tips and pointed it across the boardroom table. 'I don't think you particularly trust Currie. Yet he hangs onto his job. Why?'

'Simple.' The thin face was bleak. 'I inherited him. Years ago, we took over a small distillery business that his family owned. Currie joined us as our new sales director as part of the package, with a contract it would cost a fortune to break.'

'What was the trouble about last night?'

'His sales performance. We're barely holding our share of the market,' said Finn Rankin flatly. 'I wouldn't trust him as far as I could throw him, superintendent. But he isn't clever enough to be part of what's going on.'

Thane had other questions for the thin, bitterly angry distillery chairman. But he got no further, and sensed it was time to call a halt. Rankin produced a towel from a drawer, Thane used it as a protective cover for the whisky bottle, then they locked up and left the old Pictish stronghold.

'What happens now?' asked Rankin as they parted at the front door of Broch Castle.

'We try to catch up with where we could have been days ago,' said Thane stonily.

The man gave a small, almost apologetic gesture, then went indoors.

By the time Colin Thane walked into the welcome warmth of the Ardshona Inn it was less than an hour before midnight. Carrying the whisky bottle, Rankin's photocopied letter in his pocket, he was puzzled to find the bar deserted but went through to the storeroom incident room.

His entire team were there. They'd been waiting, their faces were serious, yet most avoided meeting his eyes.

'Where the hell have you been, Colin?' asked Phil Moss in a strange voice.

'Finn Rankin wanted to see me.' Thane laid the wrapped bottle on the table. 'He told me—'

'It can keep.' Moss cut him short. 'Something's happened at your home.'

Thane stiffened. 'Like what?'

'We tried to find you, super—' began Sandra Craig.

'I'll tell it.' Moss silenced her with a scowl. 'It's Mary, Colin. But she's not badly hurt, she'll be okay. Jack Hart and his wife have been out, he telephoned.'

'Phil – ' Thane made it a plea – 'what the hell's going on? Mary was going to be out tonight, picking up the kids—'

'She did. She took the dog with her.' Moss told it simply. 'When she got back, she was first into the house. She disturbed a burglar, he stabbed her, then the dog went for him and he stabbed the dog. By the time the kids charged in, he had done a runner.'

Thane realized he was gripping the table edge with both hands, knuckle-white.

'You said she was stabbed. How bad?'

'A wound in the neck, a smaller one in her shoulder, neither look too serious. She was ambulanced to hospital. Gloria Hart is with her, a neighbour has the kids.' Moss gave a soft, reassuring belch. 'Your dog got the worst of it – a stab in the chest – but they reckon even he'll survive.'

Thane swallowed, trying to take it in. 'I need to phone—'

'No, super.' Sandra Craig laid a firm hand on his shoulder in a way that made him look up in surprise. 'It's organized,

163

Commander Hart's orders. There's no flight out of Inverness before dawn, so we'll get you down by car.'

'I'm driving, sir.' Ernie Vass crinkled a reassuring grin. 'My speciality.'

Moss grunted with a comforting edge of humour. 'As in wrecking patrol cars?' He turned back to Thane. 'Sandra will go down with you, Colin. Don't hurry back.' As he spoke, he unwrapped the whisky bottle, stared, then gulped. 'Bloody hell, that's a criminal waste of good single malt!'

'We're ready when you are, sir,' said Ernie Vass.

Colin Thane needed less than five minutes.

7

It was a blurred nightmare of a journey, filled with the glare of their headlights. It began on mountain roads glistening with frost, then varied to broad highway, mist, and rain.

The car was a new arrival to the Scottish Crime Squad transport pool, a three litre V8 BMW 730i, metallic red, two years old, the former joy of a drugs baron until it was confiscated when a High Court judge sent him down for twelve years.

'Settle back and try to relax, boss,' said Ernie Vass as he shepherded Thane into the BMW's rear. Sandra Craig had already slipped into the front passenger seat.

It was midweek, close to midnight, and the mountain road snaking through the dark landscape was empty of traffic. The thick frost clinging to the trees reflected back their headlights. Once a startled red deer stag sprang out across their path. Sheep stood like statues at the roadside verges.

They passed a mail van toiling along somewhere north of Loch Garve, then a stationary Northern force traffic car gave an acknowledging blink of its lights as they joined the main A385 road. There was occasional traffic from then on, and thin mist began drifting in at the same time as they spotted the glow of Inverness.

The BMW sometimes swayed and sometimes lurched, but seldom slowed. There was little conversation. His sergeant and driver, sensing Thane's mood, stayed quiet.

They skirted Inverness, which was dark and empty, drew a brief blink of lights from another patrol car, then the BMW's radio began muttering. There had been fragments of other messages on the way down, directed towards the road blocks exercise on the north-east coastal route. But the new signal came in on the Crime Squad's dedicated low-band frequency. Sandra Craig used the handset, answered, listened, acknowledged, then turned and beamed at Thane.

'She is okay, sir! Stitched and packed off home!'

Thane heaved a great sigh of relief, caught a grin from Ernie Vass, then Vass tramped on the accelerator pedal and the BMW's V8 responded. Another couple of minutes, and they joined the main A9 – the fast, sometimes close to motorway standard, north–south highway which runs like a spine down most of the length of Scotland.

Thane checked the dashboard clock. Vass had carved more than half an hour off the journey time down from Ardshona.

'Ernie,' he said softly. 'Well done. Now get us there in one piece.'

Ernie Vass chuckled.

The A9 always had traffic heading both ways. At that hour it was a blend of newspaper vans and parcels wagons. A long, strange convoy of catering vans and hooked-on trailers was crawling north. Heading south, the BMW swept past road signs for Culloden and Slochd Summit, then Aviemore and Kingussie. Nothing challenged the metallic red car.

Thane dozed, then slept. When he woke again, they had come another long way, far south of Perth and nearing Stirling. It was raining, the car's tyres were hissing on wet tarmac, and Sandra and Ernie Vass were in the middle of a fierce, low-voiced argument. He heard his name mentioned, listened, eavesdropped on a discussion about who would get his job if he dropped dead, didn't think much of their candidates, and ended it by making stirring noises.

'How long now, Ernie?' he asked.

'Under the hour,' said Vass confidently.

Thane could think ahead again. There were things to be done. He told Sandra to deliver the finger in its whisky bottle for a rush examination, gave her Finn Rankin's photostat offer letter for delivery direct to the Crime Squad night shift, and told her of more digging he wanted done as soon as she had slept. She listened, nodded, then switched to studying what was left of the in-car equipment installed by the original owner.

Twelve minutes short of Vass's hour, their car crossed the Glasgow boundary and into the city's lights with Dolly Parton belting out 'Nine till Five' on a Radio Clyde country and western show for night people.

They reached Colin Thane's home a little after four a.m. Every house in the street was in darkness, but as the BMW coasted to a halt at his gate another car started up just ahead. The divisional car purred past a moment later, the constable at the wheel raising one hand in a fractional salute. Cops were human, whatever the rest of the world might think – and cops looked after their own.

Thane climbed out of the BMW, stretched his stiff muscles while the car drove away, then found his house key as he walked up the garden path. Before he reached the door it opened, and Gloria Hart looked out. The Squad commander's wife, a well-built woman with dyed blonde hair, was wearing a dressing gown and smiled a welcome.

'Mary's fine, Colin.' The smile became a frown as he came in under the light and she saw his face. Once Thane was inside, she closed the door again. 'She's awake, wanting to see you. Though your face may scare the hell out of her!'

He grinned his thanks, climbed the stairs, and went into their bedroom. Mary Thane was in bed, propped up by pillows, her neck and left shoulder bandaged, and looked at him with a small smile on her lips. Her long, dark hair had been carefully brushed until it gleamed under the soft glow of the bedside lamp, the bandaging finished somewhere under the scooped neckline of her peach coloured nightdress.

'Hi,' said Thane softly, kissing her on the lips.

'Hi.' One hand came up and touched the cuts on his face. 'So we've both been in the wars.'

He nodded soberly. 'What happened here?'

She told it in a tired voice, starting from coming back with children and dog, unlocking the front door, switching on the hall light, and coming face to face with the intruder as he burst out of the living room, brandishing a knife. Then it had been confusion – the knife stabbing, her screaming, Clyde coming to her defence like a snarling thunderbolt then also being stabbed, the young, thin-faced intruder turning and running as Tommy and Kate burst in.

After that it had been 999 telephone calls and the rest. It ended in the hospital casualty department with a cheerful young Asian doctor cleaning her wounds and putting in his 'very best, very pretty, best-quality small stitches.' Then finding Jack Hart and his wife were there to bring her home again.

'Where are the kids?' asked Thane. He didn't get an answer. Her eyes had closed and she was already asleep.

He kissed her on the forehead, tucked the edge of the bed-clothes gently around the bandages, and crept out. Downstairs, Gloria Hart was in the kitchen. She poured him a mug of hot tea and handed it over.

'Thanks for everything, Gloria,' Thane said simply, and took a swallow of tea. It was stiff with sugar and he didn't take sugar, but that didn't matter. 'What about the kids?'

'Spending the night with one of Kate's pals. They did well.' The woman saw his eyes stray over to the empty dog basket near the cooker. 'Don't worry too much about your idiot Boxer. He earned VIP treatment and he got it – the local CID whipped him away from here by patrol van to where there was a vet standing by.' She yawned. 'Your housebreaker forced the back door – one of the beat men made a temporary repair.'

Jack Hart was coming for her in the morning. She was using Kate's bedroom and Thane could use his son's room so that Mary wasn't disturbed. She yawned again, then wandered off. Thane finished his mug of tea, switched off the kitchen light, and went upstairs. The main bedroom was in darkness, and he tiptoed in to Tommy's room, where a king-sized Batman poster glowered down from a wall.

'Go to hell,' he told Batman, undressed, and slid into his son's bed.

The next thing he knew it was daylight, past eight a.m. on a grey Thursday morning, and there were clattering noises coming from the kitchen. Thane got up, showered, and went through the awkward business of shaving. He dressed, saw that Mary's door was closed, and headed down into the kitchen.

'Good morning,' said Gloria Hart briskly. She thumbed towards the table. 'Orange juice, coffee, toast. And – uh – I think you know Detective Sergeant Beech?'

'Yes.' He stared at the man already seated there. 'Sergeant, what the hell are you doing here?'

'They transferred me to this division two months ago, sir.' Sergeant Michael Beech grinned in delight and laid down his coffee cup. 'It's good to see you.'

'You're handling this?' Thane tried to keep a note of disbelief out of his voice.

'Yes, sir.' Beech nodded solemnly. 'I was here last night. I told my DI that I wanted to stay on it, that you were my old boss. He agreed.'

'Yes.' Thane silently cursed the unknown DI. When he had been detective chief inspector at Glasgow Millside Division, his team had included the notoriously new Detective Constable Beech, fresh-faced, always anxious, and the young pram-pushing father of twin girls. Beech had never been a genius. How he'd reached detective sergeant rank had been a small miracle. 'What have you got on it so far – uh – Michael?'

'Not a lot, sir.' Beech wasn't too happy. 'Chummy broke into two other houses in your street last night, also unoccupied, same MO. We're talking random housebreaking, nothing of major value stolen—'

'Value doesn't have to have a price label, sergeant,' snapped Gloria Hart, at a kitchen cupboard.

'Ah – no, Mrs Hart,' agreed Beech hastily. He switched back to Thane. 'Your dog bit him hard on the leg, tore a chunk from his trouser-leg – drew blood. Now I'd like to get more of a statement from Mrs Thane—'

'You can't, she's asleep,' said Gloria Hart sharply.

Beech blinked. 'I need a list of what's missing.'

'That can wait,' said Gloria Hart, a woman well used to demolishing detectives of any age and rank.

'You'll get it soon,' promised Thane.

'I'd appreciate that, sir.' Sheepishly, Beech got to his feet.

Gloria firmly marched him to the door. When she returned, she tidied around until Thane had eaten breakfast. Then she produced a tray prepared for her patient.

'Your turn,' she ordered. 'I heard her moving about.'

Thane took the tray up. The bedroom door was ajar, the

curtains were open, and Mary was sitting up in bed, looking more like an abandoned waif than anybody's wife or mother. She gave a smile which became a wince of pain when Thane bent to kiss her.

'How do you feel?' asked Thane.

'Punctured,' said Mary wryly. 'Sore. Mad as hell. But I slept well.' She took the tray and set it down. 'What are you going to do?' She raised a hand to stop him. 'I know. It's not your case. Did I see the original Boy Detective around last night?'

'Beech?' He nodded. 'You did.'

'Then let him get on with it – and I don't want you hanging around here, frightening the population.' She looked at him earnestly. 'Colin, you'll never know how glad I was when you got here last night. But that's it. Mack the Knife won't be back – he was probably as scared as I was by what happened. The local beatman can keep an extra eye on the house for a few days, can't he?'

'Yes.' He said it reluctantly.

'Right.' Mary grinned at him. 'Check on the kids, check on how Clyde is doing, then get back to work. Do you have to go north again straight away?'

'Probably not,' he agreed. 'There are some loose ends down here.'

'Then go find them and tie them up,' she ordered briskly.

Another hour and more passed before Jack Hart arrived, which gave Thane time to make telephone calls. The first, to the veterinary surgery which had Clyde in its care, confirmed that the four-footed Thane was 'comfortable and satisfactory'. The stab wound in his chest had required seven stitches. The other calls, including a couple to the Crime Squad headquarters building, were the kind which might set a couple of new possibilities in motion. Then Hart arrived. He brought Kate and Tommy with him, both racing upstairs to see their mother, then exploding back down wanting to know about their dog.

A couple of neighbours arrived, ready to take over from Gloria Hart. Kate and Tommy reluctantly discovered they were still expected to go to school. In the middle of it, Hart took Thane into a relatively quiet corner.

'I spoke with Mary.' The squad commander eyed his deputy quizzically. 'She wants you back at work. You go along with that?'

169

Thane nodded. 'For now.'

'Good.' Hart didn't hide his relief. 'If you need more time at home, just take it. But I hear a few things seem to be happening. You reckon this man Currie has to be in the frame?'

'Somewhere, but not on his own,' agreed Thane slowly. 'There could be family involved.'

'Be damned careful you don't even hint at that to Rankin until you're sure,' warned Hart.

Once Hart had gone, taking Gloria and the children with him, Thane used the telephone again and tried a car-phone number he knew from memory. Doc Williams, a senior Strathclyde police surgeon and pathologist, lived the kind of life which kept him on the move. He answered on the third ring of his mobile, and expressed no surprise to hear Thane's voice.

'You usually make life interesting, Colin,' he declared cheerfully over a booming background echo. 'Can you hear me all right?'

'I hear you,' confirmed Thane. 'Doc, have you—'

'Seen your famous finger? Yes. There it was, waiting to welcome me this morning.' Williams gave a cross between a grunt and a snort. 'Next time I buy a bottle of whisky, I'll hold the damned thing up to the light. Anyway, to use a time-honoured phrase, I've extracted the digit.'

'And?'

'Middle finger, left hand. Not a professional job,' declared the police surgeon. 'Probably amputated after death. The way the bone was cut it could have been done with a hobby fretsaw.'

'How long ago?' pressed Thane.

'Pickled like that? Probably not long, but how the hell would I know?' yelled Williams through a transmission break-up. 'Do you know what they did with Nelson when he died at Trafalgar? Brought him home inside a barrel of brandy!'

'What else, Doc?' asked Thane patiently.

'About Nelson, or your finger?'

'Doc—'

'At a wild guess, a week or so since it happened,' relented Williams. He paused, and for a moment there was only static. 'The state of the fingernail indicates someone certainly elderly, maybe in poor health.'

'You sent the finger on?'

170

'What else? SCRO have it now.' The police surgeon chuckled. 'About that whisky – you could probably drink it!'

'Be my guest,' said Thane stonily, and hung up.

Mary was being fussed over by her neighbours when he went upstairs. He checked there was nothing she needed, said good-bye, and went out to his pool car, a Ford Mondeo. It had been left at the rear of the house, there was no sign that the intruder had been near it, and Thane got aboard and set it moving, the screen wipers flicking to clear a light drizzle of rain.

Traffic was heavy most of the way in towards a stretch of parkland just in sight of the city centre skyline. A uniformed man was on duty as usual and raised the barrier pole which guarded a private road where a sign said Police Training Centre – which was true. The Strathclyde force carried out mounted branch and dog branch training in the same parkland area.

Scottish Crime Squad headquarters, an unobtrusive single-storey building, was located at the rear. Thane drove through to the squad parking area, left the Ford there, crossed over to the building, and went in.

'Colin' – Maggie Fyffe, Jack Hart's personal secretary, had been on her way through the reception area when she saw him and came straight over – 'how's Mary?'

'She threw me out,' he told her.

'I've got some time off this afternoon. I'll take a trip over.' She wrinkled her nose. 'I've to tell you that the Commander has had to go down to the High Court. Some judge wants to see him.'

'Maybe he'll get time off for good behaviour,' suggested Thane woodenly.

Leaving her, he went down the corridor to his office. It was small, and furnished around an old black leather swivel chair and a scarred oak desk. But it had that ultimate police status symbol, a carpet, and a window which looked out over some of the parkland towards the M8 motorway. When Thane entered, he already had a visitor perched on a corner of the desk.

'Morning, boss.' Detective Inspector Francey Dunbar gave a welcoming nod in a way that made it matter, then continued threading paperclips into a metallic daisy-chain. 'How are things at home?'

'Better.' Thane got past Dunbar and into his chair. 'Anything yet from Sandra?'

'She's been and gone,' said Dunbar dryly. 'Making busy noises and looking smug. She said she'll be in touch – I've to tell you the answer is twenty weeks and the way you thought.' He frowned. 'Answer to what, boss?'

'Just something I asked her to check for me,' said Thane vaguely. 'She's on her way to Prestwick Airport, to talk with Gina Martin and her husband.'

Francey Dunbar continued with his paperclip chain. Slim and in his late twenties, Dunbar had jet black hair and a straggle of a bandit moustache. He wore an old Donegal tweed safari jacket teamed with a grey wool shirt and grey whipcord slacks. He also possessed a cheerful brand of sarcasm it was impossible to ignore. But it now went with a heavy limp, a reminder of the car crash in which he had nearly died. The limp was also the reason for a black ebony cane propped against a filing cabinet. The cane, topped by a dented silver knob, was typical of Francey Dunbar's irrepressible attitude. He had found it in a Clydeside junk shop and had customized it by having the knob filled with lead.

A small collection of fax messages were lying on Thane's desk. He thumbed through them, made sure that none particularly mattered, then looked up and caught a waiting glint in Dunbar's eyes.

'All right, Francey,' he said resignedly. 'Out with it.'

'Something could be happening, boss.' Dunbar surrendered like a schoolboy. 'You've been homing in on Morris Currie. You've made noises about Peter Wessex, the ex-husband of Anna Rankin.' He made a brief digression. 'Uh – what's Anna like?'

'Good-looking, chestnut hair, a lawyer.'

'She may be a lawyer, but she's a lousy judge of character.' Dunbar abandoned his paperclip chain. 'Peter Wessex is a wide boy Anglo-Scot accountant. He's also a charming, thorough-going bastard. Wessex is usually London based, Currie lives in Edinburgh. But here's today's surprise. Right now, they're both in Glasgow!'

Thane gave a silent whistle. 'Together?'

'Call what we've got a hell of a coincidence, boss.' Dunbar grinned. 'I talked Edinburgh into putting a tail on Currie yesterday evening. They picked him up when he left the business centre he uses. Currie drove straight through to Glasgow then went to the Beezer gambling club in Sauchiehall Street. He stayed in the club until after midnight, then he went round to the Marriot Hotel, where he had a room booked. He's still there.'

'What about Wessex?'

'He runs his Wessex wine importing agency and a string of wine shops in London – we got that from a trade contact up here.' Dunbar hopped down from the desk, limped awkwardly across to the filing cabinet which supported his black ebony cane, lifted a single photograph from the top of the cabinet, then limped again to place it in front of Thane. 'Peter Wessex, boss. Source, same contact. We didn't get it until late last night.'

Thane touched the glossy, grainy enlargement with his fingertips. Peter Wessex had short, dark hair, a thin face and good looks marred by too small a mouth. He had slightly hooded eyes and was probably in his late thirties. In the photograph, he wore black tie and dinner jacket.

'You've a useful contact.'

Dunbar gave an almost apologetic gesture. 'A sort of distant cousin of mine. He says he has some parking tickets—'

'Serving justice should be reward enough,' said Thane piously. 'Square them. What's the rest of it?'

'The rest' had been simple enough. Ready with a story about a possible wine order, Francey Dunbar had telephoned Peter Wessex's London office to establish that Wessex was there.

He hadn't needed the script. An assistant, finishing for the night, had explained that Wessex had gone to Scotland on business for a few days. If Dunbar was really anxious to contact him, then Wessex was staying at the Hospitality Inn in Glasgow.

A copy of Peter Wessex's photograph was rushed out to the tail on Currie. But he could only say that someone who might have been Wessex had gone into the Beezer Club then had left again after about an hour.

'Two innocents, both using their own names, doing nothing wrong.' Thane went over to the window and watched the distant motorway traffic. 'I don't buy it.'

'So we keep tabs on them both?'

'We do. And remind everyone that there's a chance Banjo Kingsley might make contact. If he does, I want to know.' The name would be enough. Kingsley was both brutal and cunning. His record was known to every Crime Squad officer. Thane gently stroked a thumb over some of the tiny, healing cuts on his chin. 'Any more on Morris Currie?'

'We've been trying, boss.' Dunbar leaned his weight on the desk. 'Currie was involved in some dodgy whisky deals before Broch Distilleries took him on. The last time, he was operating a whisky investment racket, working out of a rented warehouse and selling to American tourists. He owned a few barrels filled with whisky, and a lot more filled with tap water.'

'But Finn Rankin bailed him out – for his own reasons.' Thane sighed. 'What about Anna's ex?'

'Not a lot there, but what we have, I don't like,' said Dunbar with a granite scowl. 'As an accountant, Wessex has been investigated on three separate occasions – once by the Fraud Squad, twice by professional accountancy bodies. Each time nothing stuck, but people were left mad as hell and a lot poorer.'

'What about the divorce?'

'Messy. Claims from both sides. The rest is that Wessex has a background which is foggy at the edges, but his Ophelia wine chain does well enough.'

Thane sucked his teeth. 'Any known Swiss links?'

'The Broch takeover letter?' Dunbar shook his head. 'Still checking.'

Dunbar left a few minutes later to see his licensed trade relative and talk whisky gossip. He had hardly closed the door when Thane's telephone began ringing. The call was from Phil Moss, still in the Ardshona incident room, asking about Mary then reporting that it was a peaceful day around where he was.

'Finn Rankin came visiting.' Moss's voice took a tart edge on the line. 'He wanted to know if we'd guarantee there would be no charges against Willie Adams if Adams walked in.'

'No deals, Phil,' Thane said stonily. 'Not yet. Not about Adams, not about anything. But you can hint that the world wouldn't exactly fall on him.'

After that, he had time to check the wad of print-out report sheets which had built up on his desk. For most, a glance at the heading was enough. He spent slightly more time over a Known Associates list produced by Criminal Intelligence on the two men killed in the Northern car crash. A few names seemed worth attention.

Then the telephone was ringing again, this time a local call from a carefully diplomatic Detective Sergeant Beech.

'I – uh – was out at your home again, sir,' said Beech. 'I spoke with your wife and she gave me a first list of stolen property.'

He plunged on. 'I think we'll get this one, sir. There aren't too many neds going around with a bite out of one leg.'

'What did he take?' asked Thane.

'The usual, sir. Cash, jewellery, and the memory chip from your son's computer. There's a good market for computer chips.'

Next came a visitor, Tina Redder, a detective chief inspector who had the best looking legs in the Crime Squad and who wore short skirts to prove it. Tina and her team were heavily into a drugs investigation, but she still offered help if Thane needed it. He watched those legs with what he told himself was academic interest as she walked away.

A scatter of other telephone calls came in. Some asked about Mary, prompting him to phone home and get his own update. She sounded cheerful enough. With Clyde still improving, she was more mad at what had been stolen than anything else, and had discovered a few more items missing to add to Beech's list.

'What do we need for the insurance claim?' she asked.

'Ask Beech for a note of his Crime Report number.'

'You'd better pick me up a Criminal Injuries Compensation claim form from somewhere,' she instructed. 'Gloria Hart says being stabbed could be worth a few thousand.'

When he put down the phone, it rang again. This time it was the orderly on the front desk, announcing that a Detective Chief Inspector Chester had arrived and wanted to see him.

'Not as much as I want to see him!' declared Thane.

Less than a minute later, escorted by the orderly, DCI Steve Chester arrived in his room. As the orderly left, closing the door behind him, Thane shook hands with Chester and settled him in a chair.

'Colin, you're in luck.' Chester, a lanky, balding man with thick rimless spectacles, beamed. 'That finger you sent is pure magic!'

'You've got something?' asked Thane. Steve Chester was part of the Scottish Criminal Records Office team who reigned over more than a quarter million fingerprint files.

'More than something.' Settling back, Chester let his grin linger. 'SCRO triumphs again – and I want a favour!'

'The way we all expect,' said Thane solemnly.

SCRO, a central government funded team, rented office space within Strathclyde Police Headquarters in Glasgow. For sixty years they had been collecting fingerprint records on cardboard forms and fililng cabinets. But now, in the modern IT world they operated a French-made Morpho automatic fingerprint recognition system. It had cost £1.5 million, it had been the first in the UK, and it was linked to a computerized collection of ten print marks. Searches that had previously taken hours or days could now be done in whirring minutes, drawing on the system's database.

'Of course, we're just naturally the best.' Steve Chester said it blandly, then he leaned forward. 'But I said lucky, and I meant it, Colin. Think fingerprints. What do you know about the 70–30 boundaries or the "Four I" list?' He saw Thane's blank reaction, nodded, and began the lecture.

The 70–30 boundaries and the Four I list went together. Most accused were routinely fingerprinted by police. Innocent fingerprints were later destroyed, anyone found guilty had his or her fingerprints kept on the Morpho database for a period – then these were also weeded out and discarded. Except for the Four I list and the 70 – 30 boundaries.

The Four I list involved Indecency, Insanity, Indictment or Imprisonment. Four I list people automatically had their fingerprints stored on database until they reached the age of seventy or their offence was thirty years in the past – or they died.

'The thirty years starts from age at conviction,' emphasized the SCRO man. 'So someone could go on our database aged twenty and come off at fifty, or—'

'Or go on at seventy and stay on it till he made his hundred?'

'We're still waiting for our first century,' admitted Chester wryly. Anyway' – he reached into his jacket pocket, brought out a corked plastic test-tube, and laid it on Thane's desk – 'we're talking about this.'

The finger floated lazily in a transparent fluid, bobbing a little as if it had a life of its own.

'Say hello to all that's left of the late Arden Wason – a.k.a. Old Aladdin, because he only had one lamp,' said Chester solemnly. 'He lost the other eye a long time back. He died two weeks ago, aged eighty-one, from pneumonia, and was cremated four days later.'

'Hello, Aladdin,' said Thane wrly, and grimaced. 'You checked?'

Chester nodded. 'We'd been notified; we hadn't got round to taking him off the database. Twenty-seven years ago, when

Wason was a fifty-four-year-old stripling, he attempted to rape a very small, very tough lady of sixty. She beat him up, held him until the police arrived, then he got three years for indecent assault – a Four I offence.'

'And he wasn't in trouble again?'

'Not that we know about.' Chester burrowed into an inside pocket, produced an envelope, and slid it across. 'That's a copy of the death certificate.'

Thane stared at the envelope. 'And if you want a nice, fresh finger—'

'You take it from a nice, fresh body,' agreed the SCRO man. 'Find the undertaker – it should be easy enough.'

It could be. Thane glanced towards the Known Associates list on his desk. One man's occupation was given as hire car driver. Hire cars were used at weddings – and funerals. Maybe his luck would hold.

'I – umm—' Steve Chester was fidgeting. 'I said I needed a favour.'

'Name it,' invited Thane.

'The old lad's finger.' The SCRO man meant it. 'I do some college lectures. It would make a hell of a good exhibit. So – uh – unless some relative gets awkward—'

'It's yours,' agreed Thane. 'You earned it.'

Detective Chief Inspector Chester beamed and left.

Thane put the floating finger inside a desk drawer, locked the desk, then left his office and went through to the main duty room. At that hour, it was almost empty. But Ernie Vass was sitting reading a girlie magazine.

'Idle, Ernie?' asked Thane.

'Sir?' Vass abandoned the magazine with a resigned air.

'This is yours.' Thane dropped both the death certificate and the Known Associates list in front of the man. 'Do it quietly. The death of Arden Wason – check out the name of the undertakering firm. Then find out if they employ a driver named George Eastern – he's on this list.'

'Doing it.' Vass nodded and reached for telephone and directory.

As he turned away, Thane heard a telephone ring at another of the desks, then a plump, motherly, woman officer who specialized in nailing paedophiles had answered the call and was beckoning him over. Sandra Craig was on the line.

177

'I'm at Prestwick, sir,' said his sergeant without preliminaries. 'I've seen Gina Martin and her husband, they agree the timescale, I've told them you'll probably visit, nothing more.'

'Stay there,' Thane told her. 'I'll be with you in under the hour.'

'Time enough for lunch,' said Sandra Craig thankfully.

Thane put down the phone, told Vass where he was going, then went back to his office, collected his coat from its hook and made his way out of the headquarters building. As he went out at the main door he heard a shout, then Francey Dunbar came limping over from the parking lot.

'Something on, boss?' asked Dunbar.

'I'm on my way to join Sandra.' Thane told him the rest, including the finger's place in it all. 'How about you?'

'I made out a little.' Dunbar was pleased with himself. 'All as before with the surveillance teams – Currie and Wessex haven't made a move, everyone has been warned about Banjo Kingsley. I talked with my relative and a couple of his friends. There's been a rumour in the whisky world that one of the smaller independent malt distilleries could be in a takeover mode. Broch was hinted at as a candidate.' He tapped his silver-knobbed cane on the concrete. 'And Peter Wessex could have Swiss merchant banking links.'

'Good.' It was coming together. Slowly, but it was happening. Thane reached for his Ford keys. 'If George Eastern could be our finger-chopper, I want him. But with no fuss.'

'So even his own mother doesn't miss him,' promised Dunbar.

Prestwick International Airport is thirty-five miles from Glasgow, and Colin Thane drove the distance in an easy forty minutes. The Broch Highland blending and bottling plant was a long two-storey building at the north end of the airport's sprawling perimeter, and he had to go through a manned security checkpoint before he reached its parking area. Sandra Craig's white VW was already there, and she came over as he got out.

He let her lead the way into the building. It was a noisy, high-vaulted production world of machinery; clattering lines where bottles went in empty at one end, vanished, were automatically filled with whisky, then emerged again capped and labelled.

Extractor fans gulped air, moving belts hummed, and a line of workers, mostly women, fed more bottles into the lines or packed and checked cartons which were then swept away.

If Broch Single Malt was traditional in its ways, Broch Highland Blend was the opposite. Most of the workers were too busy to notice they had visitors.

Then they were in a large warehouse area piled high with whisky cartons, a small team of fork-lift trucks endlessly busy around them. An office area was located in one corner, where a door was marked Blending Director. When they went in there, a young receptionist led them to a smaller door marked Private and ushered them through.

'This is sooner than we expected, superintendent,' said Robert Martin. 'But you're welcome.'

The sandy-haired master blender, again in a white laboratory jacket, came out from one of the two large desks which filled most of the room. His wife Gina was behind the other desk and was wearing a dark-blue maternity jacket and skirt. She watched her husband shake hands with Thane, then she rose and came round to join them, giving Sandra a small smile in the process.

'What do you think, superintendent?' she asked. 'Your sergeant told us you're worried about our security here. Do you honestly believe we could have trouble too?'

'It's not impossible,' Thane told her. 'And your father is worried.'

Husband and wife exchanged a wry glance. She sighed. 'He was making noises. But he didn't give us any reasons.'

'Because he won't have any,' grumbled Martin. 'Gina knows I like the old man a lot – but he's getting paranoid about this.' He looked at Thane. 'How about a small lie? Can we tell him you're organizing extra security?'

'Do that if it helps. And we are – just in case.' Thane was glad that Finn Rankin had not yet spelled out his real anxieties. There was also no immediate need to tell the couple that the local R Division had already been asked to put a surveillance team in place. He lied a little. 'That's why I'm here.'

'We've enough on our plate,' apologized Robert Martin. The private office had a glass window that looked out on the main warehouse area, and he gestured at the busy scene outside. 'That's an export order being readied to fly out to Tokyo, and another one for Boston.'

'And the Tokyo order is all Broch Single Malt?' queried Thane.

The master blender nodded. 'The Japanese are single malt crazy, whatever it costs. We send them a Boeing 747 freighter load every other month – that's around 4,600 cases of whisky in a load, 12 bottles to the case. But, Boston is different. Most of our American orders go out in ordinary 747 scheduled flight belly-holds.'

'Scheduled as in carrying passengers?' asked Sandra Craig, startled.

'As in pasengers,' agreed Gina Martin. 'Fly the Atlantic out of Scotland and you're liable to be sharing the trip with a lot of whisky under your feet.'

'Maybe 1400 cases on a passsenger 747,' completed her husband. 'Right now, our US market leader is Highland Blend, but demand is still weak.' He grimaced. 'It would be different if we had even a half-decent sales initiative.'

'Which is partly my father's fault,' admitted Gina. 'He's so – so damned set in his own ways it would drive you crazy!' She turned and went back to her desk, sitting down again with a sigh of relief. 'Sorry, superintendent. My resident bump is acting up today.'

Thane saw his chance. 'And somebody is going to be a very happy grandfather?'

'That's an understatement.' She grinned.

'How long now?'

'Another six long weeks.'

'Boy or a girl?' asked Sandra mildly.

'The ultra-sound scan at twenty weeks said a boy.' Robert Martin went round behind his wife and laid an affectionate hand on her shoulder. 'Either way, boy or girl, it wouldn't have mattered to us. But her father just about went into orbit with delight when we told the family, then promised to name him Finn!'

'I'm not surprised,' murmured Thane.

What they'd told him fitted with the way in which the violence had steadily grown since Finn Rankin had been told he was to have a grandson. In Rankin's world, daughters might be loved. But a grandson meant that the dynasty could continue, the arrival of a new heir should be celebrated. Nothing, family or otherwise, should be allowed to stand in the way.

They talked a little longer, then said goodbye and left. Sandra

180

Craig followed Thane out, but said nothing until they were again in the parking lot, beside their cars. A large military jet made a thundering take-off in the background.

'It's the way you thought?' she asked. 'We're talking family?'

Thane nodded.

'Poor devil,' said Sandra soberly. 'Do we know who it is?'

'Not yet. Not for sure.' Thane shrugged. 'You gave me the notion. You and Ernie Vass, in the car coming down.'

'How?' she stared at him.

'You thought I was asleep. You were talking about who would be promoted if I snuffed it. I didn't think much of your candidates – I could give you better, starting with the office cat!' He smiled at her surprise. 'I've a couple of things I want to do on my own. So go back, bring Francey up to date, do the same for Phil Moss – then you can tell Francey I'll take it as a bonus if I find that George Eastern has been picked up and is feeling co-operative.'

Sandra Craig looked as if she had more questions on her mind. But she nodded, got into her white VW, and drove away. Thane stood beside his Ford for a few moments more, looking over at the long shape of the whisky-blending plant. Then he climbed into the car and set it moving.

When he reached Glasgow, his first stop was at a South Side veterinary surgery. He stayed silent as a girl in overalls opened one of a line of kennel doors and he saw Clyde lying snoring gently on a nest of old blankets. The big tan and white Boxer looked strangely vulnerable, a patch of hair on his chest had been shaved away, and the stitched wound was very visible.

'I could wake him,' said the girl. 'He's doing well.'

Thane smiled, shook his head, and backed away as quietly as he'd come.

From there, he drove home. Tommy and Kate were still at school, Gloria Hart was back again, and when he walked in he could hear Mary telling the punch line of an explicit joke about body searches. It raised his eyebrows but brought a howl of laughter from the commander's wife.

'I'm fine,' Mary assured him. 'And don't worry about the Criminal Injuries compensation form. The Boy Detective looked in, and brought one for me.'

181

'Does he always look like a frightened rabbit?' asked Gloria Hart.

Thane grinned and retreated.

Then, at last, he made it to Crime Squad headquarters, parked the Ford, and hurried into the building through the tail end of a heavy shower of rain. When he went through to his office, Sandra Craig was replacing the telephone on its receiver.

'Inspector Moss,' she explained briefly. 'He's up to date. He says he'll sit on his hands until he's told differently. And Detective Sergeant Beech wants you to call him.' She considered Thane critically. 'Have you eaten, sir?' When he shook his head, she got to her feet. 'I'll get something from the canteen.'

The 'something' she brought back was a hamburger topped by two fried eggs along with french fries, tomato sauce, and a haystack-sized salad. Although she had already eaten, the slim redhead brought the same for herself. On cue, Francey Dunbar limped in, beamed, and began helping himself to some of Sandra's food, finger and thumb style.

'Buy your own damned food, inspector,' suggested Detective Sergeant Sandra Craig sourly. 'I'm not running a welfare kitchen.'

Francey Dunbar grinned and used one of her egg yokes as a french fry dip.

'Did you get him?' asked Thane quietly.

'George-boy Eastern, boss?' Dunbar nodded. 'He's in an interview room. We did it the way you wanted – he was lifted by a couple of uniform men on an outstanding traffic warrant.'

'Does it exist?'

'Believe it or not, it does, boss.' Dunbar beamed and took another french fry. 'All he knows so far is that he's in real trouble.'

Littled else had changed. Morris Currie and Peter Wessex were still at their respective hotels. Banjo Kingsley was losing money on horses in a city-centre betting shop where he had an after-hours arrangement with a blonde manageress slightly past her sell-by date. Anything else was fringe-style gossip – except that Kingsley had told the faded blonde they could soon be heading for the sun together.

Thane finished the hamburger, washed it down with what was left of a paper cup of lukewarm coffee, then glanced at his watch. The time had come to say hello to George Eastern. He unlocked

182

his desk drawer and took out the stoppered glass tube with its floating finger.

The interview room was a windowless hutch in the basement, the kind of place that outside sounds couldn't reach. An orderly opened the locked door for them. Thane went in, followed by Sandra Craig, then by Dunbar.

George Eastern, the man sitting at a small metal table in the middle of the room, had thin features, a hook of a nose, and protruding ears. He was wearing his working clothes – a black blazer and dark trousers, black socks and black shoes.

'First time we've met, George,' said Thane unemotionally. 'Know why you're here, do you?'

'Do I hell!' Eastern glared at Francey Dunbar, and moistened his lips. 'I'm walkin' alone when two of your thicko cops grab me, throw me in a van, then feed me some garbage story about a warrant.' He paused, moistening his lips. 'Mister, if you're the boss here, I want a lawyer.'

Thane considered him for a moment. Eastern was average height, narrow shouldered, and needed a shave. He wore a grubby white shirt and a black tie that had seen better days.

'My name is Thane. I'm a detective superintendent with the Scottish Crime Squad.' He saw the man's thin face pale and his eyes widen. 'When you need a lawyer, you'll get one – not before.'

Eastern swallowed. 'What's this supposed to be about?'

'This.' Thane reached into his pocket, brought out the glass tube, deliberately swirled it in a way that sent the floating finger into a mad dance, then laid it on the table. The man gulped and tried to shove his chair back. He couldn't. Like the table, it was bolted to the floor. But there were other chairs, and his visitors settled across from him.

'Recognize the finger, George-boy?' asked Dunbar with a heavy sarcasm. 'Of course you do. You hacked it off old Aladdin Wason before he got his ride to the crematorium, right?'

'More garbage!' Eastern's eyes couldn't leave the glass tube and its macabre content.

'Is it?' Francey Dunbar's cane swung in a quick overhead arc. The lead-filled silver head landed on the metal tabletop in a massive drum-beat. As Eastern winced Dunbar treated the man to a wolfish snarl. 'Next time, that might be your head.'

'Except I wouldn't allow it, of course, George. Presuming I was here.' Colin Thane sucked hard on his teeth then glanced at Sandra Craig. 'Sergeant, tell the little story that may save a lot of time.' He looked grimly at their prisoner. 'Your job is to listen. Just listen. Understand?'

'But—' Eastern changed his mind and let it die there.

'Aladdin Wason died from natural causes about two weeks ago, aged eighty-one,' said Sandra in a clinically precise voice. 'He lived in Seegan Square, your mother lives in the next street, and you knew Wason. In fact, you'd known him as a neighbour for about twenty years. True?'

Avoiding her eyes, Eastern nodded.

'You work as a hire-car driver and general assistant for a neighbourhood funeral undertaker, and when the old man died and your boss got the job of handling the funeral that was exactly what you needed. Sometime before you drove the hearse to the crematorium, you opened old Aladdin's coffin.' She ignored a whine of protest. 'You cut off that finger, then closed the coffin again.'

'Not too much of a risk,' mused Dunbar. 'How many people count a dead man's fingers and toes?'

'You're all crazy!' Beads of sweat showed on Eastern's face under the overhead light. 'Old Wason went up the chimney, right?'

'Most of him.' Thane took over. 'But not this finger. Banjo Kingsley wanted it. You know Banjo, don't you?'

'I—' The man cringed as Dunbar's cane slammed down again. He gave a reluctant nod. 'Yes, but—'

'What Banjo didn't want was a dead man who might have had his fingerprints on file,' said Thane. 'Right so far?' He saw a new fear growing in Eastern's eyes as he went on. 'Old Aladdin must have seemed ideal. A quiet old man you'd known all those years.'

'Except you got it wrong, George,' said Sandra Craig sadly. 'Twenty-seven years ago the same Arden Wason was gaoled on an indecent assault charge. Whatever story he told you about how he lost his eye, it happened in a prison brawl. When he was released, he moved to Seegan Square to get away from every-thing. But his fingerprints were still on file.'

'Banjo won't be pleased about this, George,' said Thane.

The thin face twitched in panic.

'You could end up seriously dead,' mused Dunbar. 'Even if you didn't, we can bring any number of charges against you. Chopping bits of dead bodies isn't really allowed. Still, if you talk now . . .'

For a moment longer the thin-faced man stared at the finger floating in its glass tube. Then he swallowed.

'Do I get protection?'

'We'll do our best,' said Thane.

Eastern began talking.

He had stayed on late at the funeral home the night before Arden Wason's body was to be cremated. All he had needed was a screwdriver and a small freezer-food saw he'd borrowed from his mother's kitchen. Afterwards, there had been no problems. He'd been paid five hundred pounds – and had supplied three fingers.

'Banjo wanted a couple of spares,' he explained uneasily.

'Why?' pressed Thane.

'With Banjo, you don't ask.' The man shrugged. 'He wanted them, I got my money.'

'Who's he working with?'

'I don't know names.' Eastern made an attempt at a scowl. 'He's being bankrolled by some English business suit – like when two of his boys were killed in that Highland crash. Maybe they met in the Beezer Club in Sauchiehall Street – that's where Banjo makes a lot of contacts.' He paused hopefully. 'I'm finished, right?'

'You could be.' Francey Dunbar delicately used his silver-topped cane as a pointer. 'You don't really want a lawyer, do you, George-boy?'

Sadly, Eastern shook his head.

He was led away. Being arrested on an outstanding warrant meant he could easily be lost in the system for a few days.

Thane went back to his office, feeling that at the very least a few more pieces of the overall puzzle now fitted together. The message 'Phone Beech' was still on his desk. He did, and Detective Sergeant Beech was preening himself when he came on the line.

'I think I'm about to nail your housebreaker, sir,' said Beech happily. 'A man walked into a jewellery store this morning and tried to sell a gold brooch like the one stolen in another of the break-ins in your street. But he panicked and ran when the

185

jeweller tried to quiz him about it. He was limping – and from the description, I know him.'

'Get back to me when you've got him,' said Thane grimly, and hung up.

About an hour later the latest set of reports from the surveillance teams came in. Morris Currie had taken himself off to a cinema, Peter Wessex was still at his hotel and had made a marathon-length business call to his office in London. Banjo Kingsley had abandoned his woman friend and was drinking in a docklands bar.

Thane made a call north to Phil Moss at the Ardshona incident room. With digital scrambler units at each end of the line they could talk freely.

Everything seemed peaceful around Broch Distillery and Ardshona. Moss had spoken with Finn Rankin, whose main concern had been that his daughter and his expected grandson were now being fully protected. Nothing else was stirring. Willie Adams might have visited his mother again, but Moss couldn't prove what he thought. Dougie Lennox was sporting a newly acquired black eye, claiming he'd walked into a door, and was staying clear of Maggie Donald – and again Moss couldn't prove what he thought.

'I'm sitting here twiddling my thumbs,' he complained. 'But it's like I'm waiting for all hell to break loose.'

Thane felt the same. He knew both Morris Currie and Banjo Kingsley, he wanted to get a sight of the third man in the equation, Peter Wessex. A little later he had Sandra Craig drive him into the city and into the Hospitality Inn's underground car park.

He took the elevator up to the ground floor of the hotel. Beauty and the Beast, two detective constables who were a Crime Squad regular pairing, were watching Wessex. Beauty was a small blonde who could have fallen off the top of a Christmas tree. The Beast was large and hairy, and waiting near a water feature in the main lobby area.

'In there, sir.' The Beast gave a slight jerk of his head towards the main cocktail bar. 'Nothing happening.'

Thane went in and sat beside Beauty, who was nursing a drink and pretending to read a newspaper in one of the screened booths. She gave him a half-smile then indicated to her right. Peter Wessex was at the bar counter, flirting with a Chinese American girl who wasn't objecting. He was taller than Thane had expected, and wearing a dark checked sports suit with a white shirt and a plain green tie. A thin man, his hooded eyes and small mouth somehow didn't detract from his line in extrovert charm.

'One smooth operator,' murmured Beauty under her breath. Then she froze, looking past Thane. 'Oh hell!'

Banjo Kingsley had walked into the bar. Thick-set and unsmiling, fair hair cropped close to his skull, expensively dressed in an Italian black leather jacket and designer jeans, the man so many feared went towards the bar counter then took the stool next to Wessex. By then, Thane had shrunk further back into the shelter of the booth and was pretending to share Beauty's newspaper.

Kingsley nodded to Wessex without any expression crossing his coarse features, then ordered a beer. He paid for his beer when it arrived. Then the fair-haired thug drank it, got to his feet, and left without another glance towards Wessex.

Thane took a deep breath. He hadn't been spotted, and Kingsley's arrival must have been an all-clear signal to Wessex. But a different result could have been a disaster.

He waited another minute, then went back out into the hotel lobby. The Beast was there with a sergeant who was one of the surveillance team watching Kingsley. The sergeant tried to mutter an apology that there had been no chance to warn anybody.

'Your fault – and a damned stupid caper,' said Jack Hart a little later at headquarters. 'Try thinking next time.'

Back from his judicial wanderings, the squad commander gave his verdict in the privacy of his own large office – a place where the coffee came in cups with matching saucers.

'Maybe you could go in now,' ruminated Hart. 'But what kind of a result would you get? No, this one you have to take right to the wire, Colin. That includes the Broch Distillery end. When you go in, the aim is to nail them all.' He paused, taking another gulp of coffee. 'The "why" seems easy enough. Finn Rankin is stubborn, old-fashioned, and sitting on what could be a gold mine of a business. People already wanted him out. But along comes the new factor, God help us. A promised grandson, a male heir. The Rankin dynasty. The man is behaving like a dinosaur! Yes, it will be years before this grandson can take over. But Rankin could set up a legally binding trust that froze everything about Broch until that happened!' He set down his cup and scowled. 'So the roots are family. Another of the sisters?'

'I think it has to be.' Thane was wary.

'Meaning you don't know who to put your money on?' Hart got to his feet. 'Right, this is an order. Go home, stay by the phone, leave this end to Francey Dunbar. Don't call us – we'll call you.'

'I can't—' began Thane.

'The hell you can't,' growled Hart. 'Do it.'

He did. When he arrived home he found that Kate and Tommy had insisted on making the evening meal, with Mary glad to supervise from a chair. Maggie Fyffe had taken the time off she'd promised and had driven them all out to the veterinary kennels to see Clyde. He was still lying down but he had greeted them with a wag of his stump of tail.

The meal was a stew, burned at the edges, but that didn't matter. Afterwards, neither of their children went out. They sat, they talked, they watched TV, and the telephone rang a few times with friends wanting to know how Mary was coming along.

The call that Thane had been waiting for came at exactly ten-thirty p.m. He tensed from the moment he heard Francey Dunbar's voice on the line.

'It looks like things have started,' reported Dunbar. 'They're all at the Beezer Club.'

'I'm leaving now,' said Thane. 'Meet me outside, tell our people we don't want them crowded.'

He hung up. Mary was watching him. So were Tommy and Kate.

'Now?' asked Mary.

He nodded.

'I repacked your overnight bag,' she said simply.

He said goodbye and left a couple of minutes later.

At that hour, the city was fairly quiet. There was a new drizzle of rain, enough to need an occasional sweep of the Ford's wipers.

Then the car radio came to life. Strathclyde control was suddenly shuffling patrol cars towards Sauchiehall Street, using a condition code which every cop knew meant a bomb alert.

Thane reached the Beezer Club to find the street lined with police cars and milling with people. Blue lights flashed, an occasional siren wailed. He parked, started walking, heard a shout, then Francey Dunbar limped through the crowd towards him. One look at Dunbar's face was enough.

'They've gone?' asked Thane.

Dunbar nodded, turning up his jacket collar as the drizzle became worse. 'Central Divison had an anonymous bomb call ten minutes ago, boss.' He shrugged at the inevitability of the rest. 'They start getting everybody out, and it's instant chaos. Our three just disappeared – they could have used a back exit. A car was seen leaving.'

Thane pursed his lips. Bomb calls were never ignored – every now and again they were for real. But at least it meant a part of the waiting was over.

A little later, they were back at headquarters. Commander Hart had called everyone into the main duty room.

'Add this to what you've got,' said Hart. 'Things are moving – Currie and Wessex checked out of their hotels before they went to the Beezer Club, Kingsley had hinted to a couple of his people that he'd be gone for two or three days, but didn't say where.' He cleared his throat. 'I'll presume that the bomb scare was just a pre-planned cut-off point. So with luck they still don't know we've been on their tails. They'll have tried to set up alibis, but right now that doesn't matter. What does is where the hell they've gone.' He glanced at Thane. 'Colin?'

'Heading north.' Thane said it automatically. 'By car – they couldn't chance flight or a train.'

Hart frowned. 'Currie and Wessex left their cars in their hotel garages.'

'They're maybe pulling the same trick as before, sir,' suggested Francey Dunbar. 'Another set of wheels bought at an auction yard.'

'Something we can't trace.' Hart swore softly. 'Yes. Anything else, anyone?'

'Sir.' Sandra Craig leaned forward. 'We presume they're heading north, we know they're careful and won't rush anything, that they want to get in and out without being seen. The best bet is they'll use backroads all the way, head for somewhere near Ardshona, then lie low during the day, and wait for tomorrow night.'

'I'll buy that, sergeant.' Hart nodded then shaped a slow, wintery smile. 'They'll lie low, like you say – and we'll do exactly the same.' He turned to Thane. 'And we mean you, Colin. Take Sandra and Vass again.'

This time there was no need to hurry. Hart turned down Francey Dunbar's plea to be included, but added a detective constable named Kerrigan as a relief driver. They drew four .38 Colt automatics from the Squad armoury. There were arrangements to be made with Moss. They ate a late supper in the Squad canteen, and Thane telephoned home.

Then, half an hour into Friday, they boarded the BMW with Kerrigan at the wheel and set off.

Overnight traffic on the main route north was busier than ever. The last of the rain died away before Perth, the sky cleared, and they travelled on under bright moonlight. Hours later, only Kerrigan was fully awake as the BMW passed Inverness then swung north-west. They were only five miles south of Ardshona and dawn was breaking when the travel-grimed red car turned off the road, went some distance along a rough, winding track and through a patch of woodland, then stopped behind a gamekeeper's cottage.

There were lights at the cottage windows, smoke came from its chimney, and two other vehicles were already there. A Nissan four by four belonged to the gamekeeper, who had a brother who was a police sergeant with the Met. The other vehicle was Maggie Donald's Northern Constabulary Range Rover. She was there, and so was Phil Moss. They had coffee waiting and the gamekeeper was frying an endless supply of thin slices of venison while his wife spread butter on thick slices of crusty white bread.

When they'd washed and eaten, Thane beckoned Moss outside. The sun was coming up, the hills around were wakening, and a couple of the gamekeeper's hens were clucking around their feet.

'Now we wait,' said Thane quietly. 'They're out there somewhere, Phil.'

'Out There is a hell of a big area.' Moss gave a gentle belch. 'Maybe you've noticed.'

Thane smiled. 'And I knew you'd remind me.'

'That's why I'm here.' Moss gave his acid grin.

'So where are they likely to surface?' Thane used the toe of his shoe to scrape three separate marks on the ground. 'There's the main distillery, though it's unlikely they'll try the same location again. There's the investment storage warehouse and the blending warehouse.' He paused, frowned, then scraped another mark. 'Then we have to cover Broch Castle. Who goes in, who goes out.'

'Four locations.' Moss kicked at a pebble and sent it flying with a kick. 'From when?'

'Now.'

'Should be easy enough.' Moss wasn't perturbed. 'And I can haul in the local Specials, ask them to keep an eye open for the unusual. No need to tell them why.'

'But whatever they see—'

'They do nothing, just report back.' Moss gave a belch fierce enough to send the hens scurrying. Grimacing, he reached into a pocket of his shapeless jacket and produced a small bottle. Uncorking it, he took a swallow of dark brown liquid and winced. 'God, that stuff tastes like death!'

'What on earth is it?' asked Thane.

'Don't shout about it near Sandra.' Moss looked round cautiously as he stowed the flask away again. 'It's an old herbal cure. Something – uh – Belle made up for me.'

'Belle Campbell?' Thane chuckled.

Moss went red and became busy. Within minutes the gamekeeper and his wife came out with an overnight bag and drove off in their Nissan, a hotel room booked for them in Inverness. Maggie Donald emerged from the cottage and started up the Range Rover. Then, with Moss aboard, she set it crunching back over the track towards the main road.

Time passed. They heard the occasional sound of a vehicle passing on the road beyond the trees. A fox appeared briefly and sniffed around the BMW. Vass produced a pack of cards and settled into a marathon game of pontoon with Kerrigan. Sandra Craig read a book she'd found in the cottage and combined it with monitoring the BMW's radio. Thane twice cleaned his .38, just to have something to do.

Lisa, with her blue Viking eyes and that scar – or Anna, divorced and bitter? Both could expect to lose if Finn Rankin chose the unborn Martin child as his intended heir. Ignore Morris Currie as a mere weak link, and either Lisa or Anna could have set aside feelings and enlisted help from Peter Wessex.

Either, or both?

He was still wrestling with the conundrum when he listened to a mid-day BBC news bulletin coming in over the Range Rover's radio. As the bulletin reported a new NATO row between the US and Europe centred on Bosnia, Jock Dawson's dog van suddenly drove in from the road and stopped. Andy Mack had come out with Dawson.

'For what it's worth, here's the update,' said the veteran Northern inspector when he reached Thane. 'I'm still around with the one and only Detective Constable Harron, our Pride of the North, and a couple of uniform men. We're sharing with your people on the o.b. scene.' He saw the question coming and shook his head. 'The Rankin sisters are out and about, so is their father. That's about it.'

'Any strangers?'

'A couple of holiday families. No one else.'

Dawson unloaded a grocery bag full of frozen meals and a couple of six-packs from the Land-Rover, and they left again.

The long afternoon began, only an occasional mutter from the Squad radio to prove that they hadn't been forgotten and that the observation squad were still in their positions. Thane walked to the boundaries of the gamekeeper's cottage garden, edged by gnarled spruce trees, twisted with age, trunks spotted with moss and lichen. The ground beneath them covered in plate-sized, red-tipped mushrooms, the air filled with the buzz of insects.

Their next visitors arrived about three p.m. in an unmarked Northern car. Harry Harron was driving. The Northern DC was hunched awkwardly behind the wheel and his Crime Squad passenger was Dougie Lennox, complete with newly acquired black eye. They came over together.

'Inspector Moss told me to deliver this, sir.' Uneasily, Lennox gave Thane a folded fax sheet.

Thane opened it, read it, and gave a soft murmur of satisfaction. The fax had originated from Francey Dunbar in Glasgow. Dunbar had evidence that Peter Wessex had positive associations with Swiss merchant banking interests – and Ophelia Holdings, which had made the Broch offer to Finn Rankin, had been part of the scene in one of Wessex's previous financial adventures.

'Fax my thanks, Dougie.' Then, fighting down a grin, he asked, 'What the hell happened to your eye?'

'A door, sir,' said Lennox woodenly.

'Dangerous things, doors,' sympathized Sandra Craig, who was beside them. She nodded to Harron. 'Any problems, Harry?'

'None that matter.' Harron shrugged. '"We are labourers together" – Corinthians Three, verse six, sergeant.'

Sandra smiled maliciously. 'Get it right, Harron. Verse nine.' She watched his mouth drop open. 'There's a Police Federation approved version. We are labourers together, but superintendents get paid more.'

Phil Moss had sent out another six-pack and some newspapers, and once these were handed over the two men got back into their car and it roared away.

Then time crept on as before, the day still warm, the sky cloudless, and BBC bulletins updating on the US–Europe row, with the UK performing its familiar sitting on the fence act.

It was after six p.m. before their next visitor. They heard the loud ringing of a cycle bell then the slim figure of Jazz Gupatra came pedalling in to join them. Kerrigan grabbed her and had hauled her off the machine before anyone could say anything.

'Nice to see you too, Mr Thane.' said the dark-skinned student indignantly when she was released. 'This isn't supposed to happen when I'm a stand-in for Pony Express. Your pal Moss sent me. I've to tell you there's a man watching the Ardshona Inn, and he suggests you stay away for now.'

'That we could have done without,' admitted Thane.

'He says the good news is they know where your Bad Guys are laid up. A Special spotted two cars behind a ruined cottage four miles west of here – where the only neighbours are sheep.' She frowned, reached into her jacket pocket, and brought out another folded fax sheet. 'Here's what he thought you'd also want to know.'

Thane took the message and read it. Again, it was from Francey Dunbar in Glasgow.

DS BEECH HAS ARRESTED A NINETEEN-YEAR-OLD HOUSE-BREAKER AFTER A KNIFE ATTACK DURING A BREAK-IN ON SOUTH SIDE OF CITY. PRISONER CHARGED WITH

ATTEMPTED MURDER OF PENSIONER. YOUR STOLEN PROP-
ERTY RECOVERED.

'Good news?' asked Jazz, who had watched his face.

'Good news,' he agreed. 'Thanks for bringing it over.'

'No problem.' The girl shook her head. 'It made a change – I spent most of my day at the Broch office while Finn Rankin yelled at his daughter.

Thane raised an eyebrow. 'Which of them – Lisa or Anna?'

'Anna.'

'You're sure?' quizzed Thane.

'Positive. Lisa was off with Alex Korski somewhere.' Jazz grimaced. 'Anna, and her father were creating hell over something to do with the Broch telephone account. He was shouting that he wanted to know why they were being billed for so much, she was yelling that she didn't know what the hell he was talking about!' She chuckled. 'Do all fathers rant about telephone bills?'

'It's part of being a father,' said Thane absently. 'Did you hear anything more?'

She shook her head. Thane let it end there, but the row added fresh fuel to the whole situation.

Sandra Craig walked back to the road with the girl, saw her pedalling on her way, and then returned.

Time crept on and the day became colder as dusk grew near. A flock of rooks rose from the trees and made the sky noisy with their wings. There was still an occasional mutter from the BMW's radio. They ate, and another BBC bulletin said that the diplomatic row between America and Europe was still growing. They were bored with waiting – but most police operations came down to hanging around and being bored. The night closed in, the moon and a thin scatter of stars took over.

It was ten p.m. before the Crime Squad radio summoned them to the Ardshona Inn. A few minutes later the BMW murmured its way into the township and parked at a discreet distance from the inn. Maggie Donald met them, and from there they slipped into the hotel and down to the storeroom incident room.

As soon as they entered, Phil Moss took Thane over to one of the trestle table desks. Andy Mack hovered at his elbow and the others gathered in the background while Moss laid out a double-sheet local map taken from some Tourist Board guide book.

'Here's what we've got,' said Moss, using a well-chewed stub of pencil as a pointer. 'The two cars were located off this back road, a few minutes away. Two Northern specials, grade one poachers—'

'Reformed poachers,' corrected the Northern inspector mildly.

'Reformed grade one poachers,' accepted Moss. 'They blend into the woodwork at more than fifteen paces! Anyway, they've been watching the cars since they were first located. Kingsley's people are using two low-mileage Fords, we've traced back the registration numbers.' He looked at Thane and nodded. 'You've guessed it. Bought for cash at an auction last week. Five men – the specials identify Currie, Wessex and Banjo Kingsley from descriptions.'

'The other two are hired help,' suggested Mack. 'One of them drove into the township a few times, like he was keeping an eye on things. But he joined up with the rest of his team again about an hour ago.'

'And now they've started,' completed Moss. He gave a frosty grin at Thane's immediate interest. 'One car took Currie, Banjo Kingsley, and one of the hired help over to here.' He stabbed with the pencil stub. 'The Broch investment whisky warehouse, right? A Northern sergeant was watching there, pretending he was some kind of a tree – and you can forget the security alarms, Colin! He saw them go straight inside, no problems. That was twenty minutes ago.'

'Thank you, Morris Currie.' Thane nodded grimly.

'Your orders were watch, to do nothing.' Moss used the pencil again. 'Well, now they're out again, they've rejoined the rest of the team, and it looks like they're all moving.'

'Heading where, we don't know,' contributed Mack bleakly. 'First thing, what do we do about the warehouse?'

Thane drew a deep breath and frowned at the map. 'If it's arson again, say some quick prayers that they're using a delayed timing device. Get some help up to your sergeant, but still tell him to wait.'

Mack gave an uneasy nod. If something went wrong, he didn't imagine there would be happy times ahead.

'Currie worked a whisky investment racket once before,' reminded Harron. His long-jawed face shaped a hopeful grin. 'If he's been at it again—'

'This could be his chance to cover up a major shortage!' Mack brightened. 'Harron, just this once I hope you're right!' He glanced at Thane. 'Superintendent?'

'It could be.' Thane nodded. A fire in the investement whisky warehouse would hit Finn Rankin hard – but the stakes were steadily becoming higher. He turned back to the map. 'How long until we know what's happening?'

He had his answer quickly enough. First Jock Dawson's voice murmured from a radio speaker. The Crime Squad dog handler had his van parked off the road on the route that led to Broch Castle, both Ford cars had just passed him at a sedate pace. A handful of minutes later a new voice murmured. This time it was Dougie Lennox, stationed within the Broch grounds. Travelling without lights, the Fords had purred in through the entrance gates and were parked behind a high hedge of rhododendron bushes a little way down the driveway. Three men had crept past Lennox and were now waiting under a tree close to the castle. The other two had stayed with the cars.

'That's it!' Thane looked round the semicircle of expectant faces and nodded.

One by one, they slipped out of the Ardshona Inn. From there they drove towards Broch Castle, stopped a few hundred yards short of its gates, and left their vehicles.

'Ready,' whispered Andy Mack. The veteran Northern inspector had produced a revolver and Harron was also armed. Thane checked his own weapon and saw his Crime Squad team do the same. Jock Dawson had brought his dog van up to join them, the dogs softly whining as if sensing they had work ahead.

'Right.' Thane beckoned and they began moving.

It worked the way he'd planned it. Sandra Craig beside him, he went forward at a low crouch and crept past the spot where the two Fords were hidden Avoiding the gravelled driveway, they were close to the silhouette of the turreted mansion when Dougie Lennox appeared out of a patch of shadow.

'No change, sir.' The babyfaced DC grinned a welcome as they crouched down beside him. 'Over there, to your right. Under the tall tree.' He waited until Thane had picked out the three figures standing together under the umbrella of leaves. 'They're waiting on something. They have to be.'

Thane nodded and took a quick glance at his watch. He saw the luminous face showed ten-thirty, and next moment he received a nudge from Sandra Craig.

'Now, sir,' murmured his red-haired sergeant. 'The castle.'

The main door of the mansion had opened and a woman had slipped out. It closed again and the woman, tall and with long, blonde hair, crossed rapidly and silently to join the men under the tree.

'It's Lisa,' hissed Sandra Craig.

Thane nodded. Standing back, analysing the facts, stirring in a couple of hunches, it had had to be.

Nothing seemed to be said when Rankin's oldest daughter joined the three men. Then, leading, she took the small procession towards the rear of the castle and the old Pictish broch.

'Radio.' Thane took Lennox's personal radio, and flicked the send switch. 'Phil, Andy – go!'

Behind him, he knew what was happening. Kerrigan and Vass were going in with Andy Mack and Maggie Donald, their assignment to take out the two drivers at the Fords. Then Maggie Donald and a Northern uniform man had their own assignment – to make sure there was no interference from Broch Castle, whatever happened.

Rustling movements coming from the rear announced the approach of Moss and Harron, along with Dawson and his dogs. The dogs were panting. Thane didn't wait for them, moving forward, staying in as much cover as he could, following the quartet ahead. He saw them reach the Broch door, heard its modern lock click, then the faint squeak of the door opening. The four went in, the door swung shut again, then a few faint chinks of light showed from inside the ancient sandstone beehive.

Thane looked around. Sandra Craig and Moss were with him, Lennox and Harron had just joined them, Jock Dawson was still those few paces back. As Lennox's radio murmured, it meant the two drivers had been taken out.

'Now,' said Thane, then cursed.

The faint glimmers of light from the broch had become harsh chinks as the main interior lighting came on. He heard a muffled cry of surprise, then a brief popping of shots from at least two different weapons.

'Jock!' he shouted. 'Secure the outside! Everybody else, we're going in!'

As they pounded across the stretch of grass towards the broch there were another few popping shots. Then there was silence. Thane reached the door, found it unlocked, pulled it open, and went through into its world of crude sandstone chambers, and the glare of naked electric bulbs. Moments took him to the door to Robert Martin's test-room office.

It lay open. As Thane went through, a single shot rang out from somewhere ahead, echoing and re-echoing through the stone chambers while the bullet whined past him in a mad ricochet.

'Armed police!' He shouted the warning, the Colt automatic somehow already in his hand, then stumbled over a body at his feet. Peter Wessex was dead. He had fallen on his back, eyes staring, two bullet holes close together high on his chest, an automatic pistol lying close beside one outstretched hand.

Thane plunged on. There was another open door at the far end, where faint traces of cordite smoke laced the air. He went through, then skidded to a halt, the Colt ready. But the people around the room stood as if frozen.

Finn Rankin had half-fallen out of a chair, slumped forward across the polished wood of the boardroom table and he was making faint groaning noises. His face was twisted, his eyes were strangely glazed yet moving, his mouth slack and wet with spittle, he showed every sign of having suffered a massive stroke. An ancient revolver had fallen on the table at his side. Standing protectively behind him, Willie Adams had a rifle covering the two other men in the room and was bleeding from a wound in his side.

Morris Currie and Banjo Kingsley were both still on their feet. Kingsley had a heavy .45 calibre revolver gripped in both hands. Morris Currie, clutching a small haversack, had total panic written across his pudgy face as Moss and Sandra, then Harron and Dougie Lennox poured in.

'Oh, shit,' said Kingsley bitterly. He was a professional and the odds were wrong. Scowling, he tossed the .45 on the stone floor. Willie Adams sighed, managed a faint grin, carefully laid his rifle on the boardroom table and tried to stay upright.

There was another small door at the rear of the stone chamber. Suddenly, Morris Currie hurled his haversack straight at Harron's head. As it fell, three separate metal boxes bound with black insulating tape tumbled out – and Currie made a wild dash to escape. He got through the rear door and vanished from sight. They let him go.

Seconds passed, long enough for Banjo Kingsley to be handcuffed. Then there was a deep-throated baying and a high-pitched barking as German shepherd and Labrador were turned loose and the two police dogs brought down their quarry. Morris Currie kept screaming in terror while Jock Dawson called both dogs off.

'Where's the woman?' asked Moss, glaring around.

'Don't know.' Willie Adams gave a grimace.

'You were here, waiting on them?' Thane asked.

'Yes. His idea.' The ex-soldier indicated Finn Rankin. 'He overheard a phone call – so he expected them. But not that she'd be with them. When he saw her' – he shrugged – 'it was like he blew a fuse.'

'You could call it that,' said Sandra Craig.

'Luck of the draw,' said Willie Adams wryly.

Then he began to topple and Harron got there just fast enough to stop him falling while Moss ran shouting for Dawson to radio for an ambulance. Very carefully, Sandra Craig lifted one of the taped metal boxes from the floor and Thane took it from her. It was a very small but very lethal firebomb, linked to a TV video timer clock, the clock not yet activated. The timer could be programmed to sleep for any time up to a month in the future, then come to life.

To record a wanted programme – or detonate a bomb. The IRA used them. Thane laid it down gently as Moss returned.

'Organized,' reported Moss.

'Take over here,' Thane told him. 'We're still one short.'

Sandra Craig went with him as he explored the maze of small corridors and stone chambers. They found Lisa Rankin on her knees in the shadows of a tiny upper cell of the broch. One hand clutched her body just below her right breast, she had another of the small, tape-wrapped metal boxes grasped tightly in her other hand, and she saw them coming.

'Stay back!' She gestured with the little bomb.

'It's over, Lisa,' said Thane quietly. In all his life, he had never seen anything to match the frustrated bitterness etched on the blonde woman's scarred yet beautiful face.

'Is it?' She swung the bomb box in a new arc as Sandra Craig tried to reach her. 'You – don't try it!'

'She won't.' Thane waved Sandra Craig back. There was blood welling out where Lisa Rankin clutched her side. 'We've sent for an ambulance, Lisa.'

199

'For me?' She gave a hoarse sound which began as a laugh and ended as a painful cough. 'I wouldn't bother. Whatever that idiot Kingsley fired at, the bullet bounced and hit me.' She grimaced. 'I'm not worried, superintendent. I don't think I'd like prison.'

Thane squatted down beside her. 'Why, Lisa? What's it all about?'

'He knows.' She gestured down below, to where her father lay. 'Damn him, he knows.'

'But I don't,' said Thane quietly. 'Is it the grandson?'

Lisa Rankin looked at him for a long moment, the tape-wrapped bomb trembling in her hand. She coughed again, blood appearing on her lips. 'No, it started long before that, superintendent.' She brought the box up to touch the scar on her face. 'He told you about this?'

Thane nodded.

'And he'd tell you that my mother was driving. Did – did he tell you that he was in the car with us? But that he couldn't drive because he was too drunk?' Her lips trembled. 'She was always terrified of driving after dark. But he went into a drunken rage and bullied her, made her. She – she HAD to do it. It was the only way she could get three small children safely home.' Lisa Rankin coughed again. 'He sat beside her, bullying non-stop, making her go fast. That – that's why we crashed.'

'I didn't know,' said Thane softly.

'Even Gina and Anna don't know, superintendent.' She gave that strange, half-strangled laugh and winced. More blood showed on her lips. 'They were too young to understand, to remember. Afterwards, he never once spoke about it. When I tried, he denied it all – told me I was talking madness. So I stayed quiet, pretended – for all our sakes. Even his, maybe.'

Then had come the plastic surgery, the presents, the attempts to compensate for the mother she'd lost.

'You came to live with it,' puzzled Sandra. 'Till now. What changed?'

'Maybe I did.' Lisa Rankin's breathing was becoming quick and noisy. 'I got tired seeing him turning down every idea anybody put up. When I tried to discuss anything, he wouldn't listen. He became totally unreasonable, totally intractable. So I decided to fight back – any way I could.' She shook her head. 'But I didn't set out to hurt anyone.'

'Even Gina's baby?'

'Never ever Gina's baby. I'd have loved – loved being an aunt.' Her voice was breaking up. 'And I couldn't have harmed my sisters – never. But then he came – came up with this crazy feudal idea of a trust. He wouldn't talk, he shut everybody out. Even Anna – Anna who is supposed to be our lawyer – wasn't told. He only told Jonesy, and Jonesy was so worried that – that she told me.'

Thane shifted to ease the cramp in his muscles. 'Did Anna know you'd asked Peter Wessex for help?'

'No. That was my idea – no one else's. It was easy enough to get Currie involved. He has his own problems.' She stopped and shuddered. 'Superintendent' – her voice sinking to little more than a murmur, she beckoned him nearer – 'I'm cold. It's getting dark. Please do something for me. Gina and Anna – tell them. Tell them I—' Her head fell, her breathing stopped after a last rasp.

'You loved them.' Thane murmured it for her. 'I will.'

He removed the metal box from her fingers. He took off his jacket and draped it over that scarred, suddenly peaceful face.

Then Thane got to his feet and followed his sergeant down to whatever was waiting below.

CURTAIN CALL.

Three days later, Colin Thane was at last getting ready to leave. He had processed a start of the formalities, he had fought off the worst of the Crown Office legal entanglements. Although there were plenty of the same ahead, the majority of what remained was being shouldered by Northern Constabulary.

The Crime Squad team was going home. To top that, he had had a telephone call from Jack Hart before breakfast that morning. The Crime Squad commander was fulfilling a promise.

'We've got that report you wanted,' said Hart briskly. 'They've finished the blood tests on the young thug who stabbed Mary and they're HIV negative.'

Thane thanked him, made other vague noises, then hung up. It was a fear which had been lurking at the back of his mind, known only to Hart. The risk had been minimal, but Clyde's bite had drawn blood from their housebreaker at the same time as Mary had been stabbed.

201

After that, he had telephoned home straight away. To find that Mary already knew because Maggie Fyffe had telephoned, and that Mary had also had the same unspoken fear at the back of her mind.

'When you get back, we'll celebrate.' He heard a familiar Boxer-sized barking at her end of the line, a barking he hadn't expected.

'Francey Dunbar brought him over this morning,' said Mary. 'What about you?'

'Sometime this afternoon,' he promised. 'Gift-wrapped.'

He heard a radio news bulletin in his room while he finished packing. The simmering row between the US and Europe over the latest Bosnian flare-up was still under way. Various heads of state were barely on speaking terms. He chuckled, wondering what else was new.

When finally he went down to the incident room storeroom, most of its equipment had been dismantled. Maggie Donald was there, neat as ever in her Northern constable's uniform, filing a last few pieces of paperwork.

'Nearly ready, sir?' She looked up at him.

'Just mopping up.' He considered her for a moment. 'Maggie, we'll have some Crime Squad posting vacancies available in a couple of months. If you feel like a change . . .'

'Thank you, superintendent.' Maggie Donald smiled. 'I'll maybe think about it.'

'Do that.' Thane nodded. 'We could use someone like you, who can handle hassle.'

He decided not to mention Dougie Lennox or his black eye. Lennox was already on his way south, sharing a car with Phil Moss and Ernie Vass. Jock Dawson had left even earlier with his dogs and DC Kerrigan. Any equipment they left behind would follow later.

There was still tragedy and chaos as far as the Broch Distilleries empire was concerned, there probably would be for a long time. Finn Rankin would live despite the severity of his stroke – but he had been broken. He would never be fit enough to return to work. Anna and Gina were already taking over, a new team backed by an ultimatum from Jonesy. The sisters, supported by Robert Martin and a suddenly decisive Alex Korski, should eventually work through it all.

Willie Adams was out on police bail, unlikely to be charged

with anything. One thing for certain was that the death of Donny Adam, wouldn't be laid at his door. But Morris Currie and Banjo Kingsley faced a series of major indictments and were ready to do deals with anyone who would listen.

That included how the video timer bombs, including those recovered from the whisky investment warehouse, had been intended as the final threat which would have smashed Finn Rankin. The investment warehouse being burned down would have covered up Morris Currie's systematic looting of the whisky stock it was supposed to contain.

Thane left Maggie Donald and the stripped-down incident room, said a few goodbyes, then took his overnight bag out onto the porch of the Ardshona Inn. He walked over to where a delivery van was unloading cartons at the inn's main door, looked at the cartons, and smiled.

The red BMW was waiting across the road, Sandra beside it. But they had a surprise visitor. The tall, thin figure of Detective Superintendent Mick Farrell, head of Northern Constabulary's CID, was climbing out of a newly arrived Northern car. He talked briefly to Moss and Sandra then came over to join Thane.

'Formal goodbyes,' said Farrell dryly. 'I wanted to say thank you.'

'Now you've got more time?' Thane smiled in a way that took any sting out of his words.

'Now I've . . .' Farrell paused, looked at him closely, and swore. 'Who told you?'

'That your Special Operation just died?' Thane's smile became a grin. 'Two of the waitress staff they poached from the Ardshona got back this morning. I'll bet every hotel between here and Inverness is getting staff back about now. There have been no more messages about traffic checks on the coast road around – Dunrobin Castle, wasn't it?'

Farrell said nothing. But the location had to be Dunrobin Castle, sprawling and impressive, with vast, lavishly furnished reception rooms and sweeping gardens, once the home of the Duke of Sutherland. There was nowhere else in the North of Scotland big enough for the role.

'I'll bet all those catering vans that have been driving north are heading south again.' Thane sighed and shook his head. 'Listen to a news bulletin, and all you hear is this row between Europe and the Americans. Put it all together and . . .'

'And even Harry Harron might get it right,' grimaced Farrell. 'That's the other thing I came to explain. All right, it would have been a nightmare. A top secret conference with God knows how many heads of state flying in. Security agencies, military, the navy off-shore, everything dumped in our lap – I was ready to cheer when they cancelled.' He shook his head. 'That's why we needed the Broch business like a hole in the head, that's why we couldn't wait to dump it on your lap. But even so, you made a pretty good guess...'

'Mick...' Thane took him by the arm and led him over to where the van was still being unloaded. One carton was open. Reaching into it, Thane brought out a pack of toilet rolls, opened one, and pulled free a length of the tissues. One corner of each sheet bore a neat drawing of Dunrobin Castle. Underneath that was printed 'International Security Conference, Dunrobin Castle' followed by the dates.

'Bottom line stuff,' said Thane with a stony face. 'Someone's busy selling it off as surplus stock.'

'Don't ask me to get in the queue,' growled Farrell. Then he grinned, they shook hands, and they said goodbye.

Colin Thane carried his overnight bag across to the BMW. Sandra Craig was already behind the wheel and started the engine as he tossed his bag into the rear seat. She set the car moving as soon as he was aboard but as they began driving out of the township for one last time Thane turned in his seat and frowned. Something bulky filled most of the rear seat space, covered over by a strip of old blanket.

'Sergeant.' He glanced at the redhead. 'What's going on?'

'Sir?' The redhead gave him her most innocent look.

'What are we carrying, Sandra?'

She gave a wary smile but kept driving. 'It came over from Broch, sir.'

Thane reached round and lifted the edge of the blanket. Two large cartons of Broch Single Malt whisky looked up at him.

Two special cartons. They had been overprinted with the Dunrobin Conference logo and dates.

'So even they knew?' He gave a long sigh. 'And no one ever said anything?'

'We never asked, sir,' reminded Sandra.

A new thought struck him. 'The other cars—'

She nodded.

Thane groaned. 'How the hell do you people expect to get away with this?'

'Research, sir?' suggested his sergeant. As she spoke, she switched on the car's wipers. The Ardshona's near drought had broken. It was starting to rain.

'Research.' He sighed, sat back, closed his eyes, and relaxed.